ALIEN CONTACT

The Queen lifte   h,
monstrous in he   e.
"Will you force   se
others will subm   ,"
the Queen rumbled. "There must."

Malye chuckled softly. "If there must be a capitulation, then perhaps you should be the one to
deliver it. I guarantee I have seen things these
others have not. Perhaps I hold the information
you seek? I and no one else?"

Strange noises sang from the Queen's throat. She
took a final step forward and grabbed Malye too
quickly for her to react. She lifted and twisted,
until she was holding Malye horizontally, straight
over her head. The Queen screamed then, a decidedly inhuman sound, and dashed the smaller
woman hard against the floor.

Malye groaned and did not attempt to rise.

"I surrender," the Queen said.

Wil McCarthy

THE FALL
OF SIRIUS

A ROC BOOK

ROC
Published by the Penguin Group
Penguin Books USA Inc., 375 Hudson Street,
New York, New York 10014, U.S.A.
Penguin Books Ltd, 27 Wrights Lane,
London W8 5TZ, England
Penguin Books Australia Ltd,
Ringwood, Victoria, Australia
Penguin Books Canada Ltd, 10 Alcorn Avenue,
Toronto, Ontario, Canada M4V 3B2
Penguin Books (N.Z.) Ltd, 182-190 Wairau Road,
Auckland 10, New Zealand

Penguin Books Ltd, Registered Offices:
Harmondsworth, Middlesex, England

First published by Roc, an imprint of Dutton Signet,
a division of Penguin Books USA Inc.

First Printing, September, 1996
10 9 8 7 6 5 4 3 2 1

ROC REGISTERED TRADEMARK—MARCA REGISTRADA
Printed in the United States of America

To Alec Perry,
who will spend his whole life in the future

ACKNOWLEDGMENTS

No book comes into being without assistance. To all the staff at Penguin Books whom I've never met, I offer my gratitude. I would also like to thank J. Storrs Hall for his foggy ideas about nano-technology, Shawna McCarthy and Amy Stout for helping this project to exist at all, NCWW for helping me start, and the Edge Club for helping me finish. Thanks also to Richard Lourie for his book *Hunting the Devil*, and especially to Sean Stewart, whose energetic feedback came at just the right time. And as always, thanks to Cathy for soldiering on. Love you, babe.

KEY TO
SIRIAN CHARACTER NAMES

In the Standard language as employed by colonists of the interstitial era, all vowels are sounded, with pronunciation as follows: *u* as in *chute,* *o* as in *rose,* *i* as in *pita,* *e* as in *kept,* and *a* as in *wall.*

Proper names ending in *e* are feminine; all others are masculine. A silent apostrophe may be employed where spelling cues would otherwise be ambiguous or misleading.

Characters are typically referred to by first name and patronym, by diminutive, or by full name. Thus, "Malyene Andreivne (mal-YEH-neh an-DREH-eev-neh, i.e., Malyene: daughter of Andrei), "Malye" (MAL-yeh), and "Colonel Malyene Andreivne Kurosov'e" (i.e., born or married into the House Kurosov) all refer to the same person.

HUMAN SPACE
circa 5000 A.D.

RELATIVE DISTANCES IN LIGHT-YEARS

	Sol	Kent	Barne	Wolf	Lande	Gate	Lute	Hasha
Sol	0.0	4.1	4.9	7.7	7.4	8.6	9.2	9.5
Kent	4.1	0.0	6.1	8.0	9.3	9.6	10.7	7.7
Barne	4.9	6.1	0.0	9.9	9.1	13.5	12.1	6.6
Wolf	7.7	8.0	9.9	0.0	3.5	9.2	16.1	14.5
Lande	7.4	9.3	9.1	3.5	0.0	10.2	15.8	14.8
Gate	8.6	9.6	13.5	9.2	10.2	0.0	10.9	17.0
Lute	9.2	10.7	12.1	16.1	15.8	10.9	0.0	13.4
Hasha	9.5	7.7	6.6	14.5	14.8	17.0	13.4	0.0

GATE SYSTEM (SIRIUS)
circa 5000 A.D.

". . . They come from Orion, from the *waist* of Orion . . . radiant phenomenon is now identified as a propulsive maneuver involving a large number of . . .

". . . Moved in on the second planet at approximately oh-seven hundred . . . The lunar surfaces are almost completely devastated. . . . Heard nothing from the Lesser Worlds in almost two days. Look, you probably know all this. You damn well should know all of this. I can't be the only one transmitting.

". . . Can't even *think* how many people have died. *Everyone* is dead, do you hear me? The whole damn colony is dead." <strained laughter> "The question has been answered, yes? The Waisters are—yes damn it—a hostile force. It's . . .

"I have to get below the surface now, but listen to me: Sirius has fallen. We are beaten, we are utterly smashed. I am Pavel Gremov, Entertainment Twelve, signing off. I repeat, Sirius has fallen . . ."

——Sirius System, Final Transmission
DCN 5328-551-5327-1839AR
(Courtesy of the Uriel Archive)
Keywords: <see index>

Chapter 1

The first thing the monster saw when she opened her eyes was a man leaning over her. Blurry, doubled—her vision refusing to focus—and viewed also through the frosted, transparent arch above her. She lay naked before him in a coffin of glass.

I'm freezing, she thought, but right away she knew that was wrong. She remembered where she was, remembered that she was in fact *un*freezing.

Shapes and colors sang across her tongue.

With a pneumatic pop and hiss, the coffin lid rose.

She vomited clear gel. Attempting to speak, she vomited again.

"Rellaxu," she heard the man say. *"Paniku nin. Thest nin dangeris."*

"My children," she finally managed to say. Her voice a yellow croak, the sound like bubbles rising in oil. And desperate. "My *children.*"

"Standard, late interstitial," the man said to someone behind him, out of view. He spoke without turning, his breath warm in her face, smelling of nothing, of the hibernation jelly still clogging her nostrils. "Congratulations; dating appears consistent."

"My children! Elle, Vadim," she pleaded. "How?" Too weak to rise, her limbs soft as noodles. Brain refusing her orders, still cold. *How are my children, please?*

The man loomed over her, spinning off colors like music at high volume. "Deep cryostasis, madam, and the machinery is old. What can I tell you?"

Another voice, from somewhere behind him: "Indications are positive, madam; there are ten bodies here, two of them children, and so far as we can determine, all of them appear safe."

Oh, Ialah. Thank you, in all your names.

Relaxing, she blinked her eyes.

The world oozed into focus, her eyes finally clearing away the gel that had fouled them.

The face above her looked much too broad at its top, much too narrow underneath, the mouth tiny, as if tooth-less. She thought this an illusion at first, but as he pulled away she noticed the eyes, staring back at her like blank copper mirrors, without iris or pupil or other visible de-tail. His hair was green, and very short, and clinging in strange patterns to his scalp. Another figure came up be-hind him, also green-haired, clad in strange, soft garments and moving in a ripply, loose-boned gait no more human than the canter of a horse. Their skins were gray-blue, their limbs unnaturally long.

"Names of Ialah," she croaked, "we lost the war."

The two figures exchanged knowing smiles, and in a moment the cryostasis ward echoed with their laughter.

"You remember the war, then?" the nearer man said to her eventually. He spoke carefully, as if Standard were a language well-known to him, memorized though not of-ten employed. "We hoped you might; it seems our risk in-vestment has been a wise one. But a long time has passed, much longer than you perhaps suspect. The war is over, the Waisters long gone."

"Wh . . . wh . . ." Where? How?

Who are you, she wanted to know. What's happened here? How did the war end, and how long ago? Her blood, still cold, felt as if it would never warm again. No green-haired people had dwelt in Sirius system, in her time or before. Nor elsewhere in human space, so far as she knew.

"We are as human as you," the man assured her, his copper eyes glittering.

And the monster knew right then and there that he was lying, and that he was *comfortable* lying, and that the truth would be a difficult thing to get out of him. But not impossible, no.

She favored him with as steady a gaze as she could muster. Cleared her throat, still slick with gel. "My name is Malyene Andreivne. With whom am I speaking?

Plainly, you are not Waisters, but what you *are* I cannot guess."

Her forwardness seemed to catch them off guard. They exchanged glances.

"In your language I would be called Crow," the nearer man said carefully. He nodded his head at the other. "This one is Plate."

She held his gaze.

Held it until he spoke again: "We're from Finders ring, Wende's six, both of us Workers. The Gate colony has . . ." He stopped, blinked. Forced a smile. "Let us not be hasty. There is much you do not know—"

"But I *will* know it," she told him. Shivering, she tightened her back muscles, hauled her nude, numb body upright. Cool slime ran off her in rivers. Her eyes held them both. Few secrets could be kept from her, had ever been kept from her, for she was Colonel Malyene Andreivne Kurosov'e of Central Investigations.

The monster.

She swung her head around in a slow, purposeful arc, taking in everything. The cryostasis ward had scarcely changed, its dozen coffins inclined, as ever, against the spinward wall. Equipment lockers all around, dead light fixtures above, a floor of bare, textured metal. But: three spheres of hazy white light hung motionless in the air, connected to nothing and yet providing illumination, and the wall which should contain the exit hatch had been replaced with a gray-white . . . membrane, it looked like.

The two men had begun to get upset, she noted. Not angry, precisely, and not intimidated either, but she had the sense that they were distracted, annoyed, finding her less convenient than they'd expected. Convenient for what?

"How long have you been at Sirius?" she demanded.

Crow frowned with his tiny mouth. "Sirius? Ah. We, that is, our people, arrived here some sixty essey past. Sixty Earth standard years, I should say. But, madam, this star system has been called Gate for over two millennia."

Malye froze. Two millennia?

Barely an hour seemed to have passed. Into the coffin, and then the choking fluid and the awful cold for a while, and then the awakening . . . *A few weeks,* she'd thought, *they'll come for us in a few weeks if they come for us at all.* Names of Ialah, two thousand *years*?

"I expect this comes as a shock," Plate told her gravely. He held a red, glittery, translucent object in his hand, like an eyeball-size ruby or a piece of cut glass, and as he spoke he pressed this against the side of his head, and then withdrew it.

"My people?" Malye asked, feeling faint, resisting the urge to lie back again in the inclined coffin and ignore all this.

Crow looked troubled, hesitant. His bedside manner nonexistent, but at least he had the good grace to be embarrassed about it. "Madam, the Sirius colony was destroyed, and was quite empty when we arrived. Until we located this facility fifty months ago, it had always been assumed there were no survivors at all."

"There are a billion people in this system," she protested. "Were. A billion people. Two planets' moons crawling with people, and a thousand hollow rocks. . . . It was a *thriving civilization*."

"Yes," Crow agreed. "Waisters are very thorough."

Oh, Ialah. Grigory, her husband, twenty centuries in his grave? Along with her whole world, yes, along with all the worlds of Sirius? She had somehow saved herself, and Elle, and Vadim. Had no one else managed to save anything? *Damn* them, damn them all!

"Madam," Plate said, "we have awakened you in the hope that you can assist us. You're an eyewitness to something we can only conjecture at. You have seen the Waisters in confrontation."

"I never saw them," she said.

"But you saw how they behaved? You know the sequence of events? The Fall of Sirius is a matter of no small importance to us."

Her eyes narrowed. The colors in the room began once more to sing. They were holding something back, still.

"Tell me why you need my help," she commanded.

Crow put a hand to his brow, looking deeply troubled, looking . . . scared? "Because, madam, the Waisters have returned. An armada of at least seventy large ships, not responding to any attempts at communication. They will be in system just over a hundred hours from now."

The world swam, shimmered. "Oh. Oh, I see. Yes, well, I will do what I can to help you, of course."

Of course.

Only now did the monster think to cry.

Chapter 2

**TYUMEN, SIRIUS SYSTEM:
JANURY 29, YEAR OF OUR LORD 3125**

They swept through the crowd like ghosts, the three of
them: Malyene and her staff, come to cleanse yet another
world, to locate and haul away the very worst of its garbage. The ferry port's exit spilled out into a vast, illuminated cavern, the crowd flowing out like water across the
floor of it. Nobody looking up around them at the great
Atrium of Tyumen, whose floor and ceiling were separated by no less than a kilometer. Nobody except Malye's
staff.

"I just don't see why Fraud gets a higher travel allow-
ance than we do," Elye was saying, her eyes everywhere
except on the causeway in front of her. "I mean, yes, they
have more people, but it's not like the local greenbars are
helpless without their *physical presence*."

"We're lucky to get anything at all," Kromov agreed,
chuckling as he took in the view. "Next year they'll
probably just ask us to put a sign out: VIOLENT CRIMI-
NALS, PLEASE SURRENDER HERE."

"That's enough," Malye told them both. Tyumen's
architecture, even what little of it they'd seen since de-
barking from the ferry, had put her staff in an expansive
mood, from which they had difficulty focusing on their
own jobs and must, of necessity, discuss everyone else's.
The Atrium *was* impressive, mammoth pillars alternating
with shafts of white light along an avenue wide and long
enough to hold an entire city, easing upward in the distance so very gradually that it was easy to forget this was
a spin-gee world at all. The Tyumenae certainly knew
how to build.

But Tyumen was the eighth largest of the Thousand

Lesser Worlds, a hollow planetoid crammed pole-to-pole with wonders, and gawking at the view would be a poor habit to develop, one that would certainly not get Kiril Gostev into custody any sooner. And anyway, right now they were late.

"Solzehn has cleared an office for us," Malye reminded the two. "If we miss this tube and arrive after he's gone off shift, you will neither of you have liberty tonight. I hope this is clear."

"As vacuum," Kromov assured her.

Alas, Malye herself was fighting a distraction of a different sort, an uneasy feeling she could not quite dispel. Her husband, Grigory, had been acting peculiarly these past few days, pacing and muttering and generally showing signs of an anxiety to which he was not accustomed. *Something is going to happen,* he'd said mysteriously, but had refused further comment. Something good? Something bad? Grigory managed a group of astrometers and chronicians, well-known and respected within their field; could he be facing a promotion, or a transfer, or perhaps something less pleasant? She wasn't going to interrogate him over it, not her own husband, but how had this distance between them arisen? Slowly, quietly, as if their two worlds were not on the same orbit after all. She wished he'd confided in her before she was called away.

The tube station now ahead of them appeared far less elaborate than the ferry dock, really just a track and a platform and a blue-tiled tunnel mouth in the wall there, matching another tiled and arched opening just barely visible on the antispinward wall at the far end of this grand, curved, columned avenue. The tube and ferry stations stared right across at one another, barely six hundred meters apart, and so Malye and her staff moved perpendicular to the main flow of pedestrian traffic, across the avenue rather than along it.

But the crowd was light, and they moved through it swiftly, not hurrying but striding beam-straight through the path their burgundy uniforms cleared ahead of them. *C.I. top silver, get out of the way.* No one would wish to be the cause of their inconvenience.

As if the monster could actually *do* anything to them, write a ticket or issue a summons. As if she would waste the time, if she could. As if they mattered to her at all, these ordinary citizens on their ordinary errands. Well, as a public to be protected, yes, but if Malye and her assistants were running late, it was their own damn problem, yes?

Still, these were peaceful people, unaccustomed to physical, personal manifestations of Authority. To them, law enforcement meant greenbars to shoo loiterers out of the shops, and Central Investigators meant . . . something else. That there was trouble, danger. That they should get the hell out of the way. Though occasionally embarrassing, the mystique was useful, and for this reason Malye encouraged her people to encourage it. Fear was not a tool she liked to be without.

Their train lay just ahead, and the crowd parted away from the train's nearest door, which slid open for them as if equally cowed. They boarded and found seats at the rear of the car, against the aft bulkhead, as far as possible from the curtained enclosure of the shitter at the car's front. Generally, nobody liked to sit near the shitter, preferring to avoid the smell and the traffic, but they liked sitting by Central Investigators still less—Malye and her staff had the rear half of the car almost to themselves. Those passengers who sat nearby cast furtive glances at them, obviously wondering: *what's wrong, what's going on?* The burgundy uniforms, so rare in their experience, at once drawing their attention and repelling it, like the scene of a nasty accident. In this case, an accident that had perhaps not yet occurred.

Just wait, citizens.

"We could have boosted directly to the capital," Elye said. They could have, she meant, if they'd had the budget. Ah, Major Elyene Izacne Boltsev'e, always ready and willing to state the obvious. In police work that could occasionally be a useful habit, but here on the tube it was simply annoying.

"Yes," Malye told her quietly. "And we would have missed this view, which has so enthralled you. Comport yourself as befits your station, please."

"Yes, Colonel," Elyene said, doing a poor job of hiding her smile.

Silently, the doors slid closed, and the great Atrium of Tyumen began to move outside their windows, the huge columns sliding past, one by one. The acceleration, mild at first, climbed rapidly, until the columns were racing by, and then flashing, and then flickering in a steady blur. Malye began to feel lighter in her seat, and then lighter still, centripetal gravity partly canceled as the train shot faster and faster around Tyumen's outer circumference, against the direction of its spin.

Outer space is barely twenty meters below us here, Malye reminded herself. For all the vastness of the Atrium, it was hollow as an eggshell. All of Tyumen was hollow, full of bubbles and voids and further hollowed by the engineers and architects who had made it a place for humans. It didn't bother her, exactly, but she preferred her worlds a little more solid.

The antispinward wall appeared huge ahead of them, and closing with alarming, deadly swiftness, the tunnel mouth invisible from this angle; it looked as if they would simply crash into the wall and die instantly. But then suddenly they were through it, the wall and the Atrium gone, all scenery vanished, replaced by smooth tunnel walls that whizzed blankly by with unguessable and rapidly mounting velocity.

"Have you no sense of play whatever, Malyene Andreivne?" Kromov wanted to know.

"Yes," she said to him in serious tones, "I have."

Kromov mused, stroking his chin and squinting at her. "Strange how we never see it. One has to wonder how your children came to be."

Elye laughed hard at that, quickly joined by Kromov himself. A few passengers turned to look.

Malye felt her ears and face warming. These Investigators, so jovial ... Two of her very finest; could they really be so blind? *You know not whom you taunt,* she thought at them with a kind of weary desperation. Indeed, despite long acquaintance they knew almost nothing of her. That Andrei Brakanov was her father? The fact had been well concealed. Elye and Kromov meant well enough; really they just wanted to be friendly, to draw her out, to tease her from her hard shell. Names of Ialah, should she give them what they so obviously wanted? Show them her sharp, vivid sense of play, so very like her father's?

No, never. The thought rolled through her in blue,

pointed waves. The train's ceiling lights played like soft music, vaguely heard.

Synesthesia. Sensory crossover, stress-induced but hereditary, somehow, at its source. *Smell the colors, little Malye, hear the shapes!* One of many marks of the beast, so very like her father.

"You forget yourselves, Majors," she said icily. Which of course only made them laugh all the harder, the peaks of their voices striking her between the eyes like pellets of hard plastic.

Later, when they'd arrived at their destination and the proper introductions had been made, Malye sat down at her new desk. Acquainting herself with the look and feel of it, allowing it to become hers, though the glass-walled office itself would of course be shared by Kromov and Elye.

Setting up in a new location was always inconvenient, for all that they did it five or ten times in a year. Becoming familiar with the equipment, with the layout of the building, with the local data systems architecture . . . But such was necessary, if Malye's people were to do their jobs.

Names of Ialah, there had been *seventeen murders* in Sirius system in the last standard year, up two from the year before, and only half the perpetrators had yet been caught. Eight cases still open, and there was the holdover from last year, the beating death for which no motive or suspect had ever been identified. Minimal DNA traces at the scene, and no lineup to match them against . . . It had been the very worst sort of crime—a random one, insoluble unless it were repeated. Possibly, many times.

The very thought sickened her, filled her with outrage. It was fortunately the only such incident on her record, but a blot nonetheless. And a reminder, most unwelcome, of days gone by.

"We won't be long here in Tyumen," Elye said to her with a solid, reassuring tone that suggested some awareness of Malye's mood. "To survive, Gostev must eventually earn some money. Or steal it. Either way, he freshens his trail for us."

"We'll get that bastard, no question." Kromov took an inventory flatscreen from one of the local greenbars, thumbed its approval square, handed it back. Nodding his thanks, the greenbar left the office and strode out onto the station floor to complete the errands from which he'd been interrupted.

Malye watched him for a few seconds through the glass wall. Tempered silicon glass, she'd been told, transparent as vacuum but not so tough as the metallic glasses with which she was more familiar. But tough enough, the greenbars had assured her—no amount of carelessness was likely to shatter it.

Alas, someone had scrawled an image of Skato, the shitting boy, in black ink upon the glass. A simple enough graffito, just four lines and four half circles, and yet the image was unmistakable: a little boy, grinning and nude, squatting to relieve himself on Malye's new desk. This was vexing, but not really all that remarkable—over a hundred years old now, Skato was one of the most popular unifying elements of Sirian culture, his picture adorning the trains and shops and corridors and offices of all but the most conservative of worlds. Malye had never seen much humor in this, but she saw little harm in it, either. She would probably leave the graffito alone, as a gesture of goodwill toward her current hosts.

As such things went, Malye supposed these accommodations were at least adequate. The furnishings had seen better days, probably as long ago as Malye's childhood, but they seemed sturdy and comfortable just the same. Mostly titanium-iron, she thought, hard and light and smoothly contoured, the desks and chairs looking like plated cushions and mushrooms. Lighting was indirect and very bright, and bluer than most people liked it, though it suited her well enough. Less like the light of Sol, which she had never seen, than that of Bee, the smaller of Sirius system's two stars, around which the Thousand Lesser Worlds orbited. A homey, familiar light, not unpleasant in the least.

The police station itself was a large one, an actual *building* huddled among several other large buildings inside this particular hollow and very large cavern. Like a bunch of privacy booths standing together, it seemed to Malye, rather than the tunneled-out spaces you'd find on most other worlds. And the staff here had proved focused and professional and had so far showed no overt signs of corruption or incompetence. Nor of the resentment that so often plagued Central Investigators when they were obliged to take over a case from the greenbars—because of the six-week deadline, usually, though in this case it was because the suspect had fled his home jurisdiction, seeking shelter and anonymity in the vastness of Tyumen. As if that could save him, somehow. But the suspect had committed no crimes here, had engaged in no public activity of any sort, and perhaps that helped the greenbars see things in proper perspective. Here were outsiders in pursuit of one of their own, and apparently welcome to him.

"I should call my family before the shift is over," Malye said. "Kromov, would you hand me that holie, please?"

He did so, letting a smile peek out under his mustache. "Be careful. They may think you have a heart beating in there somewhere."

"Oh, I have," she assured him. She felt it beating fiercely within her even now, like a violent prisoner she could barely restrain. So like her father's heart.

Taking the flatscreen from Kromov, she traced and thumbed an ID sequence, and requested a slot in the transmission queue, priority personal.

"Grigory," she said into the blank screen, "it's me. I wanted to remind you that Elle and Vad have a teacher conference tomorrow. Please send along my regrets. I hope you all are well."

Damn all this travel, anyway. Elle's last teacher had been a real bastard, singling her out for all sorts of petty mistreatment, sending her home in tears, day after day. Grig and Malye had filed the appropriate complaints, and later she'd gone to have a word with the man in person. Now they were looking for a replacement, but Elle was terrified of teachers in general. And her needs were so different from Vadim's . . .

Malye cut the link, returned the flatscreen to its prior configuration, and handed it back to Kromov.

"Touching," he said.

Malye smiled and turned away, busying herself with the straightening up of her desk. She could glare Kromov to silence if she wished, or strike back at him with calculated viciousness. With a little time and a little effort she could reduce him to tears, probing for his weaknesses and then jabbing them over and over, but what good would come of that? The monster's first rule: it costs nothing to be civil.

The flatscreen beeped, announcing an incoming message. Malye looked up.

"Your beloved's reply," Kromov said, glancing at the screen and handing it to her.

"Huh." Pinega was nearly half a light-minute away. To reply so quickly, Grigory must have been poised and ready to transmit, as if he'd been waiting eagerly for her to call. Could he be ready at last to divulge his news?

When the proper validations were complete, the holie screen acquired depth and color in her hands, like a window into another place. Her bedroom, in this case, with Grigory sitting on the edge of the bed, politely holding his flatscreen out to let it record a good view of him. His youthful handsomeness had begun to fade recently, not due to any physical deterioration, Malye thought, but more likely the cumulative stress of dealing day in and day out with *her*. Not the finest of marriages, theirs. But just now he was grinning broadly, looking more animated than she'd seen him in a good long while.

"Malye! It's good you called; I wasn't sure how to get ahold of you. I have news, finally! Do you remember that massive gamma ray burster my people recorded thirteen months ago? They couldn't explain its intensity or its duration, or anything else about it. Parallax measurements hinted that perhaps the origin was close, perhaps within as little as ten light-years, which of course would mean that it wasn't a gamma ray burster at all. Well, we've all been thinking hard about it, and now it seems we have an answer.

"The phenomenon was caused by a deliberate emission of coherent gamma rays, possibly propulsive in nature. We have a repeat occurrence now, much smaller and closer than the last, and in precisely the same region of sky—the waist of Orion. For practical purposes, the proper motion of the phenomenon is zero."

He paused, looking excited. In keeping with his job, Grigory often came home with stories like this one, obscure astronomical events that had happened long ago and far away, their light only now reaching Sirian telescopes.

She had always envied him the easy passion for his work, but had rarely shared his enthusiasm. But . . . this particular case seemed different. At least *he* seemed to think so. Was this his great secret? The point of it eluded her.

"Malye," Grigory said with all possible earnestness, "they are spacecraft. Hundreds of them, heading directly toward Sirius at approximately ninety percent of the speed of light. They haven't come from human space, not from anywhere *near* human space. The closest star along their velocity vector is Alnilam, over twelve hundred light-years away."

He paused again, looking giddily unable to contain himself.

"They cannot possibly be human!" he cried out finally. "We are being *visited* by a *nonhuman* intelligence! This changes everything, Malye. Please call me when you can."

His image vanished, a blank screen replacing once more the view of the bedroom she and Grigory shared.

She sighed loudly. Alien spacecraft. Ah. A veritable dream come true for the Ministry of Celestial Observations, and all its satellite organizations. She called up the transmission queue again, traced the RECORD MESSAGE symbols. The flatscreen beeped its readiness.

"Grigory," she said into it, "I have no time for jokes. I will speak with you in a few days."

She terminated the recording, shipped it, and sighed again. Looking up, she found both Elye and Kromov gaping at her as if she'd done some horrible thing.

"I think he was serious," Elye said. "Your husband, he doesn't kid around much."

"You have crushed the sense of humor right out of him," Kromov agreed, wide-eyed and chewing at his mustache. "Fearing your icy disdain, he would not joke about something like this. That is, I believe he wouldn't. Names of Ialah, if this is true . . . I suppose everything will change. Literally everything."

"Crap," Malye said. "It means nothing. They've made some sort of mistake, is all. They're always looking for aliens, looking for origins, looking for the footprints of Ialah out there among the stars. My husband's colleagues are . . . very excitable. Now, about Gostev's—"

"Yes, but what if they're not mistaken?" Kromov demanded of her. "What, then?"

Malye cooled him off with her gaze. "We have a job to do here, Major; a murderer is running free in this relatively innocent world. If Grigory's people are not mistaken, well, however amazing that may be, it will not bring Kiril Gostev to justice. Only *we* can do that."

"Have you no heart at all?" he marveled. He was looking at her almost as though she were a stranger now. How close to the truth he was.

"Yes, I have," she said to him, "and it bleeds at the thought of Utako's family wringing their hands in despair and frustration, their loss unavenged. Majors, we must catch this man before he causes any additional harm. We must let nothing distract us from this goal. This much should be obvious."

The two had nothing to say to that, and they wouldn't meet her eyes. Perhaps, she thought, there *was* something a little odd in her reaction. But damn it, what would they have her do? Let Gostev run around as he pleased?

A greenbar came skidding into the room, his face bright and alive with excitement. "Colonel! Majors! Names of Ialah, have you heard the *news*?"

Chapter 3

213::15
PINEGA, GATE SYSTEM:
CONTINUITY 5218, YEAR OF THE DRAGON

Malye had seen dogs before, not in person but on holies and such. Vicious or friendly, trained or naive, she had an idea they were fairly stupid, fairly emotional creatures. So why did this one, this smooth, hairless animal that had oozed through the white membrane-wall and into the remains of the cryostasis ward, eye her with such a calm, appraising air? Its head bobbed, its glance flicking here and there, taking the measure of her. Neither vicious nor friendly, nor the least bit stupid. It approached, not wagging its tail, and stopped at a cautious two meters' distance. Sniffed the air.

"Nice doggie," Malye tried, holding out a clenched fist for it to smell. Stiff and ancient, the fabric of her scavenged uniform cracked at the elbow.

"She doesn't speak your language," Plate said.

Malye blinked. She had not supposed the animal could speak any language at all. Presently, it opened its mouth and . . . fluted at her. Its voice sounded like some peculiar, breathy instrument, not quite like anything she'd ever heard before. And yet the tones were modulated, the dog's lips and throat working purposefully around them to produce . . . speech?

Her skin went cold. "Is it speaking Waister?"

"Of course," Plate said beside her.

She rounded on him. "What do you mean, 'of course?' All this innuendo, these veiled comments. What exactly are you people up to?"

Plate looked surprised, his copper eyes widening more than a human being's would. "It's nothing sinister, madam. We're good with languages—Teigo, Standard,

English, Latin, a few others ... but it's *their* language we speak among ourselves. We live in imitation of the Waisters, the better to understand them. Four sexes, two brains. ... They and humanity differ greatly; we attempt to occupy the center."

And that was not sinister? Malye shuddered, but she kept her eyes locked on Plate's, searching for the telltale traces of falsehood. "They slaughtered us without comment, never once responding to our signals. Cold, evil, uncommunicative. How do you know their language?"

"From corpses," Plate replied. "And from prisoners. A long time ago, during the infarct in Sol system, a single ship was captured outside the orbit of Saturn."

"I don't believe you," Malye said. Those ships had been seven kilometers long, seemingly limitless in their power and their weaponry. Even one of them, she was certain, would have been enough to bring the Sirius colony down.

The green-haired man simply shrugged. "It's true. Wolf system had an ansible station up and transmitting at the time of its destruction, so Sol and Lalande had nearly a decade's warning before the Waisters finally arrived. Radio signals from Sirius were not received until years later. Pity there was no ansible here."

"It was never finished. Too expensive," Malye said. Feeling dizzy, the sound of Plate's voice spinning through her like a string of tiny whirlwinds, she placed a hand against one of the coffins to steady herself. "Names, how did the war end? How could we possibly have won?"

"It wasn't won or lost, it was ... completed. It's difficult to explain. Waisters have ... a strong emotional response to new stimuli, things that haven't been, well, *tested.* But Sol system finally rolled over and surrendered, and that was the end of the war. That was all the Waisters wanted to hear."

"Until now," Malye said, her monster's heart beating with slow fear.

"Yes, until now. We don't have any idea what they want this time, why they're coming back. By our understanding of Waister psychology, it simply can't be explained."

A thought struck Malye in high, piercing notes. Her eyes narrowed, locked on the too-angular face of this

green-haired man of the future. "You say you imitate
their lifestyle, yes? Their language, their thoughts. How
do *you* feel about strangers, my friend?"

Plate locked gazes with her for a moment, and then
looked away, his expression unreadable. "I am only a
Worker," he said.

"That's one of your four sexes," Malye probed, not
quite guessing, but feeling her way by intuition.

Plate didn't deny it.

"What are the others?" she asked. "Dogs?"

"Yes. And Queens, one for each family unit. Two
Workers, two Drones, and a Dog. We call it a 'six.'"

Specialized, like insects? Was that how the Waisters
lived? In her usual manner she filtered Plate's words,
mixed them with her own observations and speculations
to formulate testable hypotheses. The Dog was smart—it
could speak, but of course it had no hands. The Dog
could not by itself do any useful work. It was not a
Worker, but Plate and Crow, who *were,* had been sent
here to wake Malye up from her long sleep. By their
Queen . . .

"It isn't your job to get angry with me, to *test* me," she
said, feeding her hypothesis back to him to gauge his reaction. "We are not arm wrestling, you and I—no domi-
nance games. I take it that is someone else's job?"

Plate looked offended, his copper eyes glaring blankly.
"You owe us your life, madam. There is no reason to be
rude."

"Am I a prisoner?" she asked calmly. *Do you have any
idea who you're dealing with?*

"No. Madam, we simply need your help."

"How fortunate for us," she observed, casting a glance
along the row of glass coffins and the nude, frozen
corpses within. "How long might we have stayed here,
otherwise?"

"Our resources are finite. We cannot simply—"

There was a rippling in the white membrane that had
replaced the north wall, and presently a human figure
stepped through it as if through a curtain. Crow. The
membrane closed behind him without, Malye thought,
the inside and outside atmospheres ever coming in contact.

Crow had a bundle of cloth in his arms, which he

dropped to the floor, save for a single strip he held out in both hands. "Will this suffice, madam?"

She stepped closer to examine it. Thin, flat, textured-looking, with bumps and ridges forming strange, bas-relief patterns.

"This is a towel?" she asked.

"It will serve as one," Crow replied, a little testily. "The fabric is soft, and extremely absorbent."

"You don't bathe?" she asked. Not so much a question as an insult, and right away she regretted it. But the two men, these "Workers," seemed not to take offense in the ways she would expect.

"Our skins do not serve an excretory function," Plate explained calmly, "and we do take care not to sully them with environmental contaminants. It's nothing you need trouble yourself about."

You, who had claimed to be human, she thought.

"I see," she said. "And robes? Have you brought those, as well?"

Crow nodded. "As you requested, madam. And one for you, as well."

They had given back her old C.I. uniform, taken from the locker where it had lain for two millennia. The black and burgundy garments, surprisingly durable, had passed the years with little change in appearance, but they had grown stiff, and if she wore them for another hour they would crack and fall away like shed skin, leaving her chafed and itchy and naked for her trouble.

"Thank you," she said. She turned back to the coffins. "I'll change in a little while. I'm impatient to begin. This one and that one"—she pointed—"are familiar with the cryostasis equipment. They helped me before, and either of them should be better able than we three to revive the others, should complications arise."

"Others?" Crow sounded puzzled. "These two appear healthy, and your two children, but the other cryogens are all sick or injured."

"Awaiting treatment, probably," Malye said. "The hospital facilities here are small. *Were,* I mean. Complex treatments sometimes had to wait. But I suppose you can treat them fairly easily."

"You do? Why?"

Because you are from the future, she did not say.

Because in the future all problems are solved, all squabbling and selfishness put aside. What a puny, stupid thought. Already, she knew that was not so.

"You cannot, then?" she asked, turning and looking at the two of them, their strange faces and bodies.

Crow made a gesture of exaggerated helplessness. "If they were of any use to us, I'm sure some arrangement could be made. But, madam, please understand, we do not have the leisure to play at medicine. Our business in this world is of the utmost urgency and transience. We will not remain here much longer."

Anger clawed suddenly inside her, seeking escape. She contained it, forced herself to reason. She would not willingly revive Elle and Vadim to face another Waister assault. That would be madness. But neither would she abandon them, nor allow herself to be abandoned here with them. If Crow's people were leaving, then Malye's children would be right at their sides, enjoying the highest possible degree of protection. Carefully, she said, "I require my children, Crow. And so, I think, do you; they are witnesses to the attack, as much as I am."

Witnesses to the inside of a rescue ball, for the most part, but these men didn't have to know that. Ialah, she felt so alone here! It all still felt very much like a dream, but even dreams could be frightening. She felt an almost pathological need to *talk* to someone, to verify that all this was really happening. And of course, she wanted her children safe and warm in her arms. What mother did not want that?

"We can speak to the Queen about it," Plate said, gently enough, the red jewel once again in his hand. A communication device? He pressed it to his head, paused a moment, then withdrew it and continued, "Certainly, your children will come to no harm in their present circumstances, and I think you will concede that the older witnesses, these two healthy males who lived through the war as you did, are much more important to us at this moment."

Malye conceded no such thing, but could think of no reply that would make her sound anything but ungrateful and petty. Perhaps she was in these men's power, after all, not a prisoner but a *debtor* who could never repay her debt. Not unless she did whatever it was they had revived her for.

"All right, then, let's get to it," she said finally.

A gasp, a gurgling scream, a labored attempt to breathe around all the cold, clear fluid. Coughing, vomiting, the young man opened his eyes.

"You," he rasped when he had his breath. His tone was full of accusation, his eyes attempting to focus not on Malye's face, but on the collar of her C.I. uniform. ALEKSANDR PETROVOT TOPURI, said the coffin's faded label in hurried, hand-drawn letters.

"Good morning, Sasha," Malye said, guessing that that was what this man's friends would call him. Not Alek, probably, and certainly not Aleksa.

"You lied to me," he gurgled. "You weren't supposed to be here."

"Take deep, slow breaths," she advised. "You have no idea how glad I am to see you."

He flared. "Don't you tell me how to do my job, lady. Don't—" The words disintegrated into a coughing fit.

"You may want this," Malye said, handing him one of the strange, thin towels. He took it.

What to say to him now? That his world was destroyed, and all the other worlds with it? That everything he'd known was two thousand years gone? How could such a thing be told gently? Not now, that was how—she needed Sasha Topuri to help her with the other coffin. She was a protector of citizens, after all, and damned if she'd let some equipment failure take the life of one of the handful of citizens she had left to protect.

"We are safe now," she said to him instead. She pointed back at Crow and Plate. "These people have come for us, Sasha. The Waisters are gone, and we are rescued."

"You lied to me," he spluttered again, now feebly toweling himself clean of the hibernation jelly.

Yes, okay, enough already. "We had no time to argue about it, Sasha. How long would the air have lasted? You might not be alive now, if not for me. Think about that while you say these things."

"Bitch."

At that, she finally took offense; her feelings of camaraderie fell away, her muscles suddenly tight and brittle as glass, and she hit him with a gaze like twin lasers. "Listen to me, sir: I make no apologies. If you feel I have wronged you in some way, take it to heart, and have a care that I do not wrong you again. There's work here for you, and I will see it done. Is that clear?"

Sasha looked back at her with wide eyes.

"Is that *clear*?" she repeated.

"Yes, Colonel," he said cautiously, his anger twisting up in visible folds of confusion, edged with fear.

"Thank you." She let her voice go soft. "When you are well enough, I have clothing for you."

"I'm well enough," he said, sitting up in the coffin.

"You recover quickly, Sasha. I'm impressed."

He said nothing, and so she handed him one of the robes Crow had brought, and watched him dress himself awkwardly. In a few minutes he was well enough to rise, which he did without complaint, though he wobbled.

"We must revive your companion next, that repairman," Malye said to him, casting a meaningful glance at Crow and Plate as she spoke, "but I am *told* we must leave the others alone for the time being."

"Alone? Even your precious children?" Sasha asked in a suspiciously polite voice.

She nodded, bristling inwardly. "Even my precious children, yes, for the time being. I will speak to the . . . authorities about it soon."

"Are you well enough to begin?" Plate asked, stepping forward as if to help. Malye held him back with a stern look: *we do not need your copper eyes and green hair upsetting him right now.*

Indeed, Sasha looked hard at the two men for the first time, and did not appear to like what he saw.

"A little time has passed," Malye said quickly. "These men are with a group you would not know. They are our rescuers, but they lack certain specialized knowledge regarding your cryo ward. You should be the one to operate the equipment, I'm sure you'll agree."

"They look so strange," he said, seeming a little more afraid.

"Yes," Malye agreed, "they really do, don't they?

I'll explain everything once the other man has been revived."

"Yes. Yes, of course." His eyes never left the two, until Malye waved a hand in his face, and pointed to one of the cryostasis coffins. VIKTOR SLAVANOVOT BRATSEV, said the crude name label.

Sasha stepped up to the coffin and activated its diagnostics. The equipment had weathered the centuries fairly well, Malye thought, but even so, only half the lights on the panel came on. Sasha frowned.

"Do you require any assistance?" Malye asked.

He shook his head. "No, no, I don't. But this equipment . . . has been damaged."

"That surprises you?" Malye asked, a bit sharply, thinking once again of her husband, of her friends. "The Waisters *damaged* a lot of things. Did you think this ward was inviolate?"

Sasha merely grunted, and began, hesitantly, to work the coffin's controls.

"We had quite a time with your own revival," she said, to mollify him and herself. "The printed instructions are not very helpful, if things are not working correctly."

He was shaking his head. "Not working correctly at *all*. The acoustic system appears to be damaged, and we can't very well revive him without that. If the backup unit is also damaged . . ." He turned, edged past Malye and the two "Workers," and began rummaging through the lockers on the antispinward wall. After a few moments he pulled out something that looked like four large suction cups joined by an X of black plastic. A flatscreen was attached at the center of the X, though, and other compact machinery beneath that.

"What is that thing?" Malye asked, partly to let him speak, to let him feel important, and partly because she was genuinely curious. She herself had never been suspended until . . . until *today*, she'd been thinking, but of course that was not right. At any rate, she knew little of the equipment and procedures that had apparently saved her life. Sasha's own revival had been mostly uneventful.

"Thermoacoustic coupler," he replied, moving back to the coffin and placing the contraption atop it, like a gigantic spider about to consume its sleeping prey.

"For heating?"

"And for cooling." Without looking up, he did things to the apparatus. Frowned more deeply. "Colonel, something is wrong; these batteries are completely dead. I'll have to run the unit off wall current."

Presently, he opened a small door beneath the flatscreen, withdrew a small plug at the end of a power cord. Unspooled it until it reached a socket on the wall.

"Why is the battery dead?" he asked, looking up fearfully at Malye. "The Waisters didn't do that." His gaze flicked down to his instruments and back up again. "This wall current is wrong, too. Wrong voltage, wrong frequency. Names of Ialah, why is your uniform falling off you in pieces?"

"A little time has passed," Malye admitted. "I'll explain when you've finished."

Sasha shook his head and went back to work, looking deeply troubled. He did something to the flatscreen, made it light up with a display of yellow numerals. The unit began to hum faintly.

"What is it you're trying to do?" Malye asked him.

He looked up at her. "This body is supercooled, vitrified like glass, not actually frozen at all. When we warm him, it must be very quickly and very evenly, to avoid thermal shock; because if his tissues crystallize, it will cause extensive cellular damage, which is difficult to repair. And if he cracks or shatters, well . . . We can hope he's lived a good life. This unit will induce a synchronized molecular vibration, and by adjusting the frequency we can warm every part of him simultaneously. A flash oven works on the same principle."

"Are you doing it now?"

"I am about to begin. I . . . need you to be quiet so I can listen for problems."

Sasha touched the flatscreen. Colors shifted across its display, and he touched it again. The ward was filled, suddenly, with low, rumbling noises that hurt Malye's teeth. The rumbling quickly became a loud hum, and then a whine. She cringed; Sasha's own coffin had made no such noises during his revival.

The effect on Viktor Slavanovot Bratsev's body was immediately apparent. Before, he had looked like a stiff manikin encased in a cylinder of transparent, vaguely blue-tinted plastic, but now the blue tint vanished, and the small bubbles surrounding him began to shiver, and then to rise. He was a rubber doll in thick, carbonated fluid. And then he was simply a naked man, drowned, violated here and there by tubes.

The fluid began to drain from the coffin. Sasha hurried around to the other side, leaned over to activate some control or other, came back up to check the half-lit diagnostic panel.

"How is he?" Malye asked with a bit more urgency than she'd intended.

"Normal, no vital signs," Sasha replied absently.

"He is dead?"

"For the moment, yes."

A green light flickered on the diagnostic display.

"We have neural activity."

Another light, and another. Sasha took the black X off the coffin and set it down gently on the floor, without once taking his eyes off the diagnostics.

"Let's see here ... cellular metabolism, transpiration ... the machine is ready to shock him ... Colonel, can I ask you to open the lid, please?"

Wordlessly, Malye stepped forward and pressed the appropriate button at the foot of the coffin. The glass hemicylinder popped and whispered up into the wall. The drowned man now lay beached in a shallow pool of slime.

"Here it comes," Sasha said.

The body jerked, spasmed, jerked again. Its chest began to heave. Malye could hear mechanical valves forcing air in through the throat tube, then sucking it back out again with wet, whistling sounds.

"And ... this patient is alive again. Ialah be praised."

The tubes withdrew, prompting gagging and retching sounds from the patient, who presently gasped and began to breathe on his own.

"Take it slowly," Sasha said to the man. "Stay relaxed. The warming process can be very unpleasant if you aren't prepared—"

The patient opened his eyes: brown, pupils hugely dilated. Unable to lift his head, he nonetheless turned it, looking around the room in dazed, sightless horror. Finally, he drew in a deep, gurgling breath, seeming to relax for a moment before he spread his lips wide and screamed.

Chapter 4

"Wait outside, please," Malye said to the greenbars guarding the interrogation room.

"I'm afraid we can't do that, Colonel," one of them said stiffly. "The suspect has repeatedly stated an intention to kill you, with his bare hands."

Malye counted the man's bars—three—and then looked up and offered him a relaxed not-quite-smile. "Sergeant, do you know how often I hear threats of that sort? I assure you, Gostev will not harm me. Is he manacled?"

The sergeant nodded.

"I'll need the key, then," Malye said, holding out her hand.

Both officers looked shocked. "Colonel, are you insane? I can't let you in there with an unrestrained prisoner. If anything happened, I'd be—"

No one else in all the worlds could glare like Andrei Brakanov's little girl. The sergeant flinched, shrank back into himself. "The key, please, Sergeant."

Reluctantly, the man dug in his pocket, produced a coin-size metal disk, and surrendered it to her. The look on his face suggested he considered this quite possibly the last act of his law enforcement career.

Malyene raised the flatscreen she'd been holding, spoke into it: "Let the record show I've ordered both guards to remain outside the room during interrogation procedures, and that I'm preparing to release Gostev's restraints. The guards have requested and received clarification of my orders, and are in full compliance."

The sergeant relaxed visibly, though he still looked far

from happy. "I hope your reputation is justified," he said. "Why haven't you at least brought your staff with you?"

She half smiled again. "They can't seem to think or speak of anything but the Waist of Orion and its supposed envoys, so I've ordered them to the nearest observation blister to watch the stars. When I spoke with them yesterday, they were very upset."

"Yes, Colonel," the sergeant agreed, his posture and tone straightening up again. "As we all are."

She inclined her head, as if in agreement. Six of the Waister ships had passed through Sirius system, slowing from nine-tenths lightspeed to only one tenth, but nonetheless looping a great, S-shaped course around the suns in only twenty hours, clearing the path ahead of themselves with blasts of coherent gamma and high-velocity dust. Unfortunately, the Lesser Worlds of Yessey and Ikarka had found themselves in that path, and had been destroyed, along with their thousand-odd inhabitants.

Grigory's very expensive messages to her had gone on about the incident for hours. Like everyone else, he'd expressed the hope that the destruction had been accidental, but from the Waisters themselves there had been no comment, no communication of any sort. "It's so damnably eerie," Grigory had said. "It's almost as if they were trying to frighten us."

Well, that might be, but unless the Waisters were formally charged with a violent crime, it was hardly the business of Central Investigations, nor of Malye herself. Kiril Mikhailovot Gostev's case remained her only assignment.

"Open the door, please, Sergeant."

"Yes, Colonel."

He slapped a control on the wall behind him, and the metal door eased back a few centimeters and then slid open.

The interrogation room was small and sparsely furnished, just a table and some chairs, all of bare metal, with Kiril Gostev sitting by the far wall, with his wrists firmly manacled to it. An expression of pure hatred graced his features, and he needed a shave and some time alone with a hairbrush.

Malye stepped inside. "Close the door, please, Sergeant."

An uncomfortable pause, and then: "Yes, Colonel."

The door sighed closed behind her.

"Good afternoon, Kiril Mikhailovot," she said brightly. "My name is Malyene. I'm going to ask you a few questions."

His eyes smoldered. "I know who you are."

Malye doubted that very much, but when she spoke, her voice was kind. "I understand you are angry with me for some reason, and have made some threats against me." She waited, and went on. "I've already arranged to move your family into protective custody, and I've taken steps toward giving them a new identity, and a stipend to replace your lost salary. They will not suffer because of your illness, Kiril Mikhailovot."

As others had suffered, under similar circumstances. Oh, yes.

"Illness?" Gostev looked puzzled, wary. He had embezzled money from the trade guild that employed him, and had eventually killed three people to cover his trail. And when it became clear that the link between these crimes and himself could not be hidden, he had fled.

"Why, yes," Malye said, still brightly. "Abnormalities of the nervous system. Specifically, of the brain's temporal lobe. Didn't you know?" She took a seat at the table, set her flatscreen down in front of her, traced up a set of files. Clucked and shook her head as she examined them. "Fistfight, fistfight, counseled for bullying, another fistfight . . ." She looked up. "These are your school records, ages fourteen to seventeen. The number of violent incidents is a marker for us, and indeed your adult life seems only slightly less explosive. Until three weeks ago, of course, at which time your symptoms worsened. Kiril Mikhailovot, I don't know how your condition has escaped medical notice for so long, but these are classic symptoms."

Gostev stared at her uncomprehendingly. Clearly, this was not what he'd expected to hear from her.

"You are easily angered," Malyene continued, "and when angry you find it difficult to slow down and think. This is when the . . . incidents occur. Am I correct?"

Uncertainly, Gostev nodded. "Well, yes. It's . . . like I can't control myself, like I'm watching myself from the outside. That's what it's like for me, like watching a holie."

Malye smiled her most sympathetic smile. "I've spoken with a medical team already, and they are very eager to examine you, to find out exactly what the problem is and how it may be corrected. We will need your permission, of course." She paused for a moment, considering, then spoke again with a more genuine candor: "My father suffered from a rare sensory disorder called synesthesia. I often wish he'd seen a doctor about it."

Of course, Malye herself had seen no end of doctors, had trumped up reasons to have her brain scanned again and again. Normal, always normal. *Smell the colors, little Malye* . . . But in a case like this, a detailed examination might turn something up, and at the very least would do no harm.

The hand of Justice would put a bullet through that brain soon enough.

"This is a trick," Gostev said, his eyes narrowing.

"No," Malye protested, with utmost sincerity. She rose, showed Gostev the manacle key. "I have no desire to trick you, nor any reason to. I'm going to uncuff you now; I'm sure you must be very uncomfortable, sitting like that."

Gostev appeared lost in his astonishment. "Why . . . why are you being so kind? I'm . . . I . . ."

I'm a killer? I killed three people?

Almost, Malye thought. Almost, Gostev had confessed to her; almost, he had not caught himself in time. But there were plenty of opportunities ahead. While uncuffing Gostev's wrists, she held him motionless with a gaze, and spoke: "Why would I be other than kind, Kiril Mikhailovot? We are not enemies, you and I, but partners in the search for a . . . solution to this mess."

The manacles sprang open, Gostev's hands tumbling out of them. He rubbed his wrists, looking at her, not angry at all anymore, but simply confused.

And the beauty of it was that he would never catch her in a lie, for Malye had spoken nothing but the purest of truth. Any fool could lie, or threaten, or raise the specter of torture and pain. And get lies in return from the suspect, or at best, hedges and half truths. But to win the suspect over, to coax his story out little by little, to build confidence and trust and the illusion of friendship *while telling him the truth* . . .

Even among C.I. top silver, not many could do it, and none half as well as Malyene herself. *Lead me to your doom, Kiril Mikhailovot Gostev; I promise I will hold your hand all the while.* No job could suit the monster better than this one, and no monster could possibly be more perfect for the job. Except maybe Father—in the back of her mind somewhere, she heard his voice, laughing softly with approval and delight.

A sharp noise.

Startled, Malye awoke to darkness. The noise repeated, an insistent beeping, and she traced it this time to the flatscreen she'd left on her night table. She could see it there, glowing ever so faintly with the star-field pattern she'd been using for an idle mode. The constellation Orion was just visible at the edge of it, the three stars of the hunter's waist standing out more sharply than the rest.

"Those stars are blue supergiants," Grigory had told her in one of his many urgent messages, "brightly visible even at twelve hundred light-years' distance, twice as hot as Aye and many thousands of times larger. In fact, you could squeeze Aye and Bee together, along with Sol and all the other colony stars, and they would hardly make a splash on the surface of one of these titans. If we dropped Alnilam, the center star, in the middle of Sol system, its surface would reach nearly to the orbit of Jupiter. Its flares might well disturb the atmospheres of Pluto and Neptune. Can you imagine what it must be like, living in proximity to such a star?"

In fact, Malye could not. What did she know of Sol system? Of stars in general? She had not bothered to reply to that message. Nor the one after it, nor probably the one after that. She wanted to tell him to stop it, to just shut up until she got the case wrapped up and came back home again. But thanks to orbital geometries, the round-trip light lag between Tyumen and their home at Pinega was now very nearly a full minute, and she hadn't relished the prospect of an argument drawn out so ridiculously, as if they were children passing notes in class. Better that the delay were an hour, time enough to conceive and dictate great monologues at one another. But of course, she had no time for that, either.

The flatscreen bleeped again, managing somehow to

sound desperate and frantic and lost. It was giving the signal, she realized, for personal messages of the utmost priority. She had only heard that sound once before in her life, on the day C.I. had come to take her father away.

She fumbled for the screen, picked it up, thumbed it, traced up the message.

Grigory's face appeared, light spilling in around it from a room she did not recognize. She squinted against the brightness.

"Come home, Malyene," Grigory said, his face looking pinched and frightened. "I know you believe your work too important for any interruption whatever, but hear me out. You've been very brave, very stoic, sticking to your duty. I love you for it, I truly do—it's stupid of you, but it shows such *strength,* and strength is something I've always admired.

"Now, listen closely. Almost a thousand Waister ships, of enormous size, have crossed into the outer reaches of Sirius system. The destruction of Yessey and Ikarka was no accident, my dearest; the Waisters are moving much more slowly this time, more methodically, and they are destroying *everything they pass.*

"Do you hear me, dearest? I think a million people may have died in the past few hours, and the Waisters are only just inside the outmost Kuiper belt. Our own geometry is not favorable, either—on their current course the Waisters will reach Tyumen in four hours, and will be here at Pinega in just over twelve. If we are separated . . .

"I know a lot more than you've ever suspected of me. I know, for example, which Andrei was your real father. Ialah, such a past you have! But Andrei Brakanov would have come home at a time like this, yes? You try so hard not to be like him; you resist even his sense of humor. Even that. But this is different, Malyene Andreivne—do not let his ghost constrain you this time. Come home now, for the children's sake if not for mine."

The image froze, then winked off.

Malyene stared once more at the flatscreen's idle-mode starscape. *Waisters will reach Tyumen in four hours.* The thought seemed to bounce around inside her, as a rubber ball might bounce around inside a hollow metal shell, ringing against its sides but leaving no impression.

She sat up, calmly sliding the sheet to the foot of the

bed. She rose then and dressed slowly, her mind cycling over and over on the same information, like the broken instrument she so often thought it was.

Crowds buffeted her as she left the tiny guest quarters behind. Angry, fearful people, milling about to no apparent purpose. The trip through the corridors of Tyumen's Capital Warren was all a blur to her, a vague dream of walking—or perhaps floating—through turns and crossings and level changes that seemed random and yet which carried her back swiftly to the police station. And still she wandered, just as aimlessly, and in no time at all she had come to the detention area.

Finding herself there, in the presence of an unfamiliar and nervous-looking greenbar guard, she blinked like a sleeper awakening. The corridor was all of white-painted metal, long and straight and brightly lit, blocked at the end with a gate of steel bars, also painted. Beyond it, she could see the holding cells, four of them, only one of which was occupied. By Kiril Mikhailovot Gostev.

"What time is it?" she snapped at the greenbar.

With quick, tight movements he checked his palm chronometer, then looked back up at her. "Four hundred hours, Colonel!" he said, then paused, eycing her expectantly. *Give me orders; tell me what I should be doing to mitigate this terrible crisis. Waisters in four hours!* Or perhaps, frightened as he seemed to be, he hadn't been told that much. As a reflex, fear was best stimulated by the absence of clear information.

"Open the gate," she said to him.

Wide-eyed and wordless, he complied.

She stepped through, moved purposefully toward Gostev's cell.

"Should I close it now, Colonel?" the greenbar called in after her.

"No," she said without turning.

Reaching Gostev's cell, she stopped. He lay asleep on his bunk, curled up among cheap, sturdy furnishings at least as comfortable as those in Malyene's own guest quarters. Except for the bars, of course, and the fact that everything was fastened firmly to the floor and walls. People were often surprised by the look of prisons and jails, functional and practical and above all inexpensive. No special effort was made to discomfort the prisoner,

and yet no energy was wasted on entertainments or con-
veniences or fancy confinement mechanisms, so that the
overall effect was at once spartan, primitive, and discon-
certingly humane—the purity and simplicity of the basic,
physical needs. The lights were never off, and yet never
bright enough to disturb a sleeper.

"Gostev," she said in a firm, loud voice.

The prisoner stirred.

"Gostev! Wake up."

Grunting in displeasure at having been so disturbed,
Gostev rolled onto his back and opened his eyes, which
immediately widened in surprise at the sight of the monster, holding a hard-projectile weapon aimed directly at
him.

"Colonel?" he said, too groggy and confused yet to feel
any fear.

"Gostev," she said to him, "it seems we've entered a
time of crisis. I do not know what's going to happen, and
consequently I cannot guarantee your inability to escape.
Opportunities may arise."

Now his fear came forth, in bright, singing waves. He
said nothing, but his eyes were wide with sudden comprehension.

Now you see, she thought at him. *Now you see what
murder truly means. Now, at last, you understand what it
is you have done.*

She pulled the trigger and held it for a moment. The
weapon coughed four times in her hand. Gostev jerked,
twitched, sprayed dark fluid, and finally gasped, drawing
in and then releasing the last bit of decent people's air he
would ever have the opportunity to breathe. The eyes
widened further, and then relaxed.

When Malye was five or six and they had lived in
Valna, the garden levels there had suffered a plague of insects. "Let us learn a thing or two about spiders," her father had said one day, laying one under his desktop
magnifier. Gently, with his tiniest tweezers, he'd removed
the legs, and then plucked the jeweled eyes out one by
one. "To let the soul escape," he'd said, but instead the
spider's body had disgorged a clot of webbing from its
other end, like a gossamer turd, and his laughter was
bright with surprise.

She heard that laughter again now, echoing inside her. *See, Papa, what your little girl can do?*

Without pausing, she reholstered the weapon, turned, and strode calmly to the exit.

"You may close the gate now," she said to the greenbar when she'd got to the other side.

And then she went out the way she had come, down the long corridor and out through the police station, into the milling crowds once more. Only later did it occur to her that she should have dismissed the greenbar, absolved him of duty and permitted or even ordered him to seek what comfort he could among family or friends. She could have done the same for every man and woman in the station. Certainly she had the authority, and anyway, what possible difference could it make? Those on corridor shift would be keeping what little peace there was to keep, and the others, who had not thought to join them in this task or who had been ordered not to, were merely superfluous.

But by the time these thoughts had come to her, it was much too late to go back. The issue would become a source of tremendous guilt for her in later times, far out of proportion, in fact, to any actual harm she may have caused, for who, she thought, would leave an innocent young man to stand guard in a white, empty corridor for the last few hours of his life?

Who, indeed, but a monster?

Chapter 5

It was all Malye could do to keep from grabbing Sasha as he stalked back and forth across the cryo ward's floor, the thin white robe flapping about his knees with every step. Grabbing and restraining him—he was driving her insane. Once informed of his true circumstances, the place and time of his revival, he had gone utterly to pieces.

"Everything's gone," he said yet again. He had stopped crying, at least, but could not seem to shut up or calm down. "Everything. Everyone I *know,* every place I've ever *been* ... My sisters are dead, and you tell me the Waisters are coming back? Names of Ialah, you ... damned evil woman. Why did you even revive me?"

"You can go back to being dead," Malye snapped him. "It isn't difficult to arrange."

Immediately, she regretted her words. *Impulse control, Malyene. Without that ...*

"Perhaps you should think of this in the other direction," suggested Viktor Slavanovot, putting a bare leg out in Sasha's path to stop his pacing. "Our survival seems nothing short of miraculous. The Waisters came, yeah, and for everyone else that was the end of it. For us ..." he spread his hands wide. "Who can say?"

Malye eyed Viktor curiously. She hadn't spoken with him before ... before a few minutes ago, but he seemed a solid fellow, the sort Grigory would have liked. He'd taken the news better than Malye herself had, and while he looked as lost and unhappy as she felt, he was also radiant with curiosity, and with a strange alertness. "The gravity's not right," had been almost the first words out of his mouth, and Plate had jumped in to explain that

Pinega's size and shape had been altered by the ferocity of the Waister attack, pieces of it literally boiling away, and its spin rate had slowed, the axis moving and reorienting as a result of the lost mass.

How a solid ball of rock and metal 650 kilometers across could be so affected, Malye could not imagine, but indeed, once it was pointed out she could feel a slight tilt to the floor, and perhaps a lightness in her head and feet as well, though it was difficult to be sure. Inhabitants of the Lesser Worlds learned to deal with wide ranges of spin and natural gravity, particularly if they traveled as much as Malye did.

An astute observation, then, under—to put it mildly—less than ideal circumstances. Viktor Slavanovot would probably have made a good criminal investigator. She was pretty sure he'd been a repairman or technician of some kind, though, and she supposed that was not really so different. Except for the methods of interrogation: *You, valve! What's wrong with you?*

In spite of everything, her dead husband and her frozen children and her Thousand Worlds gone to dust, this thought tugged at the corners of her mouth, almost enough to make her smile.

The white membrane-wall shimmered, drawing their attention, and Crow oozed through it and stepped up to them, his copper eyes glittering.

"The Queen will see you now," he said with an air of simultaneous self-importance, and of genuine allegiance and respect. Not respect for Malye and the others, no, but for this Queen, this "Wende" person Malye had insisted on speaking with. The way the green-haired men spoke of Wende, it was clear they owed her much, or thought they did, and were bonded to her not in love or in fear, but in some other, equally powerful way.

An alien way? Two brains, four sexes . . . As Malye understood it, the "Queen" was in charge of only five individuals, more a head-of-household than an officer or official of any sort. But the Queen was in charge, no question about that, and the Workers, meaning Plate and Crow, were her eyes and ears and hands, and perhaps her brains as well; this much she had gleaned from their words and their behavior, and from their body language, although much of this was strange to her, and disturbing.

Rather than nodding to acknowledge his companion's words, Plate lifted his arms and wiggled the fingers of both hands in a quick gesture, like a kind of salute. How *long* those fingers seemed, and how flexible! Like worms, almost—boneless. But when he lowered his hands again to his sides, the fingers looked normal and human enough.

"Let us go," he said to Malye in a voice that was neither friendly nor menacing, but hard. He expected no question, no reply from her. The Queen had agreed to see her, and so that was exactly what would happen.

Well, okay.

"Are you well enough?" she asked Sasha and Viktor, with gentle sadness born of a sudden and fierce sense of kinship. *We three, alone against the future.* "I can go by myself if you prefer it."

"No, I want to see," Sasha said, his own spirits suddenly deflated, his restless anger gone soft. Viktor Bratsev simply nodded, his jaw set. *We shall be together in our aloneness,* he seemed to say.

"Well, then. Lead the way," Malye said, turning to face the blankness behind Crow's eyes. She could just hear, at the faint, fuzzy edges of perception, the sound of his colors rising within her.

Viktor wondered, with a detached, horrifying lack of horror, where the rest of the hospital had got to. Outside the cryostasis ward had been the Exhaustive Care unit, up here in the low-but-not-*too*-low gravity where the patients had the best chance at recovery. He knew this because it had practically become his career to fix the plumbing and the wiring in this particular part of this particular hospital in this particular rat's nest that was fully eighty minutes from his home warren. *Get someone else,* he had always meant to tell them; from a plumbing perspective, Exhaustive Care was a damned nightmare.

But there was no EC unit here now, and no trace that there ever had been one. Behind its white membrane, the cryostasis ward lay at one end of a rough cavern, its walls of bubbled rock like pumice. Absurd, of course, because like all the Lesser Worlds, Pinega was volcanically inert, cold and solid all the way through. He flashed, suddenly, on the thousand-times memory of pipe metal flowing like water in the flame of his welding torch. The smell of it, the metal actually forming a vapor in the air . . . But that too was ridiculous; this hospital lay well in from the surface, shielded by a good seventy kilometers of high-grade, highly conductive nickel ore. You'd need one hell of a torch for that job. Names, you could probably throw Pinega into one of the *suns* and never melt it to that depth. Well, into Bee, anyway.

The EC unit was gone. A little while ago it was there, and full of people, but now it had become a cave, a gas bubble in the rock of the world. The hospital was gone. The Thousand Worlds were gone. How did one go about grieving for a thousand worlds? One didn't. That was the whole secret of it, he felt sure; one might as well grieve for all of history, all the billions who had ever lived and died. But wasn't that denial? Wasn't that simply a rationalization for cowardice, for hiding his head from very real and very serious troubles? Laughing in the face of death was one thing, laughing in the face of a billion deaths quite another.

He would find something, then, to mourn. His favorite chair, perhaps. *O Ialah, my favorite chair is destroyed!* he thought, trying it out. But no, it was false, it was nothing to him. He couldn't even recall what his favorite chair had looked like, nor, on reflection, the name of his best friend. Had he had a best friend? Yes, certainly, he'd had a lot of friends. He'd gone to parties, dances, games.

Looking inward, he found only a black, tarry mass where his grief and his fear should be. And his memories? Well, they bubbled through it, but slowly. His best friend's name was Oleg. His favorite chair was a custom recliner of blue and yellow plastic, soft and comfortable and terribly expensive. He would never see or feel it again. The pang of this thought was in some ways a relief, a confirmation of sanity, a pail of water in the face. But more thoughts crowded behind it, many more, and that black mass couldn't possibly hold them all back . . .

"Interesting, what they've done with the place," he said evenly, closing off that line of thought.

The cryo-ward attendant and the police colonel were soberly silent. Sasha and Malye, he reminded himself.

The only two people left in all the world; he should have no trouble remembering their names.

The two not-quite-people, "Crow" and "Plate," led them through the cavern and into a tunnel that was twice his height, hexagonal in cross section and relentlessly white in color, like the membrane that covered the cryostasis ward's north wall. Very artificial, he thought, and very alien. He preferred the bubbled rock of the cavern over this smoothness, just as he preferred to rest his eyes on Malye than on Crow or Plate.

"What is going on with your hair?" he had demanded of one of these men, as he lay shivering in his coffin. "Chlorophyll," the answer had been, and that one word was enough to tell him he was not waking up in the time or place where he'd gone to sleep. He'd resolved at that moment to ask no more questions, but of course he had been unable to restrain himself. Even now, the desire to *know* was far stronger than any of the other feelings kicking around in his skull.

"How many of you are there?" he asked, putting a hand on Plate's white-robed shoulder. There was a brief sensation there of cold muscle, strong and yet boneless, like touching a snake down at the petting zoo. He withdrew the hand instantly.

Plate looked over his shoulder, turned his empty copper eyes on Viktor, and shrugged fluidly. "Of me? One. Of mine? Six. I don't understand your question."

Viktor took a moment to wonder just what was going on in there, behind those eyes. And then he pressed on: "People like you. Here, in Sirius system, and elsewhere. How many?"

"Ah." Plate smiled, his eyes still on Viktor. He didn't need to blink much, evidently, nor to look where he was going when he walked. His neck looked like rubber. "Six-cubed of sixes per ring. I'm not sure how many rings, but I think about six-cubed. Certainly, not twice that many. Elsewhere in the Suzerainty, we are fewer."

Viktor ran some calculations through the black tar of his brain. Six-cubed sixes: about twelve hundred. Times six-cubed again, about forty thousand. No, about fifty thousand. Fifty thousand individuals?

Compared to the number of people who had lived here

before, that was a very small colony. Compared to the volume of Sirius system, to the vastness of human-occupied space, it was a *negligibly* small colony. But looking at Plate, walking there in the hallway with arms relaxed at his sides and his head very nearly on backward, Viktor thought it seemed like a pretty large number of these people to have around.

"Elsewhere, there are fewer of you?" he asked.

"Correct."

"In this 'Suzerainty' of yours, there are normal humans, still? People like us?"

"Tens of billions of them, yes. But Gate system is our own colony, and they will not interfere with us here. Their interests lie in the other direction, away from the Waister-controlled spaces. As if a few light-years could make a difference to their security."

Huh. Viktor didn't know whether to feel distressed or relieved—that there were normal people out there somewhere, or what might pass for normal in this peculiar era, but that they would not . . . *interfere*. Ialah. He and the others were, it seemed, rather completely in the hands of these strangers. And of the Waisters as well? He shivered, the tar thickening in his brain. Please, Ialah, let these "Gate" colonists be well armed!

"So, you belong to one of these 'rings?' " he asked conversationally. "You and twelve hundred others?"

"Correct," Plate said, giving a nod that should have broken his neck.

"And this Queen of yours is just one of, uh, uh, what, about two hundred other Queens in the ring?"

"She is not mine," Plate corrected. "I am hers. But your statement is otherwise true."

Viktor's face was less than two meters from Plate's. He forced himself to smile. "That is a *lot* of royalty. I bet your town meetings are hell."

Plate appeared to think about that for a moment, and then he shrugged again, and his head oozed back around to the front in a single smooth motion.

"Is it much farther to go?" the colonel, Malyene Andreivne, asked in a quiet voice.

"No concern of yours," Crow said without turning, in the sort of tone people use when calling an end to a conversation.

Bastard, Viktor thought. *That was a perfectly legitimate question.* The hallway, curving very slightly to follow Pinega's shape and centrifugal gravity contours, stretched on featurelessly for at least a kilometer before disappearing behind the curve of its own ceiling. A long way, it looked like, and they had *just woken up,* damn it. They had just lost their entire civilization. If this was all the sympathy the future had to show them, the future was more than welcome to shit backward.

"Have you people ever heard of the wheel?" he asked pointedly. And expected no reply, and received none.

But really, on reflection, he felt more relieved than incensed, because one of his burning questions—if Crow could be that much of a prick with that little effort, then yeah, probably he was a human being after all.

He glanced at Malyene Andreivne, who looked stiff and out of place, no doubt wishing for jackboots and a nice, high-collared uniform instead of the bathing robe and sandals they had given her. Hard to be dignified and remote when you're practically naked, he thought, but then, she seemed like the sort of person who could wither a man, so to speak, with her gaze, regardless of what or how little she was wearing.

She caught him looking, and turned, and favored him with a gaze. Not withering, not even angry, but simply appraising. After a few moments, she broke it off, and Viktor was left with a vague, curious sensation of having given something up, as if he'd spilled a secret to her. Which was crazy, of course. Probably, she'd practiced that look for years: *I've got your code, citizen. You've nowhere to hide.* She did it very well, though; he felt he should come clean about whatever it was he had done. Staring at her boobs, maybe.

"You're good at that," he said to her in a low, approving voice.

Her nod was just barely perceptible. *Yes, I am good at that.*

Well. It was comforting to know he was not the only one here who wasn't an idiot. He looked to his other side, watched Sasha Topuri stumbling down the hallway like a three-year-old on a forced march, his hair and face and robe all in disarray. Viktor had known Sasha slightly, from his many visits to that damn hospital, and had written the man off as useless, a trained monkey with no ability to operate outside his narrow specialty. And little enough ability within it, he'd suspected.

And yet, Viktor would not be alive at this moment if not for Sasha's efforts, and neither would Malyene Andreivne. She'd burst in on them, dragging that rescue ball and jamming the door shut behind her, tearing her mask off and shouting instructions ... And Sasha had done what she'd asked. And later, he had somehow managed to freeze *himself*, without assistance, a deed that must surely have required a measure of cleverness.

"Courage, my friend," Viktor said to the man now.

Sasha simply looked at him, miserably, his eyes puffy with dried-up tears.

"When you have lost everything," Viktor suggested gently, "no further harm can befall you. The secret strength of the refugee, eh? It seems like only minutes ago there was a world here, and it should still be here, we think—we should be able to hop in a tube and be home in a few minutes! But reality is not something you can deceive. When a ferry loses pressure, does the crew pine and mourn for the air they've lost? No, they would die, like fools; they would *deserve* to die, because reality does not care what you think, only what you do. And the reality, Aleksandr Petrovot Topuri, is that our world died a long time ago, and now there is only us, strong because we have nothing else to be."

That time, the message seemed to get through a little better. Sasha straightened his spine, drew a deep, sighing breath. "Life is an irreversible process," he quoted with forced casualness.

Viktor clapped him on the shoulder. Best to reinforce the good behavior. Really, though, it was hard to blame Sasha for his feelings, which were probably a lot healthier than Viktor's own. Even now he could feel the panic inside him, struggling to work its way free of the tar but unable to do so. For good measure he squashed it, stuffed it down even deeper in the mire. He had dealt with emergencies before, gas leaks and fires, a sudden divorce, and yes, even a decompression or two. Reality could change on you utterly, instantly, and you had to be ready for it.

He'd never really thought the Waisters came in peace, anyway. Too silent in those early weeks, too creepy, like stealthy animals in an Earth documentary, preparing to pounce on some helpless thing. No surprise that they'd done exactly that. Bastards. No surprise they were getting ready to do it again.

The walk continued for several minutes more, but eventually they came to a hexagonal doorway cut into the corridor's side, sinking in a hairbreadth or so before terminating in white membrane. More doorways were visible farther on, on both sides of the corridor, but at this first one Plate and Crow stopped, turned, and stepped without ceremony through the membranous covering.

The three refugees exchanged uneasy glances. Malyene Andreivne shrugged then, and followed. Sighing, Viktor went in right behind her. The membrane, just like the one at the cryo ward, felt cool and surprisingly dry, almost like stepping through a cobweb in some long-abandoned maintenance tunnel. But the surface parted without stretching, closed without rippling, touched the skin only in passing, in paper-thin cross section.

The chamber on the other side was large enough to hold a train car comfortably, though instead it held only three gray couches and three seated people, and something that Viktor thought was probably a dog, though he wasn't sure.

As in the ruins of the cryostasis ward, three hazy balls of light hung motionless in the air, providing illumination. He couldn't quite grasp the shape of the chamber at first—the walls were equilateral triangles that came together at ninety-degree angles—but with effort he was able to visualize the space as a cube with the corners entirely blocked out, the blocking surfaces meeting along the diagonals of each wall. An octohedron, then, of the same spotless white as the membrane and the corridor outside it. After all this time, the place still looked like a damn hospital, though an alien one. Or maybe a temple of some sort. The air smelled dry and faintly sweet.

He touched Malyene's shoulder, to reassure her he was there, but she shrugged him off. Her eyes were on the people who sat upon the gray couches.

On the center one sat a green-haired woman, whom

Crow and Plate approached and then turned to stand on either side of, as if at attention. At least, Viktor was pretty sure it was a woman, though a taller and fatter one than any he'd ever seen. Three, maybe four times the mass of a normal human, the skin flabby and wrinkly and loose. And yet her corpulence seemed to owe at least as much to muscle and sinew as to fat. Like a hulking athlete with pillows beneath her arms, dressed in an ill-fitting coverall of gray leather and topped off with a white robe the size of a vacuum tent. The expression on her face was sharp, almost angry.

The air immediately surrounding her appeared blurred, hazy, as if she sat in a little fog that hugged her closely. But the fog did not swirl or convect, did not appear, in fact, to move at all. At the fat woman's feet lay the dog-thing—hairless, also unmoving, looking up at Viktor with cold, measuring eyes.

The two couches on either side held men, or at least what looked like men. Again, their bodies were oversize, nearly three meters tall, but though these two bulged with muscle, their gray skins were tight and smooth and lean. Olympian godlings, they seemed, taking rest in their white palace in the sky. No, not resting, he saw; though they seemed to sprawl easily on the couches, their muscles were tense, their postures such that they could roll to their feet and spring directly to action on half a moment's notice.

Viktor felt Malyc's shoulder tense beneath his grasp as he tried once more to reassure her, or perhaps himself, with contact. Behind him, he heard Sasha step through the membrane and draw in a sharp breath. For an instant, nothing and nobody moved. It was a frozen moment, cool and tight and palpable, a moment which pressed itself indelibly into Viktor's memory: the white chamber, the couches, the accusing stares of the animal and the five strange people. And most of all that *smell*, a faint, chemical sort of sweetness he could not identify.

Nobody moved, and nobody moved, and then the fat body of the Queen shifted its weight forward a little, setting ripples down the loose skin, and the stillness was broken.

"This moment culminates long anticipation," the Queen said in a deep and musical voice.

"Hi," Viktor returned, as casually as he could.

What happened next was a blur that Viktor would not reconstruct in his mind until much later. One of the Olympians rolled off his couch, hitting the floor in a crouch and then *moving* toward him in a boneless, fluid, flailing manner, like a tied bundle of hoses rolling down a steep ramp. In absolutely no time at all the godling brushed Malyene Andreivne aside like a curtain, reached for Viktor with a huge, long-fingered hand, and lifted him.

In less time than it takes to blink, Viktor was thrown against the wall, right beside the openmouthed Sasha Topuri, still standing before the membrane-door. Viktor's feet did not touch the floor.

For a moment his shock was total. Reality could change on you swiftly and totally, yes, and you had to be ready for it, but things had simply happened too quickly for him to assimilate. He looked down the length of the Olympian's arm, at an upturned face with copper eyes and green hair and an expression he felt sure he had never seen before. The first clear thought he managed to think was that this was going to hurt, that a wave of incredible pain would slam across him in an instant or two, but there was no pain, and there was *still* no pain, and he began to wonder if maybe he'd been thrown back hard enough to kill him. Was this what death felt like, just a jerk of surprise and the wall suddenly hard against your back?

But then, finally, the pain did come, and it wasn't so bad after all. And though he was held up off the floor by a firm hand on his throat, the gravity here was not so strong, and the grip not so crushing; when he finally gasped in a breath of surprise, it was not difficult to do, nor particularly agonizing.

"That is my *Queen*," the Olympian said with slow intensity. "I am her *Drone*. You are a stranger here, and have no privilege to speak with such familiarity."

One word? Hi? That *one word* was worth this show of force? The really crushing pain had still not come, and Viktor recognized that it would not come at all if he behaved correctly, that the attack had been much more a warning than anything else. But a warning against what? It didn't seem to make sense.

"I am very, very sorry," he gurgled with great conviction. "Please tell me how I should behave."

The copper eyes bored into him. "With abject surrender," the Olympian said.

"Done!"

The great hand opened, and Viktor slid down the wall in a trail of nervous sweat until his sandaled feet touched the floor. Then his knees buckled, and he slid still farther. He wound up crumpled in a heap, with no immediate desire to rise.

Beside him, Sasha also crumpled. Fainting? Jelly-kneed with fear? Or perhaps just following along because it seemed like a good idea. But Malyene Andreivne stood her ground, and Viktor watched the Olympian turn to face her.

"Your Drone has yielded before strength. You are indefensible," it said.

Malyene's face was tight with controlled, calculated anger. "Is this how you greet strangers? Like the damned-to-Hell Waisters do it, I suppose."

The Olympian drew a breath, drew back an arm, as if he might lecture Malyene and strike her a backhanded blow at the same time, but the Queen's voice—trilling, fluting, rasping like a musical instrument being sawed in two—froze him in place.

"You, woman," the Queen said in Standard. "You will face me."

Slowly, contemptuously, Malyene complied. *I've got your code,* her face declared. *I know you, and I know your kind, and if you think I'm impressed, think again.*

"Your strength engenders admiration," the Queen stated flatly. "I have no wish to crush it for principle's sake. But neither should you, for principle's sake, move to antagonize those who have rescued your life. I trust my reasoning is followed."

Malyene said nothing. *Good for you,* Viktor thought, shaking, sweating, peering at the two through the pillar-like legs of the Olympian, the Drone, who had so easily felled him. *Play your own game, not theirs.*

"It is necessary that we end this confrontation," the

Queen went on, now beginning to sound impatient. "I require at least a token of capitulation."

"That's unfortunate," Malyene said dryly, "because you also require my help. Information, yes? The Fall of Sirius, for me only hours past? You may have the one, or the other, but understand: I will not give you both."

The Queen lifted ponderously from her couch, monstrous in her bulk and suddenly quivering with rage. She advanced slowly, loose skin bobbing with every step like fluid-filled sacs of rubber. Malyene moved not a muscle in reply.

"Will you force me to destroy you, so that these others will submit?" the Queen rumbled, looming over the much smaller woman. Her copper eyes flared wide. "There must be a capitulation. There *must*."

Malyene chuckled softly. "If there *must* be a capitulation, *Your Majesty*, then perhaps you should be the one to deliver it. I guarantee I have seen things these others have not. Perhaps I hold the information you seek? I and no one else?

"I require that my children be revived. There are several others in cryostasis as well, injured people and probably sick ones, and I require that they be revived and healed and permitted to join us before this place is abandoned. I further require that you answer *my* questions, until I am satisfied you've explained our situation to the best of your ability. These are the conditions, *Your Majesty*, under which we will assist you."

The Queen's bulk shuddered, rippled. Strange noises sang from her throat. It looked for a moment as if she might shake herself to pieces, but then, suddenly, she took a final step forward and grabbed Malye about the waist with her fat, flabby hands. She lifted, twisted, until she was holding Malye up horizontally, straight over her head. Quick, too quick for Malye to react. The Queen screamed then, a deep, booming, unfeminine, and in fact decidedly inhuman sound, and dashed the smaller woman hard against the floor.

And stared down at her with wide copper eyes.

Malyene groaned. She looked dazed, not attempting to rise.

Everything stopped; nobody moved.

Again, it was the Queen who broke the moment, this time by speaking. "I surrender," she said in a high and soft and decidedly human voice.

Chapter 6

"Are you all right?" the repairman asked anxiously, leaning over Malye, offering her a hand up.

Was she all right? Shaken, certainly, though she knew well enough how to hide such feelings. And hurt, her left knee definitely bruised.

"I am not seriously injured," she speculated, and accepted the hand. Viktor hauled her up gently to her feet. She tested her weight against the knee, but pain lanced up along her leg, and she could not quite suppress a grimace.

Chin down, Viktor cast an ugly, furtive look in the Queen's direction, his face hidden from her by a shoulder. "That bitch," he whispered softly, almost directly into Malye's ear. "She's hurt you, hasn't she?"

His kindness was touching. In a way, it reminded her of how Grigory used to be, so eager to brighten her world, to share his own. Viktor looked nothing like Grigory, but sizing him up now, she thought probably the two of them would have gotten along.

"I'll be all right," she said quietly. "Do not antagonize her. Although I thank you, Viktor Slavanovot, for your concern."

"Such formality?" he whispered. "We seem to be the last two people in all the worlds, you and I, or two of the few at any rate. You must call me Viktor, I insist. Or Vityo, even, though it's mostly my lovers who call me that."

"I am a married woman," she replied coolly, closing off that line of speculation for him. And then it occurred to her once again that she was in fact *not* a married woman, but a widow. Two thousand years a widow, and no doubts about it; she had seen Grig die with her own two eyes. The thought and the memory shook her, shook what little of her had not yet been shaken, leaving her loose and powdery as fine-ground salt within her hard exterior shell. She took care to betray nothing of this. Here and now, she would not weep.

Viktor looked a little irked, though whether at the content of her remark or the delivery or the deliverer herself she could not be sure. There were no colors to listen to just now, no overt cues as to his thoughts. But to his credit, Viktor did not sink so low as to correct her. Instead, he bowed slightly, smiled slightly, took half a step backward to make clear his lack of encroachment upon her.

"We have lost so much," she said to him. Meaning what? The comment sounded inscrutable, even to her. Grief and stress and anger could make such a jumble of everything!

Suddenly, the Queen's voice, Wende's voice, cut between them like a blade: "What you ask, woman, is difficult."

Malye and Viktor looked up, and poor Sasha as well. Wende had returned to her couch and her regal posture upon it, returned to her little fog bank, to her look of scrutiny. She did seem less angry, though, and that was good—explosive people were hard enough to deal with even in their good moods, even when they were not giants pretending to alien sensibilities. At first glance Wende seemed laughably easy to read, her ego writ large across her flabby face, and yet the specific words and phrases and actions she chose from moment to moment seemed never to be quite what Malye expected.

Dangerous. Best to keep her at a distance, yet without showing fear . . .

"My name is Malyene Andreivne Kurosov'e," she instructed. "Malyene will do."

"What you ask, Malyene, is difficult," the Queen said in the same tone as before. "In the past fifty months, Finders ring has endured considerable inconvenience to reach this place, to interface your equipment with our power distribution systems, to revive you, to keep the other rings appraised. Medical apparatus sufficient to help the sick and injured would represent an additional and considerable strain on our resources."

"I understand," Malye said.

Wende glared at her again for a few moments, and then sighed and shrugged elaborately. "I grasp your point, Malyene. This circumstance lacks convenience."

"The Waisters are returning," Malye said, now letting a share of her inward exhaustion show through, letting her voice move a step closer to the shrill tones toward which they seemed pulled. Which was a relief, really, because even a monster had limits. Even a monster could face only so much before screeching and folding up and refusing to face any more. "And we all know what bastards they are. Time is short, and you're hoping that we can give you crucial information of some sort, I don't know what. But *think*, Wende: we are only just awakened from the destruction of our homes. We need rest, privacy, information to help us feel a little more grounded here. And we need *each other*, we need to huddle together like frightened children, because really that's all we are. An hour or two, that's all I ask. That and the revival of my children.

"All these threats, all this violence, it's crap and you know it. It's not going to work." She drew a breath, glared hard at the Queen, and spoke pointedly: "You have got to treat us, *Your Majesty*, like human beings."

The Drones on either side of the chamber stirred, looking unsure of themselves, looking angry, looking . . . what? Malyene couldn't place it.

"What you ask is difficult," the Queen replied once again, her expression flat and strange. "I am here, at the nexus and interface of these events, the fate of both ring and the colony placed solidly in my hands, but understand, these decisions are not particularly my own to make. Not particularly. I am the sum of all interests through which I am constrained to operate."

Malye sniffed. "I lack the context to make sense of that remark. Is there something clear and specific you'd like to tell me?"

"No," Wende said. "Not at this time. You shall have the privacy you seek, and access to the Congress of Advisors. They can deal with you, perhaps, more gently than I."

She turned to Crow standing tall and straight beside her couch, and made noises at him, noises that were not quite musical, not quite mechanical. Fluting, rasping noises that did not quite sound like speech.

In reply, Crow ducked his head, raised his arms in a fluid gesture, and wiggled his fingers like so many loose, flexible wires.

They were brought to another chamber, empty but otherwise identical to the first.

"Is this adequate?" Crow asked indifferently.

"It will do," Malye conceded. "What is this?"

He was handing her an object, small and black and shiny, contoured like the handgrip of a pistol or a joystick. It had a stud on the top of it, something clearly intended to be pressed with the thumb.

"The Congress of Advisors," Crow said. "Be careful with it; it's very old. A relic of vanished times, like you." Then he stepped through the white membrane and was gone.

At least they did not appear to be locked in here. Perhaps they really weren't prisoners after all, but could come and go through this new Pinega as they pleased. But no, Malye's desire to explore was nil, and her desire to curl up into a ball and do nothing was very great indeed. Sasha, she saw, had done exactly that: he'd sat down by the door and hugged his knees and begun to cry once again, staring out at nothing.

Viktor threw himself down on one of the Drones' couches with an easy leap, and eyed Malye with interest. "You were magnificent," he said mildly. "You were *born* to give that bitch a hard time. I say that, you understand, as one who groveled at the feet of her servants."

"You seem awfully cavalier," Malye observed.

"Yes, don't I? I think it must be the shock. How is your knee, by the way? I noticed you limping."

"It will heal. Or they will fix me, I suppose."

Viktor grinned. "If they had their way, they'd probably just ask a few questions and throw us back in the freezer. Instead, they have you to deal with. Giving them orders! You really were magnificent."

Malye was silent, unsure how to respond to that. She simply refused to be outmonstered; it wasn't a noble thing. "I'm very tired," she said finally, and moved to the other Drone's couch. Feeling lonely, counting off the dead in her mind.

Grigory's name was, of course, at the very top of her list. He would never hold her again, never whisper soft words to her in the darkness. Ialah, she should have been nicer to him, that her memories might not be so ashen, so damning. The love of a patient man, spurned at almost every step, put off for some indefinite future when she would have the leisure to deal with it.

Well, that future was here.

The thought fogged her eyes over with tears. Not for her own suffering, Ialah knew, nor for the Thousand Worlds all gone to slag, but for poor Grigory himself, who had had the misfortune to fall in love with Andrei Brakanov's little girl.

She remembered him in the observatory on the night of their engagement. Fussing with the telescope screens, muttering to himself . . . He wanted to give her the universe, to share its vastness with her, but she'd settled for his smile and his ring. Those, at least, she was large enough to contain.

"You know," Viktor said to her back, "after all that fuss, Queen Wende will be pretty upset with the depth of my ignorance. I was right here the whole time, cooped up in the bowels of Pinega. Sasha, too, I believe. We never saw a thing. Did you?"

Malye shuddered, her eyes on the blank white wall beside her. "Not . . . not enough to know what was going on, but yes, I was outside for part of it. I saw . . . more than you, I expect."

"Really? Do tell."

"Names of Ialah, man, will you leave me alone?" She did not want to talk right now, did not even want to think. The events were so clear in her mind, so brilliantly, unshakably clear. And damning.

She heard Viktor rustling, rolling over on his couch. Saying nothing, making no further noise, making no effort, suddenly, to hold back the awful silence. Leaving Malye alone with her memories.

Chapter 7

"Destination?" she shouted hurriedly at the ferry pilot as she crowded into the bridge, waving a pair of frightened flight attendants out of her way.

"Batamay," the pilot replied crisply, then turned, saw her uniform. He did not appear alarmed.

"Changed," she said to him. "Official business. Your new destination is Pinega, flight time not to exceed ten hours."

"Authorization?" he asked calmly, rummaging for a flatscreen and then holding it out to her as if this sort of thing happened to him every day.

Malye took the screen from him, traced for an ID check, thumbed the appropriate square when it appeared, and handed the screen back again. *This is it,* she thought, *this is the end of my career.* Commandeering a ferry full of passengers for her own personal business ... But Grigory was right; she must return home. Her father's distant laughter was like thick, soft folds of velvet against her brain.

More then just her career was ending this day.

"Okay," the pilot said. His calm sang through the tiny bridge in a high, clear note. "You'll have to sit in back with the other passengers, at least during boost. Ignition in two hundred fourteen seconds."

"Understood."

She crowded back through the narrow hatchway again, turned to look down the aisle. Not surprisingly, the "Full to Capacity" lights of every cabin were lit. Everyone wanted to get away from Tyumen before the Waisters arrived to destroy it—she checked her palm chronometer—

about forty minutes from now. The first door she came to folded aside at her touch. Three men and a woman, strapped into their acceleration cribs, talking nervously among themselves. They looked up at her intrusion.

"One of you will have to leave," she said without preamble. This idea didn't seem to click with any of them right away, so she simply picked out one of the men and moved to help him undo his straps.

"What . . ." he protested.

"I'm afraid this flight is full," she said to him. "You'll have to take the next."

"But I'm going to Batamay," the man said.

"Then, you're on the wrong flight. This one has been rerouted to Pinega."

Of the four, he was the only one who appeared upset by this. Most of the people aboard, she suspected, didn't care where they were headed, so long as it was not toward the approaching armada. Pinega would do just as well as any other place. And for those others who *did* care . . .

She grabbed the man by the breast of his fancy tunic, pulled him bodily from the acceleration cradle and then from the cabin, and shoved him back up the aisle in the direction of the main hatch.

"Hurry," she advised. "I believe they're about to seal it."

"What . . ." he said again, but Malye ignored him, stepped back into the cabin and folded the door closed behind her. The countdown clock just above the window read 052, and then 051, running inexorably downward. She climbed into the vacant crib and strapped herself in.

The man and woman in the cribs across from hers looked back at her with wide eyes, as if she were herself a Waister come to destroy them. As if they wished to flee from her, but their crib restraints prevented it. Well, probably they were frightened before, and Malye had just exacerbated the problem.

"Pinega is not so hollow as Tyumen and Batamay," she said to them in a blunt attempt at reassurance. "It's smaller, but it's a good, solid rock. Probably a better place to be right now."

The two did not appear reassured. Well, diverting and defusing citizen panic was an almost reflexive part of any police work—an impulse not of kindness but of simple expedience, and hardly vital in this instance. She could always work on them later, if the need arose. The countdown timer said 021, and then 020 . . .

If the things she'd been hearing were true, these people, and Malye herself, would all be dead in a few hours anyway. *Sibir has been vaporized, Yamish has been reduced to rubble* . . . Both of those were Lesser Worlds of considerable size.

008 . . . 007 . . . 006 . . .

She prepared herself for the invisible sack of potatoes. How many today, fifty kilograms? A hundred? Maybe more than that; the flight time she'd specified was Sprint class, for emergency travelers only. She'd never used it before.

I hope he wasn't a friend of yours, she thought suddenly, looking at the people across from her. And then the ferry dropped away from its docking port in the surface of Tyumen. The view outside the window had been blank, a dark reflection of the cabin itself, but now there was blackness out there, dappled with starlight. The stars moved across the view as the ferry reoriented for boost, and briefly Malye caught a glimpse of Aye at the window's corner. It was the more distant of Sirius system's two stars, over three light-hours away—the Thousand Lesser Worlds orbited Bee and Bee alone—but it was by far the larger and hotter of the two, and the blue-white dot was fiercely bright, even the edge of it enough to make Malye squint, despite the window's rapid polarization. On the other side of the ferry, the light of Bee, dimmer but so very much closer, would be burning its way through closed window shades, illuminating the cabins bright as day shift.

One of the men in the cabin with Malye, the one who was not next to her, gasped and choked at the sudden weightlessness. She hoped to Ialah he wouldn't be sick—most Sirians took to null gravity easily enough, but there were always homebodies and delicate types who never left their spinning worlds, never ventured too close to the axis, never faced a gee level below point three or so, and many of these had chosen today for their first journeys abroad. A pity for their traveling companions, especially on the sprint lines.

But then the fusion motors groaned to life and crushed them all back in their restraints. Six-gee boost, she judged. Ialah help them, maybe even seven, and for a while Malye had nothing to worry about except breathing while the invisible sack of potatoes, fully as heavy as her own body, nestled firmly on her chest. Inhale, exhale, rest. Inhale, exhale, rest . . .

If that guy gets sick now, she thought, *he'll choke on it.* But he didn't get sick, he just gasped and panted under the invisible weight, hyperventilating until she thought he would probably pass out. But he didn't do that either, and so a kind of smothery routine settled over them all. Inhale, exhale, rest . . . Time passed neither slowly nor quickly, but with terrible effort, as if they had to heave each passing minute off their chests using nothing but lung power. Heavy gee was like food poisoning or an ethyl hangover, in that there was no escaping the misery; one simply accepted it, and waited. Praise Ialah for the oxygen-rich atmosphere, at least.

Eventually, after about thirty minutes, the pressure let up, and null gravity returned like a light switching on, and then that hapless traveler *did* get sick, as noisily and messily as Malye had ever seen anyone do it.

Damn, if only she could nap. Or at least meditate, or settle into a good state of denial from which this cowardly flight of hers might not seem so incriminating. But instead she felt the full weight of her guilt, and in fact had nothing else to think about. Guilty and *bored*! And the other passengers in the cabin kept up a steady burn of angry, fearful glares. . . . It wore her down, driving her out within a few minutes to seek the bridge once more.

Looking neither left nor right, she unstrapped herself, floated over toward the cabin door, folded it open, extricated herself, and folded it closed again. Her movements were the easy glide of a seasoned traveler, with none of the jerkiness or uncertainty that plagued so many, even in the Lesser Worlds. She got herself oriented in the aisle, and kicked off a handrail, launching herself up toward the bridge. Its hatchway tube was still open, so she simply funneled herself into it and braked against the walls with her toes and the backs of her hands.

The pilot heard her and turned around. "Hello," he said.

The view up here was much better than from the cabin's window—nearly a full 180 degrees both left-right and up-down, through seven flat windows arranged at odd angles along the ferry's sharp nose, like flatscreens somebody had pasted up in a hurry. And the instrument panel gave small, distorted views along the length of the hull, and straight out the vehicle's stern, staring past the silent engine nozzles at a starscape that included a round, shrunken world—Tyumen—hanging before the three bright stars of Orion's waist.

Presently, something flashed on Tyumen's surface, a bright flicker that came and went almost too quickly for Malye's eyes to catch. There was another flicker, and another.

"What's happening?" she asked without alarm.

"On course for Pinega, as per your instructions," the pilot said.

"No, I mean what's happening back there? At Tyumen?"

"Oh. I don't really know. There's some radio traffic about gamma-ray lasers; I guess they use them for propulsion. But those look like impact events to me. I dunno, maybe small particles sleeting in at relativistic speed. It's not just here; there's a real shitstorm preceding the Waisters everywhere they go. Which is everywhere."

Malye felt a light, cold touch of fear run down her back. "Will we reach Pinega before they do?"

"I don't really know," the pilot said again. "We have a substantial lead—believe it or not, they're nowhere near Tyumen yet—and we're coming up on our second burn in about ten minutes. But right now we're already approaching maximum safe velocity, with minimal response time for the collision warning system. If things start heating up I'll kick the burn in early, but I'm limited in what I can do because there really is a lot of particulate matter on this route, and I don't think a rescue tug could get to us if we came to grief."

"You're handling this very well," Malye observed.

"My job," he said, and shrugged.

Tyumen began to flash more brightly, and Malye

noticed for the first time that parts of its surface were glowing a dim, evil shade of red.

She thought about the young greenbar, dutifully standing watch in his empty corridor. Was he there still? Had he fled? Had he died? All those people running loose through the corridors, so many more than the ferries could ever hold. Malye had monstered her way to the front of every queue and mob, the black and burgundy uniform like a whip in her hand. So many obstacles in her way, each one a human being with his or her own life and history on the line.

Fifty million people lived in Tyumen. And she had abandoned them all.

Up ahead, through the pilot's little windows, space was clear and constant and unobstructed. All the Lesser Worlds were out there, too distant to see, indistinguishable from the starry background. No sign of Pinega at all.

"There's a lot of activity back there," the pilot remarked in an offhand way as he scanned his instruments. "Waister ships are moving in a little faster than I thought. Looks like Tyumen is really taking it in the skivs."

Indeed, the pace and intensity of the flashing seemed to have increased even as Malye watched. The ruddy glow was brighter now, covering a larger portion of the surface.

Malye shook her head, slowly feeling the color sing across her tongue like tiny hot pokers. "My job was supposed to be to help those people, but I can do nothing for them. Nothing except run away and leave them to die. I think you can be so calm right now because you know you *are* helping."

The pilot shrugged. "I don't know. Get us to Pinega, I guess—this isn't so terribly demanding. I used to fly a gas scooper out at Creta, coming off the inner moon, diving right down through the cloud tops and swinging back, usually for several passes. That's a difficult, dangerous job; people scorch it all the time. After a while, I noticed I didn't have any friends left."

"So you became a ferry pilot, nice and safe," Malye said, appreciating the irony.

"Yeah. Even sprinting like this is tea and biscuits to a scoop run. An eight-year-old could do this job."

Eight-year-old. Malye felt guilty and alone, and the words were a sharp reminder of home. Vadim was always

climbing on things. Wall, pillars, hallway fixtures . . .
"Bring me a set of traction shoes," he'd pleaded with her
before she'd left for Tyumen. "It's *almost* my confirmation day." But she hadn't wanted to encourage the habit,
and had gotten him a flash-receiver kit instead. What happened to that kit?

"I have an eight-year-old," she said to the pilot, "a
little boy, who would be thrilled to hear you say that. And
a five-year-old daughter."

"Yeah? That's nice."

Behind them, Tyumen flared so brightly it saturated the
little holie screen. Malye squinted, waiting for the brightness to abate, and eventually, after a few seconds, it did.
When she could see Tyumen again, peeking out behind
the engine cones, it took only a fraction of a moment to
see that something was seriously wrong: a huge crack ran
all the way across the cratered, gray-brown surface, its
width a major fraction of the planet's diameter.

"Oh," she said, feeling cold inside.

Up inside the crack, she could see staccato flashes,
blue-white pinpoints casting off yellow sparks, like a
welding torch. She was seeing into the planet, looking up
inside its all-too-hollow core, watching something burn
and sizzle in what must already be a near vacuum, all
breathing air fled through the sundered floors. Could that
be a meltdown, a fission core gone critical, spilling molten fuel disks out into space? A *dozen* fission cores?
What else would burn like that in hard vacuum? Or perhaps it was some weapon of the Waisters', some climbing, burrowing thing that would ferret out every living
soul from the warrens and atria of this world.

"This is happening too fast," the pilot said, his eyes on
the instruments. Malye could see the edge of his frown,
could watch it drawing deeper. "Something's moving in
past Tyumen, heading this way. I'm going to give us another kick in the skivs, okay? You have to get back to
your crib. Now."

Tendrils of unease lapped at Malye's heart, ice-blue
and flickering like nuclear fire. "Are we going to make it
out?"

The pilot turned. "Lady, I'm going to hit the engines in
about twenty seconds, whether you're in your crib or not.
Is that sufficiently clear?"

One thing about Andrei Brakanov's daughter was that if you told her something twice, she got it. Malye was back in her cabin and buckling herself in with a second and a half to spare.

Her cabin mates didn't even bother to stare at her now, didn't even bother to pant or groan as the invisible sack of potatoes settled in, as the engines flared and squeezed them all back into the cribs' soft padding. Their attention was riveted on the starscape outside the window, on the tiny, intermittent flashes of light that were visible out there. Empty space, out past Bee's stellar north. Not many worlds to destroy up there, and none at all nearby. What was flashing?

And then suddenly she knew, and wished to Hell someone had thought to close the damn window shade so she didn't have to watch this. Even a monster could know fear, could know it better and more keenly, perhaps, than anyone else in all the worlds. Fear was white, and tasted like batteries, and sounded like nothing at all.

Noiselessly, something was sweeping through the space around them, kilometer by kilometer, some great invisible beam. Destroying, one by one, the hundreds of ferries that had debarked from Tyumen in its final hours, and fled.

The rest of the flight was a blur for Malye, a confusion of spinning and falling and more spinning, of crushing weight and sudden jerking motions. She could not imagine what the pilot was doing, what threats he believed he was dodging. If the Waisters could crack open a Lesser World with so little effort, surely they could crack open a passenger ferry. Malye expected to breathe vacuum at any moment. But the hours had passed in a blur, and somehow the ferry had arrived at Pinega in one piece.

Pinega, already under siege. Malye found her way out of the ferry port and sprinted down the corridor, steadying herself against the walls when the floor shook beneath her, which was often. Breathing only in tortured gasps— she was no runner—but home was still so far away; she had to get to a tube station. She *had* to—Elle and Vadim were in danger. What she could do for them she wasn't quite sure, but by Ialah she would do something, get them to shelter somewhere. As high up in the planetoid as the corridors would take them, as far from the surface as humanly possible. If the children came to harm, it would be because Malye's body had been vaporized and could no longer serve as a shield.

Time passed. She took a tube, got out, took another. The burgundy uniform no longer a whip in her hand, no longer seen by the people who fled past her in random directions. She lashed out at them, punching, kicking, screaming at them and shouldering them out of her way. Fewer people, though, fewer with every passing minute. Everyone was finding a place to hide, a place to curl up and die as the planet boiled around them.

Malye's gasping became worse. She began to see spots and stars and shooting comets in front of her eyes, and it occurred to her finally that there was something wrong with the air. Specifically, that there was not enough of it. Shouldn't the depressurization alarms be going off if the air were thinning? But no, even the lights were dim, all the warren's systems flickering and sputtering and shutting down. How much air? It was hard to tell, dangerously hard.

She forced herself to slow down, lest she pass out and be no help whatever to Elle and Vadim. Home was close now. She turned down a familiar corridor, hurried down it as quickly as she dared, turned again, and again.

In her own neighborhood now. She slowed farther, the decision as much a physical as a logical one.

Finally, she arrived at her own front door. Jabbed it with the printed part of her thumb, and the door rolled open partway and froze. Malye threw herself against it, squeezed into the open space it left, about two handbreadths wide. She grabbed smooth walls on the far side and heaved herself through the gap, stumbling into her living room like something that had popped from the neck of a pressurized bottle.

Elle stood howling in her bedroom doorway, her face a red mask of terror and outrage. Grigory kneeling beside her, making hush-hush motions. Vadim simply stood by with his hands in his pockets, observing the scene with a detached curiosity that belied his age. He looked up at Malye as she staggered into the room.

"Mother! Papa, Mother's here!"

Grigory looked up, his face curiously blank. Malye's ears popped.

"The warren is losing pressure," she said to her husband by way of greeting. She hurried past him to the emergency locker, unsealed it, flung its little door open. The lights went red, and *now* an emergency buzzer sounded.

"Malyene?" Grigory said, clearly taken aback by her sudden appearance. He looked pale, confused.

"Don't stand there gawping," Malye snapped. "Get into your vacuum gear."

"Dearest, how did you get here? We heard ... *I* heard ... that Tyumen was destroyed. That nobody made it out."

Rummaging through the locker's contents, compact and indecipherable, every item folded or boxed or rolled into a tube, Malye finally came up with a large, round bag of tough fabric. A rescue ball, large enough even with the integral air recycler to hold a typical adult male, if he hugged his knees, or to hold two children in any unruly heap at all. Hurriedly, she unzippered the ball and, kicking strewn emergency gear out of her way, leaped to where the children stood side by side. Their father still with them, having risen to his feet but otherwise done nothing.

"Get into your vacuum gear," Malye repeated angrily. Her ears popped again. Black dots swam across her field of vision. The decompression seemed to be happening faster now. A faint but noticeable breeze blew in the direction of the half-open door. "Damn you, *hurry!*"

Vadim was eyeing the rescue ball with knowing unease. "Mother, I'm not going in there. I'm getting a mask!"

Malye didn't bother arguing, but simply blocked her son's escape, and reached past him to grab Elle, who was still purple-faced and screaming, and now struggling as she realized just what her mother intended to do. Ialah, how could she carry on like that without fainting in the thin air? But suddenly Elle folded to the floor and went limp, making a deadweight of herself, so that Malye had to hoist her and stuff her bodily into the flaccid rescue ball. At the last moment Elle began to kick and flail again, but by then it was too late; she fell fully inside the bag, her rear end thumping against the metal floor plates. She screeched again, even more loudly.

Vadim, who should certainly know better, looked ready to flee, but Malye more or less had him cornered. "I'm sorry," she said, fixing him with an intense stare, grabbing the front of his tunic, pulling him toward her. "You'll have to be brave. Keep your sister calm." And then he, too, went into the bag.

Malye zipped them in and froze the zipper in the locked position. Already, the ball was inflating. Once again, Malye's ears popped, this time with a kind of papery rustling sound.

She looked over at Grigory, who was struggling to pull a tight black pressure-equivalence garment on over his clothes. That was so completely the wrong thing to do, and his expression was so distant and confused, that at last it occurred to Malye that he was hypoxic, that his brain was not getting enough oxygen to solve even this simple puzzle. By the red emergency light it was impossible to check his skin color, but surely he was turning blue. Surely Malye herself was, too, or would be soon.

Hypoxia was a strange condition: fickle, unpredictable, because the first thing it stole was the judgment required to recognize its symptoms. Surely her own judgment was suspect, too?

"The mask first!" she shouted urgently. "Grig, put the mask on!"

Her voice was tinny in her ears. She felt dizzy. Enough! She would be no help to anyone if she didn't get into her own vacuum gear immediately. She spied her mask on the floor, snatched it up, fussed with the straps for an anxious moment before pulling the whole thing down over her head like a hat that had no top, like a tight rubber hat that pulled down all the way over the face. For a moment she couldn't breathe at all, the clear rubber pressing firmly against her mouth and nose, held down tightly by the misplaced straps, but with a yank she managed to get the thing untwisted. The mouthpiece jammed its way between her lips, and the soft rubber mask formed a tight seal around the edges of her face, with the hard, clear visor an inch or so in front of her eyes.

She exhaled sharply, essentially gagging into the mouthpiece, working against the resistance of disused valves. Nothing happened for a moment, and then the valves cleared and her breath was pulled gently from her, then forced gently back in as she inhaled. Breathing the same lungful of air, scrubbed clean by the mask's tiny filters. She tightened her straps, to make sure the seal stayed good as the pressure continued to drop. She'd need to hook up an oxygen bottle in the next few minutes, lest the air grow foul despite the mask's filters, but for the moment the need was not urgent.

Grigory's was. He had dropped to his knees and managed to find his mask, but simply held it in his hands now and stared at it like he'd never seen such a thing before in his life. Ungently, Malye took it from him and forced it down over his face. That seemed to have some effect on him; he grabbed at the mask, twisting and pulling on it. But wrongly, uselessly. They struggled for several seconds.

Malye first knew there was something very seriously wrong when she noticed the blood on her hands, hot and wet, gloss-black in the red emergency lighting. Grig's struggles intensified, becoming almost like convulsions before Malye managed to get the mask on him straight.

Breathe, Grig! she wanted to say. *Breathe, damn you!* But with the rubber mouthpiece jammed between her teeth, she could say nothing.

A final spasm, and then his body went limp in her arms, face and neck and visor smeared with blood. No rise and fall to his chest, no reaction in his wide, sightless eyes, barely visible behind the black-red smears. Malye pressed her hand against his neck, where the carotid artery would be, and found no pulse. Pressed harder; still nothing.

Grigory! She would have shouted his name if she could.

In her police and C.I. training courses, Malye had learned a number of resuscitation techniques, but all of them were years ago, the details hazy, and anyway none could be performed in vacuum. Oh, Ialah. In this day and age, death was no simple matter, no decisive, irrevocable leap into the great unknown—with proper attention Grigory Mikhailovot Kurosov could be roused, repaired, pumped full of oxygen once more, and sent happily on his way. Some people had survived several *hours* expo-

sure to hard vacuum, but there was nobody here to per-
form such miracles. There was nobody here to help at all.

She could probably stuff Grig's body in a rescue ball
and leave him here, hoping for the best . . . But today did
not seem like the sort of day when the best things happened. Was anyone's luck likely to change?

Malye's skin had begun to feel bloated, bruised with
the pressures inside her. She was farting an almost continuous stream of gas, and the skin of her hands crawled
with the slippery feel of vacuum, neither hot nor cold. If
she didn't get into a pressure-equivalence garment right
away, she was likely to hurt herself, to start hemorrhaging
or something.

The apartment shook once again, almost knocking her
off her feet. Ialah, she had to get out of here. She had to
get the door open, get the *children* out of here. She had
abandoned Tyumen, hijacked a shuttle to come and rescue
them both, and Waisters or no Waisters, they would not
come to harm while she lived.

Even Andrei Brakanov had loved his children, loved
and protected them fiercely and without reserve until the
day he breathed his last. Indeed, Malye *still* felt his love
hovering near her much of the time, like a vapor, an almost visible, almost palpable thing. Love was white, her
father had once told her on an evening's walk through the
gardens. And it tasted like batteries.

Chapter 8

Malye awoke with a start and looked around her. Confused at first, then remembering where she was: the empty chamber Wende had given them to rest in. The walls were as white as ever, the three globes of intangible light still hovering, evenly spaced, around the room's geometric center. Viktor was on the couch across from hers, lying on his back, eyes closed, chest rising and falling with slow regularity. And Sasha had moved to what would be the Queen's couch, and sprawled there now in merciful sleep, his back toward Malye and Viktor.

She should probably find out how to work the lights, how to dim them or turn them off. Actually, she should probably get up and stay up, but just now the effort seemed enormous. Instead, she rolled over and went almost immediately back to sleep.

When she woke next, it was with less alarm and confusion. She lay for a while with her eyes closed, wondering if she would sleep more, and when she did not, opened her eyes and sat up.

Sasha and Viktor sat facing one another on the floor, cross-legged, in the corner that was farthest from Malye's couch. She heard their voices, too soft to make out. They appeared to be playing some sort of game with their fingers, something quick and intense, involving counting patterns that jumped from one hand to the other and back again. Their hands fluttered and stopped, fluttered and stopped, and then remained motionless for a while.

"Oh, you win again," she heard Viktor say. "You're not bad at this, you know that?"

To Malye's eyes, both men looked a little better, Sasha

less grief-stricken and Viktor not quite so weirdly jubilant. Emotional hangover, the morning after. The process had only just started, of course—for the foreseeable future, they would all be swinging through the obligatory cycles of denial and anger and despair. And Ialah, it could only get worse when the others were revived. Elle's five-year-old temper might never subside, and Vad . . . She didn't know what to expect from him. Such an odd child.

But this moment seemed to be a respite of sorts. She wondered what game the two men were playing.

"Good morning," she said to them. They turned.

"Oh. Malyene." Viktor nodded politely. "I was starting to wonder if you'd wake up at all."

"I'm sorry. I had a very long day."

Viktor smiled at that. "A two thousand year day, heh? I must say, cryostasis did not seem very restful to me either." He paused, his smile fading. "You must forgive me, of course. You . . . said you were in the fighting before you came to us. And dragging those kids around, with everyone smothering and dying . . . A difficult day indeed."

Malye waved him to silence. *Not now, not now. Don't sour the moment.* "What game is that you're playing?"

"Oh, this?" Viktor ducked his head self-consciously. "It's called two-ten. A children's game, actually; they play it in Kaluga and Varn. *Played,* I should say."

She grunted, nodded. Those were Creta's moons, both of them large worlds with high natural gravity and a reputation for pious austerity among the citizenry. Minitarians, mostly: no spices in their food, no sweets or toys for their children, lest Ialah think them weak, and undeserving of Paradise. But the cleverness of children would overcome any obstacle; even a monster knew that. And as for Paradise, well, she hoped the Minitarians were happier there than here, because they certainly weren't likely to return.

"Would you like to learn how to play?" Viktor asked Malye.

"It isn't difficult," Sasha volunteered, politely but uncertainly, as if he were afraid of offending her.

She shook her head. "No, thank you. But you can teach my son."

The men exchanged looks, shrugged, and then began

another game. Malye couldn't quite follow it, but it looked spirited enough as the two flashed their hands up again and again. Sasha actually grinned for a moment, faintly but noticeably, and then all at once the game was over.

"Crap, you *are* good," Viktor complained mildly. He looked up at Malye. "Colonel, I tried out that Congress of Advisors thing. Fairly astonishing. You might want to take a look before we go anywhere."

"Huh. Very well, where is it?"

"I put it under your bed, there."

Without rising from the bed, she stuck her head down and looked underneath. The black handgrip was there, within easy reach. She reached.

The thing felt light in her hand, as if it were hollow. She brought it up, examined it as she moved to a sitting position. The round trigger on top of it was obviously meant to be pressed with the thumb.

She tried it.

The white room went away, Viktor and Sasha along with it. She found herself instead in a huge amphitheater, walled in with plaster and wood, domed over with dark, painted frescoes from which hung at least a dozen chandeliers. She was on the dais at the chamber floor, rows and rows of benches and tables rising up before her into the distance, crowded with thousands of human beings in clashing, outlandish dress. The lighting was incandescent, yellow and dim.

Her hand was empty, but in a distant way she could still feel the black handgrip, and her thumb holding down its trigger. Somehow, she was not sitting anymore. Somehow, she was standing, and a man was standing here with her, unfamiliar, gray-skinned but otherwise human in appearance, his red hair standing out from his head, long and straight and not quite unruly.

"Kiel kanst ye assisti?" the man asked her, smiling politely.

Startled, she let her thumb up off the handgrip's trigger.

Instantly, the enormous amphitheater became the white, octohedral chamber once more. She was sitting again, on the edge of her couch, Viktor and Sasha both staring at her expectantly.

"Names of Ialah," she sputtered. "What happened?"

"That was the Congress," Viktor said. "It's quite something, isn't it?"

"Congress? What's it for? How does it work?"

Smiling now, Viktor shrugged. "What's anything for? I don't know. Why don't you ask *it*?"

"How does it work?" Malye repeated. "I wasn't here; I was in some other place. How did that happen? Where was I?"

"I assure you, you never moved from that spot. You had that button down for just a moment, and I had my eyes on you the whole time. It does feel pretty real, though, doesn't it?"

Instead of answering, Malye grunted, and depressed the trigger again.

The vaulted Congress chamber returned.

Released it.

The white room. Viktor and Sasha.

Depressed it yet again.

Vaulted chamber.

"Kiel kanst ye assisti?" asked the red-haired, gray-skinned man on the dais with her.

"I ..." she said experimentally. "I don't understand."

"Ah," said the red-haired man. "Standard, late interstitial. Can you understand me now?"

"Yes," she said cautiously.

"Excellent, excellent. How may we assist you?"

Assist. Advise? This was the Congress of Advisors, no? Was every face out there a personal advisor?

"What is this place?" she asked, raising her arms and eyes in a gesture that took in the whole chamber.

"This place," the red-haired man replied, "is a sensory reproduction of the Senate floor on Council Station, Sol system, as it appeared during the closing decades of the Clementine Monarchy. It seats exactly five thousand, two hundred sixty-four individuals. Gravity level is zero point five two, the air a room-temperature mixture of oxygen/nitrogen/helium in five three two combination, at precisely three hundred millibars pressure. Lighting level is a spartan four watts per square meter, generated by electrical currents passing through tungsten-resistor filaments in two hundred fifty-two evacuated glass bulbs. Much of the furniture and architectural adornment you see is of mahogany, a natural wood imported at great cost from

Asia, a region of Earth that remained heavily forested at that time."

Malye gawked. The red-haired man paused for breath every so often, but he didn't fidget, didn't shift his weight from foot to foot or move through a range of facial expressions as people so often did when speaking. He looked human but awfully stiff, and he spoke . . . like he was reciting a memorized document. When police computers were made to speak in human voices, they sounded very much like that. And she got no *feelings* from him, no noises or colors spinning out from his center.

"Are you a machine?" she asked the man.

"I am part of a machine," he replied. "I am a conjugate, self-organizing data structure, which despite a highly autonomous design has been for reasons of efficiency constrained to minimal self-awareness. My purpose is to serve as a visual and linguistic interface between the user, the historical archive, the oracular extrapolation and prediction engines, and the Congressional simulacra. My official title is 'Moderator,' but the user may assign me any name, title, or other designation that suits his needs."

"I see," Malye said, overwhelmed. This . . . thing was very much like a police computer, in that every question seemed to provoke a torrent of information, the machine itself unable to distinguish between meaningful data and chaff. But it was very polished and elegant about it. Strange. "This is all very . . . Can I perhaps ask you to speak more succinctly?"

The Moderator nodded. "Of course."

Huh. That was easy enough. "Who are all these people?" she tried, pointing out at the bizarre figures seated above, in the terraced arcs of benches and tables.

"Those are the Congressional simulacra."

Malye sniffed, neither amused nor annoyed, nor even particularly surprised. Machines still did what you told them, she saw, and not what you wanted. "A little more information than that, please."

The Moderator swept his arm across the crowd. "The persons seated before you are the simulacra of pivotal figures from various points in human history, presented here as a powerful and flexible Congress of Advisors. They may be queried en masse, in groups, or individually, and may be tied in various ways to archival data and oracular algorithms as befits the needs of the user. In toto they may be regarded as representing the sum of human wisdom."

Malye peered out at the Congress, squinting in the dim light. "They all look like men to me."

The Moderator nodded his agreement. "The viewpoints and attitudes of women throughout history are preserved in archival data, and indeed, female influences on the course of history must not be underemphasized. However, many historical figures, when simulated accurately and in detail, refuse to acknowledge the validity or propriety of female opinions. This can lead to unproductive cycles of computation and dialogue, which reduces the usefulness of this unit; for purposes of efficiency all members of the Congress are therefore male."

"There is no female Congress?"

"This unit is not configured to provide such a service."

"Names," Malye cursed. Of course, women had had nothing to do with history, nothing at all. She squashed the urge to argue—what good could it possibly do?—but a pall had been cast over the credibility of this device and its makers.

This was a lot to take in, a lot to wake up to. She was tempted to release the thumb trigger again and go back to Viktor and Sasha. Such a lot that needed doing: reviving Elle and Vadim and the cryostasis patients, dealing with them, dealing with this strange future in which they found themselves. And dealing, yes, with Wende and her co-horts, telling them what they wanted—*needed*—to know before the Waisters returned to finish the colony off.

Damn it. Damn it all. She released the trigger.

Once again she was in the white room with Viktor and Sasha. They were both still staring at her, neither one appearing to have moved in the minute or two she'd been gone.

"You know, you don't have to watch me," she said to them.

Viktor smiled. "Back with us already? You can't have learned all that much in so short a time."

"We have a lot to do," she said testily. "My children—"

"Will be just fine where they are. Please, Colonel, spend as long with the Congress as you like. No time will be wasted—I'll promise to wake you if anything happens."

Viktor seemed to be enjoying a private joke, some amusing little secret he wasn't going to share until he was ready, and this clashed so sharply with Malye's restlessness that for a moment she didn't know what to say.

"The Waisters are returning," she reminded him, holding back the word "idiot" at the last moment.

Viktor nodded. "So I've heard, yes. And there doesn't seem to be anything we can do about it right now, except maybe to inform ourselves. How do we know what we want, if we only barely know where we are?"

"What do you think I want?" she demanded coldly. "I want my children."

Viktor's face dropped into a frown. "Obviously, yes. But then what? We tell these people what they want to know, and then what? Please, I'm serious: that Congress thing is powerful, and we can learn a lot from it in a very short time. How can we not? Give it a few hours, at least, and then we can all discuss what we've learned. You owe your children that much."

A few hours. Damn. Malye was nervous and impatient and sick at heart, but there were definitely things she wanted to know. A great many things. And yes, she owed it to Elle and Vadim to understand the environment here before bringing them into it.

Cursing, she pressed the trigger down once more.

"Is Ghengis Khan out there?" she asked the Moderator, casting a look out at the Congress once she was inside the vaulted chamber again. "He's a man, right? If I want to know Ghengis Khan's opinion on something, I can ask him?"

"Genghis Khan is here," the Moderator agreed, pointing to a figure in the audience. The figure stood, a black-haired man dressed up in animal skins. Not much else visible about him in the dim light.

"Ben Franklin?" Malye asked. "GovGen Xiouha of Sol system?"

The Moderator nodded. Two more figures stood.

"Well, I don't want to talk to them," she said. "I need to know where I am, what's happened to . . . I need to know about the last two thousand years. Since the Waisters came."

Suddenly, without a flicker of transition, she was in a much smaller, narrower, more brightly lit chamber, like a classroom. Only about thirty people up in the seats, though they were an exotic mix indeed. Some in uniforms, some in fancy brocades spilling over with bright metals and gemstones. One man was even naked, at least from the waist up where Malye could see him. The seated figures' skin color varied from pink to brown to blue-gray, the hair colors and styles even more varied. Only two of them had the green hair and copper eyes of the Gate colonists, though, and for this Malye felt a surge of relief, to go along with the dizzy incongruity of the scene change.

"Moderator," she asked when she felt ready, "can I speak with any of these people?"

"Indeed you can. And should you wish to adjust the parameters of the conversation in any way, I remain at your disposal."

"Thank you." She turned to the seated Congress, leveled a finger at one of the green-haired men, apparently a *Worker*, very human in appearance.

"You," she said. "And you." Pointing at the other green-hair, a vast, muscular figure crammed into a desk that appeared tiny around him. A *Drone*, no doubt. "Which of you is the more recent, historically?"

"I am," the Worker said, standing.

"You know the history of your people?"

"I do."

"Very well, then," Malye said, weaving her fingers together and stretching them back. "Let's have a chat, you and I."

Chapter 9

The Worker's interview lasted nearly an hour, and when it was finished Malye started in on the other one, the Drone, who seemed to know a lot less and posture a lot more. And when *that* was done, she spoke with another man, one Ken Jonson of Earth, who was apparently some sort of icon or figurehead to these green-hairs, these "Gateans."

Jonson seemed to want to talk about the war, though, about fighting with the Waisters when they'd arrived at Sol system, only a few years into . . . Only a few years after the attack on Sirius, a few years into what Malye still considered to be her future.

Damn. It might be a long time before her brain, wholly unprepared to lose so much so quickly, really caught up with all that had happened. How could anyone be ready for events like these? Should one scurry through life, forever expecting to be hurled into incomprehensible futures? Catatonia as the only sensible alternative? Surely not.

Ken Jonson seemed not to know the things she wanted. Or not to wish to discuss them, at any rate; he seemed consumed by strange obsessions of his own. She ended up speaking with the Moderator instead, for what felt like another several hours.

Most of what she learned in these conversations made no sense to her, things that fit into some context and reference frame that she did not and could not share. That was normal in any investigation—the police and Central Investigators knew, better than anyone, the great diversity, and yes, *per*versity, of human communication.

Within and between human societies, so *much* of what passed for mutual understanding was in fact illusion, or even outright deception. But still, she heard much that she was able to assimilate.

Sol system's Colonial Age had ended with the departure of the last of the colony ships and the collapse of the Solar economy, almost a thousand years before Malye was born. In the aftermath of the Waister Conflict, though, in what had become known as the "Suzerainty of the Human Spaces," there had been a Second Colonial Age, during which the Gateans and many other groups had departed Sol system to reoccupy three shattered colonies and to found a couple of new ones. But this Second Colonial Age was over and done with as well, the economy having collapsed once again. As in Malye's time, now known as the "Prewar" or "Interstitial" era, travel between the stars had proved ruinously expensive.

The Gate colony was allegedly founded as a diplomatic outpost, the nearest point in the Human Spaces to the Waister empire, which she gathered to be of enormous size, and very distant. She learned that the Gateans were in the business of listening for signals from the Waisters (of which there had been none), and occasionally beaming signals of their own, which would not arrive at their destinations for thousands of years. But they had only been at it for a couple of decades, had spent centuries between the stars in a long cryostasis of their own, and had rejoined the flow of history only recently.

Like Malye herself, they were an anachronism, living in their own future, acting out an idea that, she began to suspect, had never been very much in favor. *Yes, by all means, leave Sol system behind; take the long, slow journey to Gate, there to live as you please. Live as the Waisters do, yes, the better to understand them.* And yet, the return of the Waister fleets seemed to puzzle Wende's people as much as it did any of these Congressional simulacra.

Still, the overwhelming image that came out of these dialogues was of an energetic human empire, encompassing eight star systems and a huge volume of space, and linked by an ansible network, faster-than-light signals flashing back and forth between the stars in constant streams. That had been the fading dream of Malye's

"Interstitial" era: community, brotherhood, a bridging of the awful gaps of time and space that kept Sirius and the other colony stars apart. But as an engineering project, it had proved nearly as ruinous as starflight itself.

These people had followed through, though, had pinned up their sleeves and gotten the job done. It was, Malye thought, a major point in their favor.

Curiously, after hours and hours of these revelations, Malye noticed that she felt as fresh as she had when she'd started. Her voice had not grown hoarse, nor her skin greasy, nor her feet tired or sore from all the standing. But she did feel a creeping sense of guilt, of slowly building urgency—she was partly amusing herself in here, partly taking out her frustrations on imaginary people, cursing and shouting at them when she felt they were not cooperating. Partly paving the way for her children, becoming the well-informed mother they would need to protect them here. But if she were to be honest with herself, mostly she was just hiding.

"You have been very helpful," she said to the Moderator and the reduced Congress.

And took her thumb off the trigger.

Strangely, the digit was not sore from holding that one position for so long. Strangely, when the white octohedral chamber reappeared around her, Viktor and Sasha were still sitting right where they had been, still playing their damned finger games.

"Names of Ialah," she croaked bitterly. "You said you would take care of things. Have you two moved at all?"

Viktor turned and grinned at her. "I told you it wouldn't be a waste of time, Colonel; you've only been sitting there a few seconds. I know, I know. It's like forever in there, isn't it?"

A while later, when Plate oozed through the membrane-door and entered their little sanctum, the strange, quiet Dog following along behind him, Malye all but pounced.

"When will you be ready to revive my children, and the others?" she demanded.

"Why, madam, the deed is already done. Or being done, at any rate." Though no less troubled than usual, Plate's expression was smug, not at all distant or unkind.

A pair of small figures burst through the white membrane, the smaller of them screeching, "Momma! Momma!" It was Elle, and the other child with her was, of course, Vadim. They bowled into her, grabbing fiercely at her waist, even Vadim seeming much younger than himself.

"Elle! Vadim!" Malye shouted with delight, scooping them up in her arms. "Oh, my babies, how *are* you? Were you frightened? It's all right now. Everything will be all right."

Elle was wailing now, her mouth widening, eyes pinching shut, fat tears rolling down her chubby face.

"Hush," Malye said, kissing her twice, "hush, baby. It's all right." But the child continued to howl, gasping only occasionally for breath. She knew more or less what had happened to her, Malye would bet—even at five years old, Elle was no fool. News reports, alarms, decompression, and then waking up in a strange place, surrounded by copper-eyed more-than-strangers. Probably, Elle knew that her father was dead. A glance at Vadim's face was enough to confirm that *he* certainly did.

Vadim was as heavy as his expression, though. Malye put him down, and he did not protest.

"Where is Papa?" Elle asked finally, in drawn, barely recognizable syllables. She drew in a stuttering, snuffling breath. "My father, where is he? Momma, where *is* he?"

"Hush, baby," Malye repeated, bouncing her as best she could. "We'll talk about it soon." Talk about what? About Paradise? Your father is with the Minitarians, dear, drinking bitter tea every evening at shift change.

Oh, Grigory.

"But where *is* he?"

Despite her best efforts, Malye began to cry again. Plate looked on with embarrassment.

"What is the condition of the other patients?" Viktor asked, striding up to the doorway, thankfully interrupting the Kurosov Crying Chorus, giving everyone something else to pay attention to. Even Elle quieted a little and looked at Plate and Viktor, as though the answer to that question were of some personal interest to her.

"The others are being repaired," Plate said, also looking relieved. "Their condition is serious, however—none appear able to survive without gross intervention. They were suspended because they were sick?"

"I'm just a handyman," Viktor said with a shrug, and turned to cast a meaningful look at Sasha. "But my friend Aleksandr Petrovot can explain that, I think."

Sasha, sitting on his couch near the back of the room, looked up as if startled to have been consulted about anything. He cleared his throat. "Um, yes, well those were cases we didn't have the facilities to treat at the time. Two of them were about to be moved; the rest were awaiting custom surgeries or other treatments that would take time to set up. Ours was a very small hospital, and without buffering the really serious cases through cryostasis, our facilities would have been ... overtaxed ..." Like a toy, he seemed to wind down and stop. He looked around him, frowning, obviously reminding himself, *oh, right, the world has ended, and I have lost everything.*

"I see," Plate said. "Our capabilities, though minimal, are apparently superior to yours. We have set up a surgical fog that we hope will correct the macroscopic injuries within the next hour or so. At the cellular and molecular levels, repair will proceed with increasing difficulty, because the fog is intended for *our* bodies."

"But you are human," Malye said with undisguised sarcasm.

Plate shook his head. "We are not. Whatever Crow told you, we have less in common with you and with the Suzerainty of the Human Spaces than we do with the Waisters themselves. Our sole purpose is to understand them, to communicate with them."

"Yes," Malye agreed, wiping her eyes, wiping her daughter's eyes. "You understand them so very well, even though you have never seen them or spoken with them or seen what they can do. They've come back to destroy you, and in your fear and desperation you have revived *us,* apparently at great cost, even though we know so much less than you."

She set Elle down. "You have given up a lot of your humanity, Mister Plate, you and your people. But I've been watching, and I've been thinking, and I think you are far more human than you're ready to believe. If you were really Waisters, you would not be speaking with us now. If you were *really* Waisters, you would be making war on those who are different from you: making war on the Suzerainty of the Human Spaces."

Plate flinched minutely. His sounds and colors shifted, his posture stiffening ever so slightly, and Malye received the message loud and clear: *who says we are not?* But when Plate actually opened his mouth, what he said was, "We don't know that they've returned to destroy us. We don't know anything about this at all. Madam, we have been running machine simulations of Waister neural activity for thousands of years, since before the war even ended. We know them very well indeed, and I tell you that this coming back, this returning to the scene of the conflict, is not in their nature. Their confrontation with us is complete; we *should* be of no further interest. And yet, here they are. We don't know what this means."

"And you believe we can help?" Viktor asked, echoing Malye's sarcasm.

Plate looked at him and sighed. "We do not *expect* that you can help, but we hope that some chance of help exists. Did they do something unusual here the first time? Or *find* something, or *learn* something? This is what we need to know. We are Finders ring, what you might call archaeologists, though that term is not a good description of what we actually do. But many of the other rings have doubted our usefulness to Gatean society, and in finding *you* we have proven them wrong. Now, we find ourselves the subject of considerable attention."

"How wonderful for you," Malye said. Behind her, Elle began to cry once again. "Excuse me, I must tend to my family."

"And I to mine," Plate echoed.

He and the Dog slipped out through the membrane once more.

"Do you mind if I follow them, Colonel?" Viktor asked Malye. "I'd like to see this 'surgical fog' they're talking about."

Malye glared. "You ask me? I am not *your* mother, Viktor. Do as you please."

"All right. But I thought you were . . . our leader. After all, *Colonel,* who is more qualified? Who is it that put Queen Wende in her place? Not I."

"There's no need for leaders here," she said angrily.

"How many people do you see? Go. See the surgery, and leave me alone."

Grinning, Viktor clicked his heels together and saluted. "Yes, ma'am! Sasha, you should probably come with me. It will be good for you."

Viktor practically had to drag Sasha with him to see the surgical fog, which turned out to be a kind of aerogel suspension of microscopic machines that would surround and penetrate the patient, working small miracles on the inside and out. Similar to the "security fog" that surrounded Queen Wende, Plate informed them. But it wasn't much to look at; it really did look just like fog, like a hazy blurring in the air around the patient, and whatever it was doing was much too small and slow to see with the naked eye. Like watching a food plant grow.

The thought prompted Viktor's stomach, and when he asked about food, Plate brought them a basket filled with things like muffins, cold and soft to the touch, and tasting more like potatoes than like bread.

"These should not prove harmful," he said reassuringly.

And then, with nothing else to do, Viktor and Sasha returned to the *utterly charming* company of Malyene Andreivne Kurosov'e, and waited for the arrival of the newly revived. They came, one by one, healed and disoriented and beginning to suspect how very long they had been frozen. Many had never heard of the Waisters, had entered cryostasis too soon to hear news of them. Of those who had heard, none had been frozen after the start of the attack. Which meant, of course, that they knew nothing of how they had come to this place.

One by one, they asked their questions and shed their tears, but thankfully, all Viktor had to do was hand them food and show them how to work the shitter. It was Malyene Andreivne who got the job of comforting them, of answering them, of introducing them to one another.

There was Svetlane Antoneve Vdovin'e, who did not find the rhyme in her name at all funny when Viktor pointed it out, and who seemed even in the depths of her grief to be showing off the body she had so thinly clad in one of the Gate colonists' white robes. Not a bad body to show off, Viktor supposed. The woman had been a restaurant hostess in her previous life, but had been struck down by a sudden and virulent cancer, she said, that began in her stomach and spread quickly to her other organs. Sasha, who had of course attended her cryo-suspension, was able to confirm the story.

Next came Konstant Aleksandrovot Bulgakov, a bureaucrat of some sort who kept asking who was in charge, who was in *charge* here? He'd fallen from a high balcony and landed on his head, and woken up to the sight of Crow leaning over him. Must have thought he was in Hell. And really, what was there to disprove it?

Next, a woman: Ludmile Vitrovne Drozd'e, who had somehow located a wide strip of green cloth and had tied it around her waist in a broad sash. Two decades older than Svetlane Antoneve, she had not ever had a profession, had been a kept woman all her life, and seemed obscurely proud of the fact. She also had suffered a rare cancer, though not the same one as Svetlane Antoneve. Here and now, she seemed utterly devastated at the loss of her home, which, she said, had contained "everything of importance" in her life. Viktor tactfully decided to assume she included her lover on that list. Or keeper, or whatever.

Next, a man: Nikolai Ilyovot Kuprin, call-him-Nik. Nik had suffered a stroke deep inside his brain somewhere, and then another one a few days later while he was undergoing treatment, and had been frozen to give the doctors a chance to determine the cause, lest a third stroke come along and strike him dead. He was a construction foreman specializing in indoor zero-gravity structures, which seemed to Viktor like a pretty interesting job. The man was over ninety, though, coming hard on retirement age, and he didn't seem interested just then in talking shop.

And finally there came another woman, one Vere Sergeivne Seydkh'e, who also worked in construction, as an "excavation engineer," which probably meant "driver of digging machinery" rather than "designer of excavations," though Viktor wasn't completely sure. She was a little heavy and coarse for his tastes women-wise, but person-wise he took an instant liking to her—she had laughed at one of his jokes, and of all these people, these (he counted) ten human beings who had made it through the Waisters' attack unscathed, she seemed the only one who really appreciated her good fortune. "Goodness," she said sadly when the situation had been explained to her. "And I thought my lucky bracelet didn't work."

Chapter 10

"Mother," Vadim said to Malye, "what are we going to do when the Waisters come back? Will they destroy everything, like they did before? Is that pretty much what they do?"

Malye put down the muffin she was eating, and motioned for Vadim to sit beside her on the bed. "Baby, I don't know." She hugged him, kissed his forehead. It was such an intelligent, appropriate question, but really she had not thought about it much, had not wanted to. What was there, really, to be done?

"Can the people here help us?"

"I don't know," she said, shaking her head, acutely aware that she was speaking for an audience. It was "afternoon" just now—she'd been awake for about eight hours—but really it was a kind of bleak, hopeless morning for the newly revived, so that they all stumbled around like sleepwalkers, unable to operate in this new world. Malye convinced them at least to take turns at the sink and the shitter, cleaning and emptying themselves so that they might feel at least marginally more human. Nobody talked much—not even Viktor—and Vad's words had drawn everyone's attention.

"I don't know, baby, but I hope so. Do you know the one called 'Plate?' He says there may not be any fighting at all. He and his friends know a lot about the Waisters, about how they think and what they do, and he says they can do the right things to avoid a conflict."

"Because they have funny eyes?" Vadim said, and there was such bitter irony in his voice that Malye wondered if he were simply repeating someone else's words, someone else's opinion. But no, his eyes held the fierce, bright glow of sincerity—he did not trust the Gateans any more than Malye did.

Such a strange, *knowing* little boy. *Do you hear the colors?* she wanted to ask him sometimes, but a terrible dread always held her back. That dread sang through her right now, yellow and massless and indestructible. Andrei Brakanov had been a collector of mismatched shoes, many of them quite small. "Look, Malye," he would say in that same, knowing way as he strode through the doorway, "I've found another!" And she would hear his laughter, clear and joyous. Not a monster's laugh at all, but high and friendly, and therein lay its greatest danger.

"Is there any chance we could run?" one of the new men asked: Konstant, the bureaucrat. His voice was red with stymied anger, his eyes clearly hunting for someone or something at which to direct the emotion. The universe had hurt him, and on some level he wanted to hurt back. But his tone was controlled, his hands folded behind him as he paced, and he at least displayed more energy than any of the others. "Do these Gate people have fast enough ships to get us out of here? We *have* to get out of here."

"Not in time," Viktor said, stepping away from the sink, wiping his hands off on the thin robe he wore. "And not at all if the Waisters chose to pursue. I got the Congress to run an analysis for me: those Waister ships were faster, tougher, many, many times more maneuverable. It was like a joke, like target shooting."

Pause.

"So what are we supposed to do?" Konstant asked finally, angrily.

"Nothing," Malye said to him, not darkly but as a flat statement of fact. Get used to it, citizen.

He favored her with a contemptuous look. "That is quite a fatalistic attitude, miss, and one I don't happen to agree with."

"Fine. You may agree with whomever you like."

Konstant frowned, not liking that answer, either. "Miss, you don't seem to understand what's happening here. Our world has been destroyed. We can't just sit on our thumbs, and we don't dare cooperate with these people without knowing—"

"I suspect," Viktor cut in irritatedly, "that the *colonel* understands our situation a little better than you do. On the one hand we have the Waisters, and on the other, the Gateans, and in between we have *us*, dressed up in sandals and bathing robes."

"We will cooperate with the Gateans," Malye said quietly, "because we've made a bargain with them, and they have kept their part of it."

Everyone was silent for a few moments, looking at her, so she continued: "This is difficult for all of us, but for the moment we have no choice but to place ourselves in these alien hands. Do I trust them? No, but they understand far more than we do, or claim to at least. Are we to face the Waisters' wrath without them?" She pointed around her at the white walls, the ruins of Pinega. "We already know how that will turn out."

She watched all the somber and hopeless and puffy-eyed faces react to her words. The message appeared to strike deep—even Vadim was nodding. But Konstant still glared at her, unsatisfied.

Would you still look at me like that, the monster thought idly, *if your eyes were punctured and ran down your cheeks like tears?* For a moment the room took on a reddish tinge that rang in her ears, but then it was gone and oh, Ialah, oh, *Ialah,* she thought she had this under control. She thought she'd found *productive channels* for all this crap, found ways to make it *serve the greater good,* but here it was flowing back into her again, mental sewage pumped the wrong way through the pipes of her brain.

Damn you, Papa.

At least it did not flow into her hands, at least she had not actually *done* anything. Yet.

"Don't stare at me like that," she said, looking away, feeling sick. "Don't you dare."

At that moment the white membrane over the doorway rippled, and then the Dog was stepping through, and Plate behind her, and one of the hulking Drones behind him, none of them moving quickly but all managing nonetheless to convey a sense of urgency.

Everyone turned to look.

"Madam," Plate said, looking directly at Malye, striding about a third of the way into the room before stopping, "you must come with us. You must come with us. All of you must come with us now. Bring whatever you will need, whatever you have, if you have anything, because we must leave now and you will not be returned to this location."

Malye blinked. "I beg your pardon?"

"No delay!" Plate flared, looking genuinely angry for the first time since Malye had first laid eyes on him.

Back at the entrance the Dog stiffened, and the Drone raised his head almost to the three-meter height of the doorway, his copper eyes bright with a terrible alertness, his muscles tense and ready. Thick neck twisting and straightening, twisting and straightening in a kind of spasm, or tick, that was more sinister and terrifying than anything Malye had yet seen in this strange, future time.

"What has happened?" She asked Plate with forced calm. She would not show fear to these ... creatures, though even at that distance the Drone could race forward and snap her like a wafer before she could so much as breathe. *But the children are in the way*, she thought, and that fact filled her with cautious dread. No sudden movements.

Plate grimaced. "There is fear that Finders ring may be hoarding information. Not true, not true, not the slightest bit true, but Wende has been summoned to Holders Fastness for an accounting. You are a part of this. You. You are a part of the accounting, and you will not be the cause of the Queen's delay. You will come with us *now*."

Malye had acquired a blanket that morning, and cautiously, she now took it up in one hand, and pulled Vadim to her with the other. "We're coming," she said. Elle was out of reach, staring at the monsters in the doorway and beginning to cry, to wail. "Come to Mother, Elle. Now!" She looked around at the others. "Did you hear him? We must go with the Queen. Get your things, now! On your feet, we're leaving!"

At this, Plate appeared to relax a little, and with him the Drone and the Dog, and Malye finally got her arm around Elle and pulled her out of the line of danger. Why they were so angry she could not imagine. Not anger, even, but some other emotion, some needful urgency that would not be denied. Without understanding, she mimicked the posture, dragging the protesting children forward, half wrapped in the blanket, and glaring at the adults as if she would treat them all in the same manner if she had to.

It appeared to be the correct response; the tension ran right out of Plate and his companions, and after a moment the Dog and Drone turned to vanish once more through the white membrane.

"Forgive me," Plate said, and smiled wanly.

But he stood there waving his hands, urging them all through the doorway, reminding them with his mere presence that an order had been given, and that disobedience would simply not be an issue they were going to worry about.

Dutifully, Malye made a show of hurrying toward the exit, of shushing Elle's wailing, of making sure that everyone else was following behind her, however reluctantly. But as she brushed past the green-haired, small-mouthed, jelly-boned Worker, she could not resist whispering to him: "Does Wende's surrender mean so little?"

Indeed, it was no wonder the Waisters had returned, if this was their idea of capitulation.

But Plate declined to reply, or in fact to respond in any way. In the parlance of Central Investigators, he had "sealed his locks," his mouth still smiling mechanically, his eyes simply staring back at her like copper mirrors, reflecting the forced blankness of her own expression, an emotional vacuum that filled the space between them as between distant planets.

But nature abhors a vacuum, she told herself. A simple truth that was nonetheless one of her most powerful interrogation tools, because people were not pressure vessels, were not evolved to hold back against the force of a vacuum for any length of time. Sooner or later, that emptiness would fill itself, would draw an emotion out of Plate again. Or even, Ialah help them all, from Malye herself.

And then the eye contact was broken, and Plate was impatiently shooing her through the exit, and she went without further complaint.

Viktor didn't much like the direction things were heading, but Malyene Adreivne seemed willing to go along with it, at least for the moment, and so he did so as well, hurrying silently down the long corridor and urging the others ahead of him, like schoolchildren in an evac drill. This time, the walk was not so long before they came to . . .

Well, I'll be painted, he thought.

In the old days, twenty-odd hours ago, ferries had docked only at Pinega's equator, where centrifugal force could fling them away if any problems arose, if they were leaky or burning or found to be carrying something dangerous. But here, at forty degrees south latitude and eighty kilometers inward depth, the Gate colonists had carved and smoothed and polished a cylindrical chamber some fifteen meters across and several hundred high, just barely larger than the dimensions of the ferry that hung stern-down within it.

At least, he assumed it was a ferry. All the ones he'd ever seen had been boxy in shape, lined with windows and covered over in layers of thermal LCD that danced with shifting, deep-contrast patterns of black and white. This one was quite different, long and slender, shaped like a sausage with six longitudinal wires running down it, invisible but pulling tightly against the skin so that it ballooned out between them. And yet, the thing was clearly no balloon, no soft, pliable surface held in by strings. Its windowless hull was the orange color of iron oxide, and looked at least as solid. Indeed, the whole thing gave off an impression of tremendous, unspacecraftlike mass—a pillar of stone, perhaps, carved into some ghastly alien phallic symbol.

But it had big fusion engines projecting down from its stern, and little steering jets visible here and there on the skin, and anyway it *smelled* like a ferry, that acrid, oily smell that was always the same, wherever you went. The smell of lubricants, he supposed, and coolants, and pure hydrogen leaking slowly from its compression tanks, reacting with everything in sight, one molecule at a time. It was a holiday sort of smell, one that spoke of trips to faraway places, and in spite of himself, Viktor felt a flush of excitement.

Was that so bizarre? He had been to Yercha and Kaman and Tyumen, had once even visited far Vyazma, that mightiest of Lesser Worlds. It amazed him, always, how very different the worlds were on the inside, how people who spoke the same language he did, the language of nearly all humankind, could produce so many things he would never have thought of, never even have imagined. In Yercha they kept it hot and humid and ran around naked—or nearly so—and kept the gravity so light you could sleep comfortably on the ceiling, held up only by straps of friction cloth. In Tyumen they built everything fifty times larger than it needed to be, just because they bloody well felt like it, and unlike the naked Yerchans, a smile and a wink would tumble their women into bed with hardly a second thought.

Where would he be going, this time? Holders Fastness? That was no world of the Sirius colony. Some shattered place, then, that the Gate people had claimed for their own? Ah, Yercha. Would he even recognize the place if he saw it? It hit him once again that *everything* was gone, that the Sirius colony simply didn't exist anymore, nor any appreciable trace of it. He'd asked the Congress about it, and had been shown image after image, world after broken, sterile world, until he exited, unable to stand any more. He would not grieve for a billion souls, snuffed out in vacuum, in fire, in molten rock. He would *not*.

Already, he had traveled to a new place, called Gate system. A place where the people looked like children's drawings, and behaved like them, too. *Well*, he thought sourly, *what a wonderful adventure it's been so far.* The brief elation had turned to ashes in his gut.

The corridor opened out to a wider ledge, from whose center a translucent bridge extended, reaching out to a circular hatchway in the ferry's hull. The bridge, though it had a flat walkway and a handrail on each side, did not appear any more solid than if it were made of cobwebs, or smoke. In fact, it looked like a visual illusion, some trick of refracting light. But the "security fog" and the "surgical fog" had looked a lot like that, too, and the Congress had assured him that despite their vaporous appearance, both were exceedingly tangible, capable, in fact, of stopping projectiles, or throwing them, or tearing them apart into microscopic pieces. Perhaps this bridge was a *structural* fog, equally solid, equally malleable.

He was in no hurry to try it, but Plate was urging the refugees forward, out onto the ledge, and the Drone that

was with them (wasn't his name "Line?") went right out
onto the bridge, crossing it neither cautiously nor reck-
lessly, but with the quick ease of familiarity. He paused in
the hatchway, craning his head inward on the end of that
enormous, almost prehensile neck, and then vanished inside the ferry.

And then, Plate was urging Malyene across. "Go on,"
he said, "the Queen will be here momentarily. We mustn't
delay."

"I don't understand this sudden urgency," Malye said
back to him.

Plate simply shrugged in his soft, inhuman way.
"When you see Holders Fastness, you may understand.
Holders ring is . . . very influential. Now, please, go in the
transport without further delay."

Viktor watched her approach the bridge, a dubious expression on her face. At her sides the children (Vadim and
Elle, he had to remember their *names*) reached out to
touch the railing. Their hands appeared to touch solid
matter, and Malye copied them, and once satisfied with
the corporeality of the bridge, set out gingerly across it.

Unaccountably, little Elle began to cry again. She'd
pretty much been crying all day. But her brother crossed
willingly enough, and after tarrying a moment at the
ledge, she hurried after him, screeching for him to *wait*!
Their mother disappeared through the hatchway, and a
second or so later so did they.

The bureaucrat, Konstant, went next, trailing his hand
along the rail, gaping at it with mingled wonder and dis-
approval. And then came Sasha, and then the gray-haired
Nik and strong, stocky Vere, who still struck Viktor as the
two "realest" people among the newly revived. Together
the two of them made a point of kicking the bridge and
railing struts sharply several times, grimly satisfying
themselves that the structure was sound before they
would step across. Even so, Viktor saw the woman com-
pulsively fingering her "lucky bracelet." And when they
were across, Sasha followed, and then Svetlane Antoneve
and the older Ludmile Viktrovne, looking neither up nor
down, but at one another with sad, fearful eyes. There
was an edge of indignation there, as well. *Oh, this future
world is so awful, so frightening, such a terrible burden*

to us personally. Well, he supposed they were entitled to a bit of selfish emotion.

And that left Viktor himself to bring up the rear, with Plate's wormy fingers and snaky arms practically shoving him out onto the bridge of fog.

"Come on, she will be here in just a moment!"

Viktor snarled: "I'm going, Plate. Take your hands off me."

The bridge felt solid enough beneath his sandals. Very solid, in fact—almost unyieldingly so, as if it were cast from a single crystal of quartz or diamond. But through it he could see, far below, the cylindrical chamber's floor, a flat and fragile-looking sheet, like the white membrane doors, only scaled up to a much larger size.

He could not fight down a sense of dizzy near-panic, a light tingling in his feet. He was supported here by a thing he did not understand, a thing whose true characteristics he had no way of guessing, and he realized suddenly that this had never happened to him before, never in all his life. From earliest childhood, he had been in the habit of taking things apart, of demanding explanations and demonstrations, of knowing how things were supposed to work and how they actually *did*—the two were rarely the same. But here, he was not given much chance to ask, to be demonstrated to, to make demands. And truthfully, he was not entirely sure he wanted to know. What if things had simply come too far, raced out ahead of his intuition, into some strange, incomprehensible realm? What if he simply *couldn't* understand?

High above, the rust-colored ferry hung from the ceiling by . . . another fog of some sort. He couldn't quite make it out. Names of Ialah, at least the ship itself was built of solid matter. He wasn't sure he could stand having nothing but fog between himself and the great vacuum.

And then the bridge was behind him and he was stepping through the ferry's hatchway. Inside, it was much darker; his eyes took a second or two to adjust.

Purple. Inside the ferry was an octohedral chamber, much like the ones back in the cavern, only smaller, less adorned, and a whole lot more purple. Even the lights, the usual trio hovering motionless in the chamber's center, were more violet than white, vaguely painful to look at despite their dimness. There was a hexagonal opening in the ceiling, webbed over with pale lavender membrane, but with no ladder leading up to it or through it. But then he noticed a ring of fog surrounding the opening; ladder on demand, perhaps. Or maybe a staircase, or maybe the fog simply extended a friendly hand and lifted you up through the hole.

Plate crowded in behind Viktor and urged him farther into the chamber, which was already crowded, the enormous Drone seeming to take up by himself nearly as much space as the other nine humans put together.

"Make room," Plate said, "here she comes."

Viktor crowded off to the side, and turned just in time to see the lighted entryway eclipsed by a massive form. Not Wende, but the other Drone. "Mark," he was called, though whether it was the noun, as in marks on a holie flatscreen, or the old Earth name, as in Mark of the Gospels, Viktor didn't know.

Mark hulked in through the hatchway, his hands extended before him and then sweeping out in wide arcs, clearing a path. His arm, when it brushed against Viktor's chest, was as large and cold and solid as a high-pressure waterline, and his head bobbed improbably on that great rubber neck, copper gaze seeming to flick suspiciously from one person to the next.

Viktor was reminded sharply of the prime minister's personal bodyguards, who had always behaved exactly this way at her various and numerous public appearances. As if the crowd were somehow dangerous, as if she must be insulated from them as much as possible, lest their touch corrupt her.

And right behind the giant Mark came the even more giant Wende herself, blocking the light from outside almost completely; her round, flabby body filling pretty much the entire doorway. Ialah, was there even room in here for such a creature? Viktor decided this would be a good time to crowd himself up against the wall and look small.

Mark made his way four meters or so to the chamber's center, and then—

And then he disappeared. More properly, he ascended through the membrane-covered opening in the ceiling, so quickly that Viktor's eyes could scarcely determine what had happened. Mark's body was not still during its rise, but had flailed its arms and legs in a peculiar way, not alarmed, not climbing, but ... something. Graceful, like a high-gravity pool dive performed in reverse. The membrane opened and closed for him in its usual way, leaving no trace that he'd been standing there on the deck just an eye blink before.

"Ialah!" somebody said, startled.

Now Wende came forward, moving slowly and rather more gracefully than Viktor would have imagined, her platter-size sandals slapping quietly against the hard purple floor. Her green hair and the thin white robe she wore did not bounce or flap as she walked, or rather did not do so at normal speed—they seemed imprisoned, moving jellylike through the near-transparent layer of security fog that surrounded her, following her every move and jiggle.

Viktor felt his hair standing on end. What a ghastly figure she cut, marching along like that, her surfaces undulating with such underwater slowness! Like a ghost, a fat, flabby ghost, except that he could *feel* her solidity even from a meter away. She seemed to displace the air, to displace spacetime itself around her.

Her gaze also wandered, her head— so very much like a melon draped with folds of gray rubber—swinging nearly a hundred eighty degrees one way and then the other as she moved, as if nothing anchored it but skin. When her eyes met Viktor's, he saw with a chill that she was smiling; a cold, reptilian grin that did not belong on a human being's face.

Her legs were longer than they looked; she reached the chamber's center after only a couple of steps. And then she, too, was waving her arms, and raising them, and kicking hard against the deck as if leaping. Which was ridiculous, of course, but she became airborne just the same, a flicker of structural fog surrounding her like a winding glass helix. And then the membrane absorbed her and she was gone.

Right behind her was Crow, who also flashed up through the opening, and the Dog came in behind him, and then Line stepped back into the chamber's center again and vanished in the same way.

Which left Plate the only Gatean remaining. All eyes were on him.

"Thank you for your cooperation," he said.

The hatchway irised shut with a faint whispering sound. The ferry began to hum.

"This is probably somewhat disconcerting," Plate noted wisely. "I'll try to answer any questions you might have before Wende comes down to speak with you again. If she chooses to, that is."

Viktor could not suppress a nervous chuckle. "I have a question or two, yes."

But at that moment there was a great banging noise, and without warning the gravity vanished, leaving them all in sudden free fall. As one, the refugees gasped as their feet skidded along the floor, losing contact. The ferry had dropped! The ferry was falling through the membrane-floor of its holding chamber, falling through some deep shaft below that, falling, *still* falling, and Viktor found that he was too busy screaming to ask any questions after all.

Chapter 11

CONGRESS OF ADVISORS:
UNIT 312293, 8642nd SESSION (PARTIAL)
CONTINUITY 5218, YEAR OF THE DRAGON

"What is wrong with these people, these Gateans?" Malye asked the ghost of Ken Jonson. "They look up to you, even though you're nothing like them. What did you do that they admire so much?"

The chaos of the ferry's interior was gone, vanished with the flick of a thumb trigger. A few questions, a few commands, and suddenly she and Jonson were sitting in a tiny conference room, walls covered in a heavy beige cloth of some sort, the chairs and table of steel and red plastic, the floor of some sort of tile, not ceramic. Between them sat Mediator, who apparently could not be dismissed for fear that she, the user, might be confused or misled by the opinions of a simulacrum, which of course were not facts, nor even necessarily good advice. Though how Mediator thought he could tell good advice from bad, she wasn't at all sure.

Jonson, in a military uniform she did not recognize, was a small-framed but muscular man, pale-skinned, his age indeterminate except for the streaks of gray in his brown hair, particularly at the temples. He had no emotional aura, per se, no complex mélange of smells and tiny involuntary movements to indicate his mind's inner workings. He was, after all, a machine, a simplification of the gist of the original persona, or so Mediator had informed her. And yet, there *were* nuances of the sort that a sculpture or still portrait might capture; a good portrait, not like an arrest-record holograph or the sort of hasty flatscreen scan people took of their friends and relatives. The image of Ken Jonson that the Congress projected was one of confidence, of weariness, of a man who had seen too much, done too much, been repudiated and vindicated and repudiated again, many times over the course of his life. He looked, in some obscure way, like Malye's father had in the closing days before Central Investigations had come to take him away. The monster at the end of his career.

"That question exceeds in part the historical boundaries of this simulacrum's experience," Moderator cautioned. "It is possible to feed archival data to the simulacrum in order to obtain its analysis, its 'opinion,' if you will, but the result must be considered highly suspect."

"I just want to know what he thinks," Malye said.

"You wish to link the simulacrum to the archive?"

"All right, yes."

"And to the oracle?"

Oracle? "Um, no. I don't think so."

Ken Jonson smiled at her with weary politeness. "To answer your question, Colonel, I need to step back a few paces. Are you familiar with the term 'aggressor?' " When Malye shook her head he went on, "It comes to us from the late English, a word meaning 'enemy' or 'attacker.' But in its later meaning there is a subtext to it, a nuance of deceit, of camouflage. The aggressor is the one who poses as his own enemy, who lives and thinks and spits like his enemy."

"The better to understand," Malye said, echoing what Plate had told her.

Jonson nodded. "That's exactly correct. The people you call Gateans are members of what is more generally known as the Aggressor Cult, individuals who for various reasons have elected to live like Waisters."

"And you founded this cult?"

Jonson made a face as if something bitter had dropped into his mouth. "God, no. I was drafted into it, long before it was anything like a religion. The navy made me do it, put a Broca web in my brain and shipped me off to a secret base near Saturn. The jewel of Sol system." He snorted without amusement. "I was very good at my job. The war ended when it did because we followed our instructions precisely. Because *I* did. Becoming the enemy, fighting against our own kind, surrendering to the Waisters . . . It worked, but it's not something I'm proud of."

"But the Gateans are," Malye observed.

Jonson leaned back in his chair. "You know, all my life I was accused of going too far, of taking things too far. I was a translator for twenty years, and I tried to pull across every nuance I possibly could, every concept for which there was common ground for understanding. And people said I was making it up, reading too much into it; the information couldn't possibly be that dense. I can't count the number of times people said I was crazy; it happened all the time. 'Jonson has shed his humanity, Jonson has ceased to be a reliable source of information. Jonson is a fucking whacko.' On and on. But by Aggressor standards I'm extremely conservative. I always was."

Malye could not help smiling, if grimly. "What would they think, these people who said you were crazy? What would they think if they could see the Gate colony now?"

Jonson simply nodded—she had clearly touched the core of his identity, of his self-image. The cautious man, who knew full well the dangers that he faced. How far down that road could you travel without losing sight of your original goals? Without losing sight of who you were and what you were really trying to accomplish? How long could you keep it up without becoming a monster?

"I have the feeling," she said, more slowly and guardedly now, "that the Gateans mean some harm to the human 'Suzerainty.' They are so far from it, so very far, I can't imagine what they have in mind . . . But I've dealt with rebels all my life, people who refuse to recognize any rules but their own, any *needs* but their own. I know the look, and I find it here."

Jonson was nodding again, sitting up straighter in his seat. "Yes. You have to understand, they view themselves as quite distinct from humanity, and rightly so. Their bodies are filled with machinery from the molecular level right up to the macroscopic. Fantastically efficient. And genetically, they've adopted a number of nonhuman attributes—the hypermobility collagens and collagenated bones, for just one example, and the chlorophyll to reduce their nutritional requirements . . ."

"Yes? So? I never thought they were human."

"They would certainly agree with you about that, and because of their perceived novelty they have a desire to confront. They *expect* to be confronted. And the Suzerainty of the Human Spaces has changed and evolved in their absence, in the centuries they spent traveling to Gate system, so that is a new thing, also."

Even the Human Spaces had changed? Well, of course they had, but Malye couldn't help wondering just how different things could be, just how lost her own worlds and cultures were in the fog and distance of time. There hadn't even *been* an interstellar community when she was alive, not really.

"How different is it?" she asked.

Jonson seemed to understand the meaning behind her question. His voice was gentle. "I'm not really qualified to answer that. I've been dead a long time. But it seems to me that human history is a cyclic phenomenon; we build and build and build, striving and struggling toward these fantastic goals that seem just out of reach, everything moving better and faster and smarter, but then we fall back. The Clementine Monarchy, the collapse of the Second Colonial Age. The Fall of Rome, the Fall of America."

"The Fall of Sirius?" she asked, not quite sure what he was getting at.

But he nodded. "I think so, yes. The collapse never seems to come from within; it's always some external force that triggers it. But it always comes, doesn't it? Something catches us off guard. We notch up a little higher on every cycle, but we never reach that breakthrough point when all the curves go vertical, when everything becomes easy for us, and the universe is our playground. Maybe we never can."

Malye doubted that, and shook her head to show it. "The Waisters. Ialah, they were *so* powerful, melting whole planets . . . There was nothing we could do against them. They've crossed that line. It can be done."

"I doubt it," Ken Jonson said, and now he was smiling again, once more the tired man who had seen too much. "I could write everything we know about Waister history on my thumbnail and still have room to chew the white part off, but in dealing with them I always sensed a certain . . . stagnation, I guess. They seem very old, very set in their ways. Their civilization has been around a long time, several million years at least, and if I had to guess,

I'd say their history isn't cyclic at all. I'd say they're approaching their breakthrough point asymptotically, or possibly even retreating from it. It would disturb them, the idea that they might become something new, something incomprehensible to their present selves. There's no way to confront a thing like that, not without experiencing it. But how could they experience it without confronting it first? They'd be very uncomfortable with the paradox."

Malye thought about that, and decided the information was nothing she could make use of. What was it she wanted to know? What questions, specifically, had she come in here to ask? Suddenly she wasn't sure. Everything was so new and so frightening, and no amount of Congressional advice seemed to make her feel any better about her position here. Where were they going? What was Holders Fastness, that it held such sway over the minds and hearts of Wende's six? These were not questions Ken Jonson's ghost could answer, nor anyone else in the Congress. The answers lay, rather, in the real world from which she was presently hiding.

"Thank you very much for your time," she said to Jonson, with a respectfulness that felt right, however unnecessary it might be. And then she released the thumb trigger on top of the Congress, and returned at once to the hold of the Gatean ferry.

She'd only been gone a moment, it seemed—she tumbled weightlessly through the chamber, Plate floating calmly in the corner across from her, serene amid chaos.

Everyone else was still screaming and thrashing in the air, their eyes bulging, white flickers of terror dancing around them. Weightlessness was one thing, but they were *falling*, still high inside the world of Pinega and dropping outward toward Ialah knew what. If they hit anything . . . well, assuming the ferry itself survived, they would all be smashed together in one happy splatter, and there wasn't a damn thing Malye could do to prevent it.

The thought struck her as obscurely, obscenely funny, and for the first time in almost two standard years, she threw her head back and joined her father's voice in laughter.

* * *

"So how long will this trip take?" Malye asked Plate.

Once the engines had fired, everything had settled back to the deck once more, and fortunately, nobody had vomited in the interim. They had fallen, Plate said, through an eighty-kilometer shaft that followed a Coriolis curve all the way out to Pinega's surface, before reorienting in open space and beginning their burn. And the engines on this ferry (or "transport," as Plate preferred to call it), unlike the ones she was used to, fired continuously at low thrust, so that there was no crushing acceleration, no invisible sack of potatoes pressing down, and also no weightlessness during the course of the trip. Which seemed like a good thing, because they'd all had their share of it already, and there were no cribs here, no safety straps, no handrails, nothing to hold onto at all except maybe the shitter.

And really, the light acceleration was very comfortable. Generally, people had always stayed away from low gravity in Pinega, it being considered a kind of effete addiction, akin to overeating. Low-grav sports had never been very popular there, nor high-grav ones for that matter, since the very worst Pinega had to offer was 0.9 gee. But yes, the *reason* it was considered effete was because it was so pleasant—you could easily lounge and play in an environment like this for months or years, until your bones went soft and required medical attention.

Still, people in many of the worlds simply didn't worry about it. There had been a few Lesser Worlds that had no spin-gee at all, just the whisper-soft gravitational pull of the rock itself, and those people either gobbled medicine to keep themselves strong, or else consigned themselves to those few worlds for life, too weak to survive in the more normal environments.

And then again, there had been some high-gravity worlds, with equatorial spin of two gees or more, whose citizens grew up strong and short and arrogant, carrying the invisible sack of potatoes with them every day, everywhere they went. A lot of crime in those worlds, at least by Sirian standards, and a lot of accidents as well, simple scrapes and falls turned deadly in the heavy gee. If Malye had to pick an optimal gravity, it would probably be somewhere around 0.75—enough to hold everything down (like the children, for example, who tended to bounce around maniacally in low gee), but light enough to let you feel free and alive. But here, at barely 0.3, she was comfortable enough for the moment, if a little giddy.

So, it seemed, was Plate—he had wedged himself into one of the octohedral chamber's many corners, his head at the intersection of two triangular walls, his sandaled feet flat on the deck, his back and legs entirely unsupported. In higher gravity he'd have broken his spine. Or perhaps not—he seemed so often to be made of rubber, of bean curd, a life-size but boneless doll from some anatomy classroom somewhere.

He smiled at her in a very human way, though, and said, "We should be in Holders Fastness in about fifteen hours, I think."

"You're much calmer now," Malye said.

Viktor, who was sitting cross-legged beside her, nodded. "Yeah. You know, I've worked on emergency life-support controllers that changed operating states slower than you people. Hot, cold, pressure up, pressure down ... What exactly is your problem?"

"We are not in need of repair," Plate said with guarded amusement.

Malye cleared her throat, summoning her Investigator's voice, her I'm-on-your-side-so-why-don't-you-let-me-help-you voice. "Tell me about Holders Fastness."

"It orbits close to Small White, the star you call Bee."

"Holders Fastness is one of the Thousand Lesser Worlds?" Viktor asked.

Plate nodded. "Yes, almost certainly, although I couldn't tell you which one. I don't think any among us could; our knowledge of your time is very patchy and imprecise. Many of the old worlds have shattered, anyway; Holders Fastness may simply be one of the fragments. Its shape is very irregular."

"Irregular like a hat? Like this?" Viktor said, sketching out a three-dimensional shape with his hands.

"No."

"Like a bird's wing?" He made another shape. "Two hundred kilometers long? Tumbling end-over-end once every six minutes?"

Plate squinted his copper eyes for a moment, then nodded. "Yes, like that. You have familiarity with it?"

"It's called Artya. There's—there *was*—a lot of heavy industry there."

"What I wanted to know"—Malye cut in, but immediately she had to turn away and shout: "Children, stop it!"

Vadim had invented some sort of game that involved hurling his sister up to bounce among the crazy planes and angles of the ceiling. She was attempting to sing a song Malye couldn't quite make out, her voice shrieking with delight. She held her robe down fastidiously against her knees as she flew, but she wasn't looking down, and Konstant sat by the two of them, speaking in low, urgent tones to Sasha and Nikolai, and Elle's second landing had very nearly been on top of their heads. Konstant glared now in Malye's direction, as did Vadim. *How dare you interrupt me, Mother,* his eight-year-old eyes said.

Though she threatened punishment, in truth it warmed Malye to see the children behaving so outrageously. They clearly missed their father desperately, and were frightened and horrified by all that had happened to them since his death, but they simply couldn't sustain their grief for more than a few hours at a time. They still had childhood energy that needed burning, one way or another.

"Be good," she warned, though, for propriety's sake, and after a moment Vadim dropped his eyes. One such warning should suffice; Malye's punishments tended toward the severe, sudden twists and holds that, while not immediately painful, could become so without effort and therefore encouraged instant obedience. And Vadim would especially hate to be so treated in front of strangers—there was a lot of dignity bound up in that small body. Indeed, he seemed prouder and more defiant with each passing year, so that it was not difficult to imagine the day when he would simply stare his mother down and go on about his business, when he would slip away from her punishing hands, when he would begin to conceive revenges and punishments of his own . . .

It was Grigory's chin he thrust out at those moments, but the eyes were purely Andrei Brakanov's. *Do you hear the colors, Vadim?* Oh, Ialah. But for the moment, thankfully, he was still very much in her power.

She turned back to Plate once more. "I wanted to know why you were so anxious before, when you rounded us up. This Holders ring, it's a group that holds power over you, over Finders ring, and over Wende herself, correct?"

"Not power, no. Influence, obligation; the word is 'giri' in Teigo, the language of the Suzerainty. Please understand, madam, that without the efforts of Holders ring, there would be no Gate colony at all. By contrast, *we* have done very little for the common good, and so we are deeply in their debt. Everyone is deeply in their debt."

"Including us," Malyc said. "So when they call, we must come running."

Wedged in the corner as he was, Plate couldn't nod, but he grunted his acknowledgment instead. "That is essentially correct. They expressed a concern that we were withholding information, or that you were. They feared knowledge existed that was not being shared. The accusation, which probably came originally from Talkers ring, is untrue and unfair. By presenting you and your fellows in person for a full accounting, Wende hopes to demonstrate our contributive nature and to allay any further suspicion."

"And with all possible haste," Malye observed. "Why is that, Plate? What exactly will they *do*?"

Plate shrugged, which caused him to slide a few centimeters down the wall. "I don't know what to tell you. Talkers ring is spreading rumors, to draw attention away from their unauthorized communications with the Suzerainty. The Waisters will be here in ninety hours, and everyone is working to secret agendas. Everyone but us."

"How very noble," Viktor said, sniffing with amusement.

It struck Malye, how very un-doomed everyone was acting—even she herself. Could it be that on some level, they all really did have some kind of backhanded faith in the Gateans? Or were they simply weary of their fear, simply taking a rest from it while stuck on this ferry?

Even as she thought this, she saw Konstant getting angrily to his feet, leveling a finger at Plate.

"You," he said. "Get your Queen, please. I need to speak with her right away."

Plate stiffened, sliding another several centimeters down the crease between the walls. "Concerning?"

"Concerning our treatment," Konstant flared. He turned his pointing finger toward Malye. "This woman negotiated in bad faith, without consulting the rest of us, and I must *insist* that Wende hear our demands."

"*Your* demands," the elderly Nikolai corrected, from over where he was sitting with Sasha. In another corner, the three women looked up.

Sighing, Plate snapped forward into a cross-legged position and settled to the floor. "Wende is occupied, and could well remain so throughout our voyage. What is your concern?"

"My *concern* is that we are free citizens, entitled to come and go as we please, and this woman, Malyene Andreivne, has no business dictating our fates. And neither do you, and neither does your beloved Queen."

Before Konstant had even finished saying the words, Plate was up and moving, his feet seeming to skate in the low gravity without ever quite touching the floor. He skidded into Konstant and stood in front of him with arms spread and waving in a fierce display.

"Do you *confront*?" he asked with hot clarity. "Are you a new thing, untested? Is it your desire that I call down the Drones and watch them crush you? This woman, Malyene Andreivne Kurosov'e, has made peace with Wende. If that peace does not include you, tell me now."

To his credit, Konstant flinched only slightly and then held his ground. But his face was crimson with rage.

"Are you and the woman at peace?" Plate demanded to know, and though his build was slight and rubbery, he held himself with full confidence, as if nothing could harm him, as if he could crush Konstant with a thought.

And this, Malye reminded herself, was the peaceful member of the family.

Konstant's anger blazed out from him in crackling red waves, but after a moment's thought he turned to Malye and said, "You have them well trained, *Colonel*. It seems we are at your disposal."

"Names of Ialah," Viktor said disdainfully, "will you people just follow Malyene's lead? The Gateans *respect* her, and if you thought about it for a moment, you might wonder if maybe you should, too. I shudder to think where we'd all be right now if not for her. If she hadn't bullied her way into that cryo ward when—"

"Viktor," Malyene interrupted, "shut up. Konstant is

quite right; I have no authority to run your lives, nor any desire to. Plate, if you've been regarding me as some sort of leader, then stop it now. I won't stand for it. Really, I refuse to be responsible."

Plate turned his head almost all the way around to face her, and shrugged with deep fluidity. "Madam, I'm afraid that choice has already been made. Such as you are, such as you've done, it is in our nature to accept you as a known and tested quantity. These others . . . if they are not yours, then they're new, and we will break them. I thought this was understood."

"We are hers," Viktor declared, bowing slightly to Malye. "We are definitely, *definitely* hers. No breaking necessary, thanks very much."

"Damn you," Malye said to Viktor, tasting white fear on her tongue. "You don't know me at all. You don't have any idea what you're doing."

"On the contrary," Viktor said, staring back at her with calm, serious eyes.

I could kill you for this, she thought fiercely, and indeed, that was the whole problem. In this time and place, all the monster's careful routines were shattered, her balancing mechanisms jammed. She *wanted* the power, and that frightened her more than anything else, because she had no idea what she wanted it for.

"The authorities can take your property, your freedom, your life," her father had told her once with a laugh, "under circumstances they themselves dictate. What a fine thing it must be, eh?"

The palm chronometer was a kind of animated tattoo, ticking off the seconds and minutes of the day, or else presenting a date when tapped twice in the proper way. The refugees' dates were hopelessly confused—they'd all been frozen at different times, and clearly some of the chronometers had continued counting for a while afterward, while others had simply been randomized by the process, or by the long years that followed. Malye figured it would just be too depressing to figure out what the date actually was, but she did suggest they synchronize to a particular time of day, which activity consumed everyone's attention for the next several hours as they tried to deduce and/or remember how this rare feat was accomplished. Normally, the chronometers would synchronize automatically to broadcast standard time. Normally.

Surprisingly, it was little Elle who knew the most about the subject, having learned about it in one of her nursery classes, before the Bad Teacher had entered her life. She'd gotten a lot more practical-type instruction than Malye ever had at that age, which would have been wonderful had not the society it was practical *for* been so promptly destroyed.

When all the chronometers had been set, though, Plate produced food for them from somewhere in the transport's upper spaces, and they talked and ate and talked some more, until their self-declared "night" began to draw near. Moods crashed at this point, arguments flaring up with little provocation, most of them ending in tears, and Malye finally asked Plate to turn the lights down for them, declaring an early bedtime.

Surprisingly, Plate did not go back up to join his family, his "six," but elected to remain here with the refugees, claiming he needed just as much rest as they did, and preferred to take it in their company.

"I have been charged with your care," he explained.

Viktor found the lighting controls and reduced the three ghostly light globes down to bright stars, night-lights for the ten of them, who lay sprawled on the floor in the easy gravity. First night here for some of them, though for him it was the second. And tomorrow the third, and the night after that, the fourth. How long would it be before he lost count? Would he live that long?

Conversation died with the lights, though the weeping and moaning grew louder. *Oh, we poor refugees!* They had not yet realized that the way to deal with their various tragedies was not to deal with them at all. It was a difficult concept, he supposed, and even *he* had broken down a time or two the night before, surging awake with screams of horror trapped in his throat. In his dreams, it was not so easy to be flip, nor was it while lying around in the dark with nine miserable people, two of them children.

Still, he was pretty damn tired, and sleep found him quickly in spite of it all. And dreams, oh, yes.

* * *

"Can I look out the window?" Elle asked Plate brightly. Morning again, a time for the hurt to retreat a little.

It was usually difficult to get Elle to eat anything but fruit and soya mash, but she had eaten the Gatean food willingly enough this morning. She'd complained several times about wearing the same robe two days in a row—at some point while Malye was away on business, Elle had become fanatic on the subject of clean clothing—but even this mood was short-lived, quickly overcome by her curiosity.

"Of course," Plate replied, imitating her tone. The better to understand her, Malye wondered?

The chamber's floor was triangular, met by six triangular walls in a confusion of right angles, three of them joining the floor at their points, the other three at their edges. Of these three walls, one held the sink and shitter, another the hatch through which they had entered. Plate walked up to the third wall, which was blank and purple and shiny-looking, and rapped on it sharply with his knuckles. This produced a muted, solid sound, as if he were rapping on stone, but an opening formed where he touched, and in a moment it had expanded to a circular hole.

Malye felt a stab of fear when she saw stars, and her heart hammered even when she realized that the transport was not decompressing, that the hole was not really a hole at all. The other refugees startled similarly, except for Elle herself, who seemed not to realize the potential danger. Perhaps her education had not been so practical after all.

But the window was secure, Malye saw: a thick, transparent plate, held firmly in place by the even thicker metal of the transport's hull. One edge of the window frame outside caught blue-white sunlight and reflected it fiercely, brightening the transport's interior.

"Where is Holders Fastness?" Elle asked, hopping excitedly to the window in the low gravity. "Can we see it?"

"I don't know," Plate said, craning his neck inhumanly as he peered through the transparent material. "I think . . . well, yes, there it is." He pointed in a generally downward direction.

Elle clapped. "I see it! Momma, Vad, I see it!"

Never one to miss out on a good view, Vadim moved to join his sister at the window. And so did everyone else, crowding forward with a distinct lack of composure, their veneer of adult calm stripped away by the promise of *actually seeing something.* Something other than blank white chambers, or purple ones, something other than green-haired, gray-skinned people who looked like nothing human. And Holders Fastness, formerly known as the world of Artya, was something they might actually recognize, something that had come forward through the years from a much earlier time, just as they themselves had done.

Malye couldn't see it clearly, didn't want to force her way through the crowd for a better view, but Viktor shoved right up to the window, scanned for a moment, and then . . . froze.

"Wait, no," he said. "That isn't Artya."

"It is," said Vere Sergeivne, craning her thick, muscled neck. "Look, you can see the Promontory Ridge running, um, down the spine of it. At least, I *think* it's the Promontory Ridge. The shape is not quite . . ."

"This planetoid had been partially melted and then re-solidified," Plate said carefully, "at the time of the Waister infarct. We surveyed the body when Holders ring first occupied it—and by 'we' I mean Finders ring, including myself—and we found no definitive signs of human habitation. This is typical of the entire system, though, and by itself means nothing."

"Oh, Ialah," someone groaned. It seemed the only possible comment.

And finally, Malye *did* push forward to the window to peer down at the object herself.

She didn't know what to look for, wasn't really sure how Artya was supposed to appear, but the small world that lay at her feet was a dual-lobed body like a cucumber that had been stepped on, and notched deeply in the middle with some not-too-sharp implement. The harsh light reflecting off its dayside revealed a surface that was smooth, almost shiny, and quite free of the pitting and scarring you would normally expect to see. It looked bad, not at all like any world Malye had ever heard about. It looked exactly like factory slag, like something that had been partially melted and then resolidified.

As for signs of human habitation, the night side of the world had been striped with dotted rings of light, unwinking, the individual light sources looking alien and unnatural somehow. Too big maybe, and too dim for their size, and looking as if they did not quite touch the world's surface, but hovered motionless a slight distance above it. And they were all one color and one brightness, and they were spaced so evenly that the whole thing might pass for some quick-and-easy computer enhancement, a grid wrapped around an irregular object to highlight its features more precisely.

"Names," another voice echoed.

"No, I'm afraid Vere is mistaken," Malye declared firmly, and with a deliberately false air of expertise. She pushed her face almost up against the window, looking down and sideways for the clearest possible view. "This isn't Artya. It isn't any of the Thousand Lesser Worlds at all. Obviously this is a new world, previously unknown to us."

People were breathing all around her, breathing in the sharp, heavy way of those who are about to speak. But no one spoke. No one felt like contradicting her declaration.

She turned away from the window, fixed her eyes on Plate. "How soon until we dock?"

"Not long," he said, looking back at her, and for some reason his copper eyes were sad, as if he had begun to comprehend the magnitude of their loss, to sympathize with it, to realize there was no comfort he could possibly offer.

You, Malye thought impatiently, *who claimed not to be human.*

Chapter 12

HOLDERS FASTNESS, GATE SYSTEM: CONTINUITY 5218, YEAR OF THE DRAGON

The new world proved just as alien on the inside as on the out. High gravity, for one thing; probably very nearly two gee's, which came as quite a shock after relaxing in a tenth that much aboard the transport. There were white, hexagonal corridors just like the ones in reclaimed Pinega, except that here they wound together in a twisted mess that quickly stymied Malye's sense of direction. Like noodles in a bowl, almost, and also the corridors here were crowded with Gateans, mostly Workers, who moved about unhurriedly but with palpable self-importance, their chins held high.

Everywhere, she heard the fluting, huffing, scraping sounds of the Waister language, aesthetically compelling and yet seemingly neither musical nor linguistic in its patterning. Really it was just noise, like modulated static. But it was everywhere, echoing through the crowds, filling up the breathing air with its alienness.

Plate had told her that this whole world was not hollowed out and occupied pole-to-pole, as Tyumen had been, nor inhabited superficially, in its near-surface crustal layers like Pinega. The shape and composition of the planetoid didn't lend itself to such projects, and anyway the cucumber tumbled end over end, producing a fierce spin-gee gradient between the center and the outstretched tips, and it was the high-gravity portions the Gateans preferred to occupy. Just like Waisters, of course, the better to understand them.

"Holders Fastness" was in fact just a warren of tunnels and chambers at one of the cucumber's ends, the whole complex no more than five kilometers from top to bottom. Which relieved her, because at this population density the world could easily hold hundreds of millions of Gateans, and that was something she'd rather not have to think about.

The refugees marched in more or less the same way they had in boarding the transport that morning—Crow and Wende and Mark and the nameless Dog filling the space behind them, with Line and Plate leading the way ahead. The children, evidently not bothered by the heavy gee, amused themselves by running out ahead and then running back to badger Plate and Line with questions. At first Malye worried about this, about what Line might do if the children managed to annoy or upset him, but in fact he seemed to be ignoring them almost completely, and Plate actually appeared to enjoy their attention, so she decided to let them be. They would spend their whole lives in this future, however long or short it proved to be for them; best that they enjoy themselves when they could.

And so Malye found herself, as in the much quieter and simpler time that already seemed many days distant, walking between Viktor and Sasha, and speaking with them in low tones.

"I think I could almost get the hang of this," Viktor was saying. "The Gateans are strange, yes, but it's just a matter of deducing their operating states. Do this, they behave that way. Do that, they behave this way. That's all emotions are anyway, just a change of operating states. You see that in any machine."

"People aren't like machines," Sasha cautioned in his usual defeated tone.

"No, they're not machines," Malye said, "but Viktor is right; there's nothing random about them. We are not powerless here, not quite, but what influence we have, we don't know how to use. We've benefited thus far from luck and intuition, but that has to change; it *will* change. Intuition is worthless without understanding."

It went on like that for a while, not exactly idle chatter but not focused either, not productive. They didn't know what was going on, or what was expected of them, or anything, really.

The walk was long, a kilometer at least, and through

endlessly twisting hallways, but eventually they came to a membrane-door that led them into what was clearly an elevator, a large white platform at the bottom (or middle?) of a hexagonal shaft which rose to dizzying heights above them, terminating in a flat ceiling just barely visible in the distance. When Wende and her entourage oozed through the membrane, crowding in behind the refugees as they had in the transport's hold, the air smelled close and sweet. *I wonder how we smell to them?* she thought suddenly. Probably, she didn't want to know. The platform began to hum.

"Don't lean against the wall," Plate cautioned, his voice echoing and echoing upward, and then they were rising, slowly, the membrane doorway sinking beneath the floor, many others moving down the shaft toward them on the six walls. Everyone was silent. The ascent took several minutes, and covered what must surely be a hundred meters or more of vertical distance.

And then the platform stopped again, and Line hulked his way through the crowd to exit the membrane first, Plate trailing behind him as if in tow. Everyone followed. They were getting good at this; it was starting to come naturally. Was that a good thing or a bad?

The new corridor looked just like the old, and snaked about so much that floors twisted around to become walls and even ceilings. Any surface might hold a doorway, its orientation only approximately horizontal. Malye began to suspect that the laser-straight corridors Wende's people had built at Pinega were more a matter of expedience than of aesthetics—clearly this place would be, in every way, just as the Gateans wanted it. How did they find their way around?

This time, it wasn't long before the group came to another membrane that Line and Plate stepped through. Malye, who found herself at the front of the queue again, followed them, trying not to shiver as the faint, dry touch of the membrane kissed across her skin, across the thin robe that covered it.

On the other side, there was a . . . throne room?

A perfect white octohedral chamber, of the sort so very much in fashion these days but significantly larger, and with three smaller chambers sticking off it in three directions. It was through one of these lobes that Malye had entered, but the whole space was open, vaulted, a hollow cathedral of the sort you might once have found in Tyumen, though perhaps not quite so grand.

And it was absolutely *full* of Gateans, a hundred of them at least. Malye stepped out of the way so everyone else could get inside, and the chambers filled up even farther.

At the chamber's center was a dais, about a meter and a half higher than the surrounding floor, on which sat three couches, and a truly enormous Queen, who outweighed Wende by a good thirty percent, with two equivalently proportioned Drones lounging on either side. At their feet sat a pair of Workers, with a Dog curled up between them, apparently asleep.

It didn't take a lot of brainpower to figure out this Queen was top silver, that she and her six were members of the dreaded Holders ring, perhaps even the leaders of it. Did rings have leaders? There was so much Malye didn't know. But enough to get by, perhaps, if she stopped playing along and started making the rules up herself. *The best defense,* her father had once told her, *is a vicious attack to the eyes and genitals.*

Ialah help them all.

She rounded on Wende, puffed herself up as best she could, squared her shoulders, and held her arms away from her sides to create a false impression of mass. It felt somewhat absurd, but absurd tricks like this were common in the animal kingdom, and as often as not they worked, at least a little. Or so she'd been told. And whether or not they were human, the Gateans were certainly more animal than mineral.

"Wende," she said calmly but forcefully, "stay here. Keep everyone with you."

And then, without bothering to gauge the Queen's reaction, she turned and started for the dais. The crowd, who had all turned to face her, fell into startled silence, and stepped aside to make room for her as she advanced, holding them back with her eyes. She moved through a sandaled, white-robed corridor of fat and thin and muscular and four-footed bodies, of Gateans, Aggressor Cultists, green-haired, gray-skinned people who looked like something a child might conceive with a flatscreen and a mismatched set of drawing sticks.

Shapes and sounds marched across her tongue. Blues and yellows, uncertainty and opportunity and the sharp angles of surprise all around her. But there was no bitter, electric white to spoil the flavor—she was not afraid. Her mind was as clean and clear as a glass of water: free of plans, of recriminations and self-doubt, operating on pure instinct.

The monster was free.

On the dais, the Queen began to look a little alarmed, and her Drones stiffened, ready to roll off their couches and drop into action at any time. They didn't know what Malye was up to, and they didn't like that. It was *new*, and they didn't like new things one bit. They *crushed* new things, untested things, whenever possible, yes?

But nobody had ever accused the monster of being stupid. Three meters from the dais, she suddenly threw herself down, kneeling, arms extended until they touched the floor, her forehead following, nose flattening against the warm, slick, seamless ceramic.

"Oh, great Queen!" she called out without raising her head. "I, and all who attend me, surrender before your great strength!"

These had been the first words to enter her head, the only words, and she said them without reflection, without recrimination or regret. That was pretty much how things were done, when the monster was on the loose.

Apparently, it had been the right thing to say, or nearly so, or else it had been so outrageously wrong as to stun the Queen and her attendants into almost total paralysis.

In any case, the Queen burst out laughing, and did not stop for a long, long time.

As it turned out, most of the Gateans assembled here were members of Finders ring and something called Talkers ring, though there were some Holders in the crowd as well.

It seemed—Malye wasn't quite sure about this—but it *seemed* that any Queen could be entrusted to act with full authority on behalf of her ring. Not a democratic or anarchic structure, but rather one of pure expedience and mutual trust, like a police district in which any greenbar could serve as Coordinator if the circumstances required it. It seemed a little too convenient to actually work, and Malye couldn't quite bring herself to believe it. Not of these people, no. But certainly, the other Finders Queens greeted Wende briefly and simply enough, with neither deference nor arrogance nor formality.

But the *other* Queens, the Holders and the Talkers and the one or two from still other rings, were making noise and waving their fat, flabby arms at Wende. The Drones and Workers seemed less animated, though far from motionless, and the Dogs had begun to wander slowly through the crowd, their hairless heads and tails held down.

It was difficult to know what was going on, what it all might mean; all the conversation was in Waister, all the emotion in some alien realm, some operating state to which the refugees themselves were not privy. Malye had never stood in the middle of a flock of screeching, strutting geese, but having seen them on educational holies, she imagined the experience might be very similar. Occasionally, Plate would lean toward her with boneless grace and whisper the odd detail in Standard; that Wende was explaining the mechanics of the Pinega excavation, that Tempe (apparently the name of the Holders Queen) was soliciting opinions of some sort. But the action taking place here was too complex to be explained in this way. It was like a warren meeting, like a church service, like a drama and a dance and an ugly mob preparing to beat the crap out of some poor citizen. It was an environment that maddened Malye's law enforcement instincts—if this were a human crowd, she would have dispersed it immediately.

But there was nothing human about this, and Malye was not at all sure of her position. Something between a guest and an observer and a pet, she thought, and in no way entitled to enforce her alien ideas of law and order.

Eventually, though, things seemed to settle down, the cacophony dying away, and at this point the Queen, Tempe, turned her attention on Malye and addressed her in Standard, in a deep, scratchy voice: "Woman, you are here to provide information at a time which is now. You will begin."

"Momma," Elle said, "is that fat lady another Queen?"

"Hush, baby," Malye replied, touching her daughter's arm. "We'll talk later." She squared her shoulders and faced the enormous Queen, calling out across the distance between them. "Tempe, my name is Malyene. We have come to provide information, yes, but we do so as a gift to you, in order to help. We will not be coerced or exploited. Do you understand this?"

The Queen fidgeted liquidly on her couch, as if considering Malye's words. "Malyene," she said after a few moments, "what you say has been comprehended."

"What will happen when the Waisters arrive? What will you do with the information we provide?"

"Talkers ring," said the Queen, "will communicate with the Waister fleet."

"What will you do with the information we provide?" Malye repeated. "If it's useful to you, what will it change? Will it prevent another war?"

The Queen seemed to inflate slightly. "No infarct will take place. Newness is absent here. Talkers ring will communicate in the manner we recommend."

And she said nothing more after that. All the Gateans had stopped moving, seemed to have stopped even breathing.

What will they communicate, you fat sack of shit? What is it you intend?

But that was not a question Malye really felt like asking right now, so she took a deep breath instead, and launched into her own personal account of the Waister attack, of the destruction of Tyumen and Pinega, of the fall of the Sirius colony at the hands of an unknown and merciless enemy.

And when she was done, Viktor took his turn, and then Sasha, and then the children, and then even the prewar cryostasis patients were asked to come forward and tell their stories, irrelevant though they might be.

And strangely, as if the air here were infected with some alien spore that killed off human feelings, not one of the refugees wavered or wept in the course of testimony. Too tired, too empty, too self-conscious under the gaze of these hundreds of copper eyes ... It was as if they had discovered all at once how much *effort* it took to be human, and how liberating it could be to set that aside, if only for a while.

Malye, of course, had learned this lesson long ago.

Chapter 13

Plate stood quiescent before the Queen's dais and strove to appear humble and contrite.

"*#Your project is/will be constrained?#*" Tempe demanded of him in the Waister language, its tones fluid and grating, like sand raining down on hollow tubes. Plate had been listening to the Holders Queen's voice for a thousand heartbeats as she discharged her frustrations at him, and for the first time in decades, he heard the strangeness of it, the alienness. Sounds no human throat could produce, framing thoughts no human would understand.

Or would they? The Sirian colonists had engendered almost continual surprise in him since their revival. Strong, intelligent, flexible . . . all the things humans were supposed not to be, else why had the Aggressors retreated here to Gate system in the first place? His memories of the Suzerainty were dim and fragmentary, the memories of a child swept up in events too vast and convoluted to be understood in any but the simplest terms: a government corrupted and crippled by its own introversion, unable to address or even recognize its vulnerability. Populations of blindness and ignorance, wholly unfit to deal with the promise and threat that the Waisters embodied. Unfit even to understand that the problem merited study.

But how much of this had he actually perceived for himself? Malyene Andreivne Kurosov'e would have no place in the Suzerainty of his memory. Even her *children* were cleverer than he'd imagined a human could be, and could human nature have changed so much in two millennia? It seemed unlikely.

"#*The humans are/have been constrained physically/ spatially#*" he replied without emotion. "#*They/their capacity-for-disturbance is/has been constrained#*"

The word for "human," translated literally, meant "small and stupid," the Waister designation for a species too bellicose and territorial to yield before an overwhelmingly superior rival. The term had been applied to one other species, now extinct, and it occurred to Plate that the human race, being the first to survive its initial encounters with the Waisters, had perhaps earned the right to be thought of more charitably. But such, of course, was not his place to suggest.

By "constrained" he meant that he had placed the humans in a remote corner of the Fastness, weighed down by heavy spin-gee and adjacent to nothing important, with no visual cues or other assistance that might help them find their way out. Tempe might wish for more, might wish to punish the humans for the high cost of their testimony, or perhaps simply for being human, but he would not willingly help her do it. Let her punish *him,* instead; let her rage against the inanity of his ideas and projects and self.

Finders ring had undertaken the tunneling and retrieval and revival projects at Pinega, consuming colony resources extravagantly, and Wende's six had played a larger role in the work and planning than most others. Plate himself had had tremendous influence over the course of it all, had in fact discovered the ancient cryostasis ward himself, and had been the first to propose its excavation. And all for nothing, as Holders ring had predicted from the start. What could the frozen humans know that the Gateans themselves did not? Very little indeed.

So here Plate stood, absorbing the blame, deflecting as much of it as possible from his six and ring, and from the Sirians themselves, for whom he felt a certain proprietary interest and even a kind of sympathy. For all their imperfections they were certainly blameless in this matter, so let Tempe interpret "constraint" in any way she liked; he would not explain more precisely without specific instructions to do so, and he had been maneuvering the discussion to avoid this ever since it had begun.

Deliberate ambiguity was an antithetic trait not found in Waisters, nor sanctioned here in Gatean society, but then, neither was scapegoating. Wende had enthusiastically shifted the blame onto her Workers, who after all should have known better, and Crow had deftly shed his own portion, leaving Plate to stand here alone. The annoyance this caused him was yet another antithetic trait, a holdover from a less controlled, more human past.

But "human," while still an antithetic concept, no longer seemed to him quite the epithet it once had been.

"#You/individual are causing/have caused disturbance#" Tempe said. "#You/ring are/was/has been stupid-because-of information/ideology having-originated from you/individual#"

"Yes," Plate agreed, switching to Teigo for the sake of its brevity and precision. Waisters knew all about "no," but its opposite was not a concept easily expressed in their language, and Plate was in a mood to speak compactly.

But Tempe scowled—she didn't approve of that.

The convergence chamber was still bustling with activity, representatives of five separate rings still exchanging information and speculation, trying to identify every possible datum and activity pattern from the accounts the Sirians had given. Many hands clutched Congress units, thumb triggers going up and down as their owners passed in and out of session, seeking the programmed wisdom of the dead. Appeal to authority, to history, to the ancient oracular algorithms—the last refuge of those who could not think for themselves. Suitable, no doubt, for the Suzerainty, but here? Was their situation so dire? Had it come to this? It puzzled him; why should the dead understand the situation any better than the living?

But presently, a particular sense of alarm seemed to break out among the scattered groups, as if they had all heard the same troubling news at the same time. One knot of Queens and Workers broke up, and a single Worker, a representative of Talkers ring whom Plate did not know, stepped forward and signaled for Tempe's attention.

"#You/you will explain you/your information/ideology at time-now#" she said, recognizing him formally.

In his agitation the Worker reverted to Teigo, as Plate had done: "Tempe, Holders ring shall be reminded that Talkers ring has been signaling the Waister fleet for several months, without response. Holders ring shall be informed that a response has now been received, in the form of a verbal radio message that Talkers ring is now recording."

A response? A *verbal response*? Plate felt a rush of excitement, of more-than-excitement. The purpose of his life, of the entire Gate colony's life, was to communicate with the distant Waister empire. But the signals had always gone out, out, through a thousand light-years of silent space from which no reply could be expected in his lifetime, if ever, and the empty frustration this engendered was something Plate had never truly recognized until this moment, when it suddenly vanished.

It echoed the winning of a prize, the cheating of death, the recognition of one's ring and six for extraordinary contributions. A human being would have jumped in the air and shouted and waved his fists in triumph at such a moment, Plate felt sure, but jubilation was not a Waister emotion, nor often a Gatean one, and so he simply touched his face, running his fingers down the side of his jawbone as if to confirm its solidity. Many around him were doing the same.

Tempe looked surprised and curious, but tightly controlled. *"#You/you will explain-with-detail at time-near-future#"* she said to the Worker, leaning forward slightly on her couch. Holders ring had not achieved its pervasiveness by overreacting to unexpected news. And really, this contact was more premature than surprising, given that the Waisters were less than seventy hours outsystem. Eventual contact was inevitable, however uncertain the Gateans might be as to its form and outcome.

As if echoing his thoughts, Tempe signaled to a Queen from Watchers ring, and said, *"#Beginning-of-events occurs at time-now The weapons will be/will be brought-to-readiness at time-now Ring (Testers) shall take/hold/execute responsibility for weapons You/individual overlay you/six/ring shall take/hold/execute responsibility for bringing-to-readiness#"*

The Watchers Queen, now effectively a military general, turned and departed the chamber without comment or delay, to execute Tempe's orders. *Suggestions,* Plate reminded himself. Holders ring possessed no genuine authority, no more than any other group, and Watchers and Testers rings knew their business well enough without such advice. Gate system's armaments were intended for much weaker opponents than Waisters, for much smaller and stupider ones, but there had always been the possibility, however remote, of a new infarct, and the weapons' keepers had prepared for this as best they could.

Well enough? Doubtful. Two millennia of research had done little to reveal the principles behind Waister technology. Tanks of liquid gallium, circular plates of boron and rhodium ... Bizarre but rudimentary mechanisms that nonetheless seemed able to alter the characteristics of the space around them. To a Waister fleetship, rest mass and relativistic mass seemed perfectly interchangeable, regardless of the intermediary energies involved. Sustained power, in the hundreds of terawatts, could be summoned from mysterious sources, channeled in mysterious ways before vanishing once more into nothingness. Or so the theories went, at any rate; not much had fallen intact into human hands.

Human technology had never been a match for this. Sol system had damaged the Waisters, even held them off for a time, but only through the application of overwhelming numbers. A hundred mass-produced ships swarming in on every attacker, backed up by planetary beam and projectile weapons, and millions upon millions of individual soldiers trained to ram and board and kill. Human and Gatean science had come a long way since that time, but here and now, in the decades-young colony at Gate, overwhelming numbers were simply not available. If they had to fight ...

Plate blinked, suddenly aware that his attention had been wandering unacceptably. His thoughts had lately lacked both focus and relevance—no doubt the effect of excessive human contact—but this was hardly the time or place for such distraction! He forced his attention once more on the Holders Queen before him.

Tempe had returned her gaze to the Worker from Talkers ring. *"#You/you will explain-with-detail at time-now the received signal#"* she said.

The Worker signaled both his understanding and his contributive nature. But when he spoke, it was again in Teigo, the primary language of humanity. "Holders ring should know," he said excitedly, "that I personally determine the signal to be an unmodified Waister voice operating in Waister-normal environs. Holders ring should know the consensus of Talkers ring, just reached, that the signal has been broadcast via coherent, frequency-modulated radio emissions at twenty-seven million cycles per second, a communications medium employed by human societies of the late Interstitial, now long obsolete. The opinion of Talkers ring is that this signal was intended to be heard. The opinion of Talkers ring is that this signal represents a deliberate, contributive transfer of information by the approaching Waister fleet."

Now Tempe began to look impatient. "Would you play the signal for me, please?" she snapped, in Teigo.

Obediently, the Worker produced a comp jewel and pressed it against his forehead. His face went blank for a moment, and then his mouth opened, and the sounds of the Waister language began to emerge.

But . . . strangely. The cadence was slow, almost poetic, the mix and order of the words . . . unfamiliar.

# contemplation-of-error	# returning I/universal	#
# in principle/ideology	# to states-of-ambiguity	#
# fragmentary but in	# reveals nothing with	#
# fixture-not-so we find	# absence revealing not	#
# an end to contemplation	# this/these ideas to us	#

Plate watched Tempe as she listened to the strange voice. She looked down with furrowed brow at the Talkers Worker, cocking her head when he'd finished. Then, slowly, she rose from her couch and seemed to float across the dais toward him. Plate stepped deferentially aside for her, thinking she might be about to step down, and indeed, her next step carried her off the edge of the dais. She crashed heavily to the floor, her feet slamming down flat and hard, but she appeared not to notice. Her attention was fully on the Worker before her.

Casually, and with a somewhat distracted air, she raised
an arm across her body and then smashed the back of her
hand across the Worker's face. A frustration blow, not
hard enough to knock him down.

"#*What new thing is this?#*" she demanded quietly.
"#*I/I express surprise   Express dissatisfaction   Express I
not-have understanding do#*"

Wisely, the Worker remained silent, as did Plate, as did
everyone else in the chamber. Word had finally come
from the Waisters themselves, not an attack or infarct or
accidental emission but a deliberate signal, meant to be
understood, and directed toward those most able to understand it.

And yet it had sounded like total gibberish.

The refugees' new quarters were a group of small
chambers joined together by a short hallway. For the first
time they had access to some semblance of privacy, and
so in an off moment when they wouldn't likely be
missed, Malye led Viktor to an empty chamber and asked
to speak with him privately.

Once the membrane-door had sealed behind them, she
pushed him up against the wall and attacked him with her
lips, kissing as though he were her only possible source
of oxygen. He reacted at first with startlement, but
quickly relaxed in her grip and began returning her ardor,
his large hands digging into her back, wandering slowly
downward . . .

She broke it off. The room, though unrelentingly white,
sang with shapes and colors and bright, wavy streamers
of noise. What in Hell was she doing?

"What's wrong?" Viktor said, appearing puzzled but
not terribly surprised by her sudden change of mood.

"I can't," she told him, backing away.

He shrugged. "Okay. I didn't expect that you could."

"I just can't," she repeated, as if he hadn't spoken. Her
mouth was running on automatic. Her mind, her body . . .
"I'm sorry."

Now Viktor looked sympathetic, damn him, a classical
specimen in his flowing white robe, impervious to surprise, to harm. Had she wanted to harm him?

"It's a very trying time for us, emotionally," Viktor
said gently. "We're all confused."

She shook her head. "No, no, you don't understand. I'm having a problem here. With impulse control, the thing that separates the law-abider from the criminal. These ... Gateans are undermining my impulse control."

"Yes?" he looked politely concerned.

She wanted to make him understand. And yet, she didn't want him to know ... There were a great many things about her she didn't want him to know. How could she explain? How could she *explain*? Frustrated, she put a hand in her mouth and bit down hard.

"Hey!" Viktor said, stepping forward, grabbing her arm. His other hand closed on her jaw, squeezing, forcing her teeth apart until he could pull the hand free without tearing it. "Ialah's names, woman, what's wrong with you?"

"I'm trying to tell you," she said, spitting on the floor. No blood, a fact she found strangely disappointing. The room's sounds and colors shifted subtly toward the pastels, toward pink and blue and pale, quiet yellow. Her mood shifted again.

She put her hands on her breasts, cupped them, fondled them. Made an attempt to smile alluringly. It would be so easy to drop the robe. "I want you," she said slowly, her face only inches from his. "I'm drawn to you. But you must understand, I'm drawn to a lot of things. I've learned to resist being drawn. I've had to."

Viktor simply stared, as if unsure what he was looking at.

"What would people think?" she tried, feeling and sounding plaintive. "Ialah, the *children*. Two days ago, their father was alive. What would they think?"

At that, Viktor came back to life, a sarcastic grin planting itself on his face. "Lady, if that's the only thing holding you back, I'd be happy to take you by force. Is that what you want? A thousand years ago you were a widow, and a thousand years before that, and here we are with nothing to support us, nothing to comfort us. You want me?" He chuckled humorlessly, spreading his arms with visible effort in the high gravity. "Here I am."

"Touch me and I'll break you," Malye warned, tensing. "I'll break every part of you."

Viktor sighed. "Well, then, I won't touch you. Far be it from me to undermine your sense of impulse control."

"You don't understand," Malye insisted. "You really don't."

"No? Really? Well, why don't you enlighten me? What exactly is your problem?"

She breathed, lungs swelling and emptying in uneasy rhythm. Could she tell him? Would it be better, after all, if he knew? She'd never told anyone, not even Grigory, but then, where had been the need? *What is your problem?* No one had ever come straight through and asked her that before.

"My father was Andrei Brakanov," she blurted. Committed now, the words impossible to retract.

But Viktor did not seem to have a reaction. He blinked, waited, an expectant look on his face as if she had not finished speaking yet. Could he have misheard?

"Andrei Brakanov!" she repeated.

Still nothing. The room a storm of colored static through which she gaped at his still-impassive expression. "The Monster Andrei! Rapist, murderer of children! All Sirius trembled at his name! Even when thcy'd caught him and killed him, still there was fear. There was no knowledge, no understanding of how anyone could ... My father. My dear, beloved father. Oh, damn you, Viktor, will you say something?"

She watched the light of recognition flow into his eyes, just before he closed them and lowered his head and brought a hand up to pinch the bridge of his nose. His body spasmed slightly, shuddering with the impact of her news.

So that was it. Her naked soul lay quivering before him, its last defenses stripped away. Ialah, why had she brought this out? What could possibly be gained? Had her impulse control simply failed her again? Yes, obviously it had.

"Viktor," she said, wanting to reach out to him but not daring to.

But when his eyes opened up again and locked on hers, she saw that he was laughing.

Laughing? Bright rage stabbed through her. How dare he—

"Oh," he gasped, tears trembling in reddened eyes. "Oh, goodness. I finally understand! I've got your code now, lady. Guilt as a . . . hereditary trait. I'm sorry, I don't mean to mock you, Malyene Andreivne, but *really*!" He broke out in a fresh wave of laughter.

"Damn you," Malye said, feeling hard and empty inside, the singing of the colors echoing through her hollowness. "Listen to me! My father had certain . . . abnormalities. Which I share. Neurological abnormalities. I have inherited that monster's brain. I have these . . . urges, and . . ."

Viktor's laughter died away. "Urges," he said.

"Yes, urges! To harm, to injure, to kill! Horrible urges. All my life I've fought for control, and now . . ."

"Oh, Malye." Viktor's smile was gone, a tired and serious look in its place. "You poor, stupid woman. You think you're the only one? You think other people never get the urge to drop a wrench through someone's skull? The mind is an ugly place, full of garbage and noise, and none of it matters a whit. Can I hear your thoughts? No. But I can see your actions."

She flared. "Actions? You don't know me, citizen. You don't have any idea what I've done."

"Killed?" he asked, unimpressed.

"Yes! Twice!"

"Were they children? Did you enjoy it?"

"No—"

"Was it in the line of duty?"

"Yes, but—"

"But nothing," he said, his eyes gone cold. "All this time I've been wondering about your . . . operating state, wondering what made you act the way you do, but now that I see it . . . Well, I can't tell you how disappointed I am."

"Will you listen?" she nearly screamed at him, "I'm telling you that I am dangerous! When you hear a warning buzzer, do you ignore it? When you feel the rush of escaping air, do you ignore it?"

He shook his head. "Stop it, Malye. Don't do this. You've had your little fit, shown me all the rage and turmoil inside your skull, and the message has been received. But you're not the only one under stress."

"I shouldn't have come to you," she said, turning away. But Viktor grabbed her arms and turned her back to face him again, and for a moment she was too shocked to think of resisting.

"Petty self-indulgence," he said, shaking her firmly with each word. "Ialah's names, lady, look at yourself. Without you, these people would eat us alive."

He released her, then turned and stepped away, moving toward the exit as if she no longer interested him in the slightest way. But at the doorway he stopped, turned, looked over his shoulder. "The Gateans have made you our leader, Malyene Andreivne. You should consider acting like one."

Then he stepped through the membrane and was gone.

When things got moving again in the convergence chamber, they did so swiftly and dramatically.

Someone pointed out the signal's parallels to the Waister Departure Song, which had taken a team of skilled translators years to decipher. Someone else pointed out that the signal might not be complete—more information might be forthcoming at any time. Yet another person suggested that the brief, obscure speech had been a deliberate attempt to confuse them all.

At this point, and with Tempe's consent, Plate stepped in with an observation of his own. "I have some experience dealing with the revived humans," he said to the assembled crowd, "and they are not at all what one would expect. Let Finders ring remind you all that culture and behavior and predisposition are three very discrete phenomena. Even if we emulate the Waister mind perfectly, Finders ring reminds you that we live in a different place, that we use different tools. It is entirely conceivable that our society here at Gate resembles the Waisters' own no more than the Suzerainty of the Human Spaces resembles the Sirius colony that once occupied this system."

And *that* comment provoked a storm of rebuttal and dispute that went on for many hundreds of heartbeats. Plate took the opportunity to press a comp jewel to his head, which had the effect of transmitting the full context of his thoughts and experiences to Wende's six, and an abbreviated packet of same to the rest of Finders ring. In return, he received the information that Wende wished him to remain close to the center of controversy, so that

Finders ring should not be without voice at so pivotal a time. She would join him here as soon as circumstances permitted.

He was still standing very close to Tempe, and amid the tumult he leaned forward and spoke to her quietly. "Perhaps we engender our own difficulties here. Can Talkers ring send a reply in the same format, asking for clarification? If the Waisters want to talk, then probably we should talk."

"We must yield before their strength," Tempe replied in a much louder voice, so that a dozen nearby Queens and Workers could hear her. She raised her voice higher still, shouting above the crowd: "We must surrender! There is a newness here that demands it of us. Talkers ring should prepare and send a capitulation message immediately."

"Tempe"—Plate cut in, his manner antithetic and inappropriate but, he thought, necessary under the circumstances—"at least ask for clarification while you're at it."

She turned and struck him hard, stinging the side of his head.

"*#Urgent-request listen#*" he insisted, signaling for her full attention but stepping backward a pace to avoid another blow. "*#Request-for-information consumes null-resource Invokes null-risk Creates-possibility-for benefit I/my function-to-advise constrains I/me in activity of advising Comprehension is crucial#*"

Tempe flared at him, obviously tempted to smash him into oblivion, but she held back. Instead, she turned slowly to face the lone Talkers Queen present in the chamber, and said to her, "*#Leshe Urgent-request initiate compilation-of-reply We yield before strength We request clarification of signals We express desire-to-contribute regarding you/your objectives#*"

Leshe, the Talkers Queen, signaled her understanding and pressed a comp jewel to her forehead.

"Talkers ring points out that it will be ten thousand heartbeats until the signal reaches them," her Worker reminded the assembled units, and then grinned irreverently. "Perhaps nine thousand, if we remain unusually quiescent."

Plate considered that remark. Jokes were antithetic and disrespectful, of course, but they could sometimes jolt one's thinking into new channels. He dared to laugh.

"Mother, are the Gateans angry with us?"

"Oh, Vadim, I just don't know. I don't think they were pleased with our stories. I don't think we helped them in the way they hoped."

"What will they do with us?"

"I don't know."

"What will *you* do? It seems to me you don't want to be in charge, but I think you should. Doesn't somebody have to make decisions?"

"Ialah's names, Vadim, where are you getting these thoughts? You're a little boy, you should be thinking a little boy's thoughts. Go and keep your sister company."

Pause.

"Mother?"

"Yes, Vadim?"

"Is Viktor Slavanovot going to replace our father?"

```
 "  #     Additional errors require compensation     #
    #          Require repetition-of-effort          #
    #                  Which annoys                   #
    #                                                 #
    #     Concepts presenting strange difficulty      #
    #               Now appreciated                   #
    #     We express satisfaction at the state of     #
    #           existence we identify here            #
    #                                                 #
    #          But what state? What state?            #
    #     That you surrender to a thing not new?      #  "
```

"#I/We request instruction Request clarification Your strength dominates I/Us You approach How can I/We contribute toward you/your objectives?#"

```
 "  #     Something moves awry in this exchange.      #
    #          Requiring repetition-of-effort         #
    #                  Which annoys                    #
    #                                                  #
    #     Are you stupid-ling of this space-region?    #
    #          Pile stones beside the water            #
```

```
#          Are you things-of-newness?          #
#                                              #
#          We do not arrive with               #
#          Preparation-to-confront             #  "
```

"#Of confrontation null   We surrender   We surrender   We surrender#"

```
"  #      This exchange carries no information      #
   #                                                #
   #                   Surrender?                   #
   #    Null-war concepts have been comprehended     #
   #         We approach in null-war state           #
   #                                                #
   #    Completed confrontation equates surrender    #
   #      Where newness implies confrontation         #
   #                In precedence thereof             #  "
```

"#Stupid-lings have been similarized toward you/your
information/ideology   Toward you/your sensory-discrimi-
nation Toward you/your life operative status   I/We are
not stupid-lings#"

```
"  #   Fragmentary comprehension has germinated    #
   #      Do you pile stones beside the water?       #
   #      In under-air where water has visited        #
   #                                                #
   #             You are not stupid-lings             #
   #    Confrontation-of-newness can be achieved       #
   #                 With difficulty                   #
   #    We are prepared to offer your destruction      #  "
```

"#No   No   No   Of destruction null we surrender   We
surrender#"

```
"  #             Comprehension bifurcates            #
   #         If stupid-lings are-present then           #
   #                  Newness is not                   #
   #           If newness is-present then               #
   #    Confrontation must precede all activity          #
   #                                                #
   #         Surrender follows confrontation            #  "
```

"#Urgent I/We possess null capability-to-survive confrontation Urgent Confrontation engenders null-state concerning I/We Urgent Stupid-lings are here Stupid-lings are here Stupid-lings are here#"

#		#
#	*Comprehension has been accomplished*	#
#	*Learning differentiates from inanimacy*	#
#	*Ergo we learn even from stupid-lings*	#
#	*Even from stupid-lings*	#
#	*Null-war interests us*	#
#	*Exchange-of-information interests us*	#
#		#
#	*Difficulty*	#
#		#
#	*We will exchange information with*	#
#	*Stupid-lings in proximity-context*	#
#	*We arrive time-soon to exchange*	#
#	*There is much to accomplish*	# "

"#You/you will-speak with I/Us? We have-prepared time-long time-long We have prepared to speak with you#"

#	*We will speak*	#
#	*With the stupid-lings*	# "

Tempe removed the comp jewel from her forehead, her scowl echoing, Plate thought, the rage and frustration of all the Queens of Holders ring. Of all the Queens of Gate. Of Gate itself.

We will speak with the stupid-lings? We will speak with the stupid-lings? Plate could scarcely believe what he'd heard. Could the Waisters really be so impossibly naive? Could they be insane? Here were lifetimes upon lifetimes invested in the Waister language, in the Waister mind and habits and viewpoints, in the very idea of *speaking with Waisters.* Didn't that mean anything?

But Talkers ring had posed the question in several different ways, and each time the answer had come back unequivocally. The Gateans were either "new," meaning that they should be attacked, or they were subordinate to the stupid-lings, the humans, meaning that they were redundant and useless, that they had wasted the past two millennia perfecting skills for which no need existed.

"Painting the inside of the air tanks," as the colonists of Kent and Barne would put it.

This place was only one of many where the subject was being debated, where the incoming signals were being interpreted and the Gatean response formulated. Wende could perhaps have achieved greater influence in another chamber, with another Holders Queen, but thankfully she had chosen to come here to support Plate instead. He leaned on her now, drawing strength from her bulk and her confidence. She was his Queen, and he would die for her if the need arose.

Presently, she cleared her throat, and spoke to the assembled units and to Tempe in particular: "*#Refusal-of-reality engenders null-benefit Finders ring will prepare stupid-lings for exchange-of-information#*"

Ripples and murmurs of discontent ran through the crowd. Tempe's scowl deepened.

"What do you propose for the rest of us," she demanded in Teigo. "The entirety of Gate colony, what goal?"

Wende shrugged. "I do not know, really. I believe it will be possible for you to contribute."

And with those words, Plate felt a palpable shift in the balance of influence. Tempe appeared diminished, reduced, disempowered, while Wende seemed to grow and harden beneath his touch.

All eyes were on Wende. All thoughts were on Wende. All conversation had stopped, so that Wende's voice might be heard more clearly.

The taste of the moment was foul; all they believed in and stood for had been dashed to waste and nothingness. And yet, through the wreckage of the Gatean dream, the Waisters themselves had hurled Finders ring to utmost prominence. All expenditures vindicated, all theories confirmed . . .

It should have been the happiest moment of Plate's life, but instead it made him feel heavy and weary and ill, as if his stomach were filled with rocks. *We will speak only with the stupid-lings?*

He dared to weep.

Chapter 14

Bleary-eyed and yawning, Malye staggered out of the chamber she shared with her children and toward the communal washroom. Fortunately, the facilities there had changed little in two thousand years, a fact for which she gave silent thanks several times a day.

Great Ialah, merciful Ialah, let us thank him for this shitter. Amen.

She would have stumbled right back to her couch when she'd finished—her palm chronometer gave her nearly two hours until lights-up—but through the corner of her eye she spotted movement out in the dayroom, and for whatever reason, she found herself wandering in to investigate.

The movement turned out to be a Dog, hairless and pink, quietly sniffing and snuffling in the many corners of the room. Looking up, it noted Malye's arrival with cold eyes. Its tail did not wag. Was it Wende's Dog? The Holder Queen's? Some other animal entirely? No way to tell.

On the far side of the room sat Viktor, his jaw slack, body conspicuously not moving. He had his back to a wall and his hands in his lap, and Malye might have thought him asleep but for the fact that his eyes were open, and his right thumb was holding down the trigger of the black Congress of Advisors unit. This was nearly the same position she'd left him in eight hours before.

Edging nervously past the Dog, she went to Viktor and shook him gently. No response.

"Viktor?"

She tried flicking his thumb off the trigger, and that

worked instantly, his eyes blinking, posture shifting, throat clearing noisily. He looked up at her.

"Oh," he said hoarsely. "Hello. Malyene."

"Hello yourself. Have you been sitting there all night?"

The question appeared to confuse him, until he put his thumb back on the trigger again, quickly pressing and releasing it. His eyes lost and then regained their focus on her.

"All night," he agreed, "yes. Straight through."

A wave of fear swept through her. She'd only been joking; every moment of real time was stretched to impossible lengths inside the Congress. In addition to its simulacra of history's great minds, she'd been told the Congress also formed a computational ghost of the user, which was capable of operating much faster than any biological system like a brain ever could. When the session was over, the dense experience of the ghost was dumped back into the user's brain just as though it represented genuine memory. The illusion of time was perfect.

"Oh, Ialah," she moaned, "you're not serious. Eight hours in there would be ..." Forever.

"Eight hours, twenty-one minutes, thirteen and a half seconds," he said. "A long time, yes. The subjective record averages five thousand times actual chronology. That would be, what, about five standard years?"

He looked up at her, his weak grin spinning off slow curlicues of blue.

Her stomach went into freefall. Five years? Time enough to earn a trade degree! Except that the user simulacrum would never tire, would never need to take a break. Time enough—O Ialah!—to earn a *stack* of trade degrees. Time enough to interrogate every single Congressional simulacrum for half a shift, then turn around and do it all over again. All 5,264 of them.

"Shit, Viktor! Oh, shit, are you all right?"

"I'm thirsty," he croaked, still smiling. "My thumb hurts, and my arm. I have to pee." He reached up, patted her on the hand. "It's good to see you again."

"Ialah." She turned, shouted: "Sasha! Aleksandr Petrovot, get in here! Now! Sasha!"

"It's all right," Viktor said, waving a hand dismissively. He looked drunk, drugged. "I'm fine. It's just a little different, having a real ... Would you help me up, Malye? I can't seem to work my legs."

She continued cursing.

The hallway filled up with people, and Sasha came forward into the light.

"*Don't* try to get up!" she snapped at Viktor, who was leaning and rocking, attempting woodenly to get his legs underneath him.

"What happened?" Sasha said, his voice and motions jerky with alarm.

"He spent the whole night in the Congress of Advisors. Five years! Shit, Viktor, why did you do this to yourself?"

"Just wanted to help," Viktor replied meekly. His smile seemed painted on, a permanent feature. "I think I was a little hard on you ... yesterday, and ..."

Penance? Repayment for the sin of trying to help her?

"What do you want me to do?" Sasha asked of Malye, holding his hands out to the sides as if to say there was nothing he *could* do at a time like this, no relevant skill he could apply.

Ialah take him, Malye had had enough of this false helplessness. If Sasha had been competent to hold a job in times gone by, he would damn well hold one now.

"You're the doctor now," she told him flatly in her best no-nonsense tone. "Take him. Help him." She placed the knife edge of her hand right up against his jaw, to quell the protest she saw rising there. *I could strike you*, the gesture said, *though it would bring me no joy.* "I mean it."

Sasha blinked, flinched away. "I guess ... Get off me! I guess he could probably use some sleep."

"Sleep," Viktor said reminiscently. "Oh, that would be nice. And I have to pee."

"Help him," Malye repeated, locking gazes with Sasha. He looked away quickly, nodding.

Malye snatched up the Congress of Advisors from where it lay beside Viktor's leg. "And this," she said, holding the unit up for Sasha to see, "is dangerous. Flush it down the shitter."

"We might need it," Sasha protested. "I might need to—"

"All right, all right," she snapped. She looked up at the

other refugees, still crowded in the doorway. Showed them the Congress. "But nobody is to touch this thing without my permission, and without a buddy watching."

Malye rounded on the Dog, still standing in the far corner, observing the proceedings emotionlessly. Its eyes might as well be tiny flatscreen recorders.

"You," she said. "You are not welcome here. Get out. And tell your Workers that one of our people is injured."

The Dog stared back, not moving.

"I said get out!" She repeated, taking a step toward it.

That got through, whether the animal understood Standard or not. It turned, with surprising speed, and leaped through the membrane covering their outer door. Its tail flicked and vanished, the white surface closing seamlessly behind it and freezing in place, as if solid

"Look, I take full responsibility for this," Malye said for the third time, looking around her at the assembled refugees, feeling curiously as though she was on trial. "He'd been using the Congress more and more, and I should have seen the warning signs. Ialali, it might have been any of us—it might have been the children!"

She grabbed up Elle and hugged her like a doll. Elle, who had held the Congress several times in her hand! Who had not even lived as long as Viktor had spent in that imaginary amphitheater!

Konstant didn't seem to be buying it, though. "Your leadership," he said, "does not seem to be getting us out of danger here. Rather the opposite."

"He did it to himself," one of the refugees offered. Vere Sergeivne, the tunnel digger. "He said he wanted to help."

Malye nodded. "Yes, and that may be my fault as well. We argued, he and I, and I think—"

"I think you both have missed my point," Konstant cut in, his voice rising, not loud but nonetheless demanding attention. "What I'm saying is that we need to get out of here."

"Out of where?" someone asked.

"Out of Artya, for a start." He speared Malye with an accusing stare. "How could you let them bring us here? We need to go someplace safer, more isolated. Back to

Pinega, maybe. Better yet, we need passage out of Sirius altogether. What's closest, Sol system?"

"Another hundred years in cryostasis?" said Nik. "No thank you, not me."

"And where are we supposed to get a ship?"

"We can start by asking!" Fuming, Konstant jerked an elbow in Malye's direction, pointing, making an insult of it somehow. "This woman isn't asking for anything. 'Yes, Plate. No, Plate. Of course we'll see your Queen, Plate.' We all saw it. Ialah's names, she was groveling on the floor."

Malye sighed. "Citizens, be realistic. As we speak, Gate system is being invaded. Even assuming we survive, what kind of help we can expect from the Gateans? Just how important do you think we are?"

"Perhaps more than you think."

Everyone looked to the dayroom's outer entrance, in which stood their old friend Plate. Slim and supple as ever, Malye thought, a collection of elastic cords in the shape of a man. And yet, he seemed flush with some exertion that had left him feeling weary but empowered, as if he had run a race. As if he had *won* a race.

"May I come in?" he asked, the air around him pink with tension.

"Why so polite?" Malye inquired, setting her daughter down. "Why not simply barge in, as you always do?"

"I apologize for that," he said, nodding liquidly. "I try to be sensitive to your ways, but I have little experience. The, ah, the Dog told me what happened. Who is hurt?"

"So your Dogs speak Standard after all," Malye said.

His large copper eyes met her gaze. "No. But they recognize a problem when they see one. Who is hurt, please?"

"It's Viktor," she said. "He spent the whole night in the Congress of Advisors."

"Ah." Plate nodded again, his neck bending, almost folding double before it straightened once more. "Yes, we have that problem with our own people, sometimes. It's . . . less serious than it may appear."

"Will he recover?" Sasha asked.

"His body should be fine," Plate replied, turning now to look through the doorway toward the sleeping rooms, craning for a glimpse at the victim. "The physiological

stress is not in any way unusual. Like any sort of pro-
longed labor, I suppose, like walking, or perhaps sitting at
a comp station all day. Mentally . . . well, an eight-hour
session is quite a lot to absorb. Much information, much
subjective time crammed into that space. There will certainly be . . . personality changes."

That phrase rang a cold, clear note in Malye's core.
Personality changes. "Serious?" she asked quietly.

Plate shrugged. "Possibly. He's been out of connection
with reality for many thousands of hours. His personality
will likely reassert itself in short order, but the residual
effects may well last the remainder of his life. Attention
inertia, we call it; he will be slow to react, slow to change
the course of his thoughts. Or to put it another way, his
attention span has been increased. And of course, he'll
know a lot more than he did when he began."

"You make it sound like a good thing," Sasha said dis-
approvingly.

Plate shrugged "The process carries no moral objec-
tivity."

Malye tasted gray ambivalence, like dust on her
tongue. A single moment of trauma, she knew, could
haunt a person forever, coloring every thought and action
from that time forward. And yet, she had once known a
violent offender who'd been sentenced to ten years in
prison with nothing but a library flatscreen to keep him
company in his cell. In the end he'd emerged a quiet,
contemplative man, ready to take his place among civi-
lized people. Changed, yes, and yet also the same, his
hard corners smoothed and polished. And he himself
agreed that he was smarter.

That Viktor had no crimes to atone for, at least so far
as she knew, mattered less than the fact that he'd chosen
his prison willingly. And if there was no lasting harm, per
se . . . Well, so be it.

"So he will recover," she said, feeling better. But she
eyed Plate cynically. "What of the rest of us? What will
you do with us, now that we've . . . performed the function for which we were revived?"

"You have been assigned a new function," Plate replied
gravely. "You're to begin in thirty-six hours."

"And what would this function be?"

Now Plate's tiny mouth split into a grin that revealed small, flat teeth, evenly spaced. "It's a surprise," he said.

She sensed no menace from him, only a sort of weary snugness and an almost reflexive impulse to withhold information. From her? From humanity in general?

"And if we refuse?" she asked.

"You will not," he replied simply, his grin never wavering.

Well, at least it was something.

When Konstant was through quarreling with Malye, he quarreled with Svetlane Antoneve, and then fell into bed with her and, to Malye's relief, remained there for the rest of the day and night. Vere and Nik, the two construction workers, had also taken up together, though more discreetly. Perhaps the age difference made them shy, though what scandal it could generate in a population of ten was not at all clear.

The children quarreled as well, with the adults and with each other, saving the day from what would otherwise be a mournful and apprehensive silence.

Time passed, in short, as time had always done: heedless of anything.

Chapter 15

"So, how are you?" Malye asked Viktor. After two hours in the washroom following nearly two full days of sleep, he'd emerged scrubbed and fresh, his amber skin almost glowing, his hair and beard neatly brushed, though they could use a trim. Soon, they would all have to start worrying about things like that. Haircuts. Did Gatean hair even need to be cut?

"I'm ... fine," Viktor replied with slow sincerity. "It's all a little unfamiliar, but ... it's coming back to me."

"Are you fit to travel?" she asked him, nodding sideways toward their escort: Plate, Crow, and a pair of hulking Drones. Not Wende's Drones, but rather spares from two other Finders Queens, here to—assist them? guard them?—on the way to their new assignment.

"Travel where?" Viktor asked, eyeing the escort thoughtfully.

Malye shrugged, not bothering to conceal her apprehension. "They won't say. But they want all of us, at least for now. Our 'new assignment.' Are you well enough?"

Viktor blinked, formed and released a frown. "I suppose I am, yes." He turned to look at the other refugees, who stood in a tight knot near the exit as if preparing to leave. But they were apprehensive as well, the air around them pink, and a gulf of several meters separated them from the knot of calm but clearly impatient Gateans. "I remember all of you."

Little Vadim spoke up: "Viktor, do you remember how to play two-ten?"

"Yes, I do," Viktor said slowly, and after a lengthy

pause. He made symbols of his hands and held them up to show.

"I think he'll be okay," Vadim said to Malye, in what he probably thought was a voice too quiet for Viktor to hear. But in fact, all the Sirians overheard him, and laughed, releasing their tension for a moment.

"Are we ready to go now?" Crow asked them all. A slight edge to his voice—of anger? No, of something else. Resentment, perhaps, but of what? They had nothing worth coveting.

But Malye nodded. "Yes. Lead the way."

They cycled through the membrane-door, quite accustomed by now to being led like children, with the heavy Drones trailing behind them like a threat. Out in the corridor, a wide red stripe had been painted along the floor, with black chevrons crossing it every few meters as if to point the way. It stood out sharply against the whiteness of everything else, buzzing in Malye's brain like a too-close look at the fractal-moiré surface of a fingerprint lifter.

"This indicator," Plate said, pointing to the line, "will lead you from the interface station to your chambers. Should you become lost or disoriented, simply look for the indicator to find your way. Do not seek assistance from passersby."

"Or what?" Malye inquired.

Plate did not deign to reply, which told Malye even more than his words had done, even more than his deferential behavior, even more than the presence of the painted line itself. Somehow, something had happened to increase the refugees' importance, to make a tangible asset of them. They mustn't be lost or even inconvenienced. They mustn't be allowed to fall into unfriendly hands.

And yet their escort was not so fearsome. There was no direct threat against Finders ring, nor against the refugees themselves. It must be more a matter of leverage, of social maneuvering. Sometimes a local greenbar commander would attempt to seize a prisoner from Central for similar reasons or, more rarely, to force an unwanted prisoner upon them. But the refugees were not prisoners here, not precisely. That much had been made clear, in both word and deed.

Malyc sighed. For all that had changed in the past two millennia, politics nonetheless seemed alive and well.

Vadim, who had edged his way forward until he walked alongside Crow, his little legs pumping almost twice as fast with the effort of keeping up, now spoke again. "Crow," he said, "I noticed that all the Workers are named after things, except for you. Why are you named after an animal? Are you special?"

The question impressed and intrigued Malye, and she made no move to intervene. Indeed, she wanted to hear the answer.

The Worker looked down, as if astonished to learn that Vadim could speak. "A crow is an instrument used for prying," he said without reflection, as if explaining the obvious. "A plate is an instrument which physically separates objects that have been pried apart."

"I told you!" Vadim said, turning partway around to address his sister, half a pace in front of Malye.

"No-oh!" Elle replied. "You said it was for opening doors."

"That's the same thing."

Crow's head turned backward to face Elle. "Your sibling is correct; a crow may be used in that manner." The head snapped around toward Vadim again. "Our names were chosen by Wende when her six was formed, and are appropriate to us. There is nothing special about me."

"Oh," Vadim said. "How old were you then?"

"What? I had lived four standard years. That is a strange question."

"Four?" Vadim said, sounding impressed for some reason. "Ialah, that's young. Are there other children around here?"

"No."

Crow's tone was final, dismissive; the conversation had interested him briefly, but no longer. To his credit, Vadim seemed to recognize this, and dropped back to speak more quietly with his sister. He knew better than to force his luck.

"Your children are very bright," Viktor remarked. "I've been dealing with stubborn simulacra for five years. The change is welcome." His voice was a little slow, a little strange, but he hovered at Malye's elbow and appeared to have no trouble keeping up as they moved through the

twisting corridors. They were going uphill, at least—
gravity was getting lighter.

"Yes," she said, appreciating the compliment. She
reached forward to ruffle Elle's hair. "They do surprise
me at times. Vadim once put a pressure regulator back together without instructions. And Elle can name the hundred largest worlds in alphabetical order."

"They will barely remember the Interstitial period at
all," Viktor went on distantly. "They will be children of
this era. I wonder what they will call it, when all is over
and done?"

"Depends on what happens in the next few days,"
Sasha said from behind them.

After a pause, Viktor grunted and nodded. "Yes, that's
so."

Disparate feelings flickered through Malye. Had
Viktor's mind been damaged? Had his soul? She still felt
that pull toward him, that alarming, uncontrolled attrac-
tion, but now it was tempered with sympathy, and guilt,
and perhaps a tinge of fear as well. What had this man
become? What was he feeling behind that slow, distracted
exterior?

"What did you learn," she asked him, "in all that time
with the Congress? What questions did you ask them?"

"Oh," he said, and the word was rich and deep and textured, conveying a sense of burden, of sacrifice, of ac-
complishment. "Oh, I asked them so many things. About
history, at first, but the more you look at history, the more
it comes apart, the more it seems to be the history *of* a
million different things. You can't see history from the
outside; you have to pick something caught in the flow,
watch the way it changes and is changed by the events
around it. History of language, history of economics, history of warfare . . . I once followed the development of
lighting and illumination technology through fifty centuries of human endeavor, and I became convinced, *convinced,* that lighting was the key to everything. And it is;
I can make a very good case for it. But the processing
and recycling of waste is also the key to everything, and
so is transportation, and religion, and the social status ac-
corded to adolescents. Everything is the key to everything
else."

"That sounds a little abstract," Malye said, despairing

quietly, within herself. Had Viktor simply become a mystic, doomed to see everything as some useless holistic jumble?

But Viktor chuckled and nodded. "Abstract! Yes, exactly! I followed that line of inquiry for a long, long time before *finally* concluding it was a dead end. Looking backward, at events that are fixed within the continuum, there are simply too many connections—they choke, they constrict. When everything is connected to everything else, what use is knowledge? What use is free will? There *is* no free will in the past, because the past can not be changed. This is the great fallacy behind the Congress. And yet, many of the simulacra understood this shortcoming in themselves, and advised me not to heed their advice. A paradox! It took me all that time to find that the Congress itself is a paradox.

"So, disheartened, I turned to the physical sciences, exploring them through the archive, through the recordings and limited simulacra of some of the best teachers in human history. I was a repairman, a mere technician, but in the leisure of timelessness I found I could apply myself fully, and I came to understand even some of the more difficult concepts. But it was the simple concepts that proved the more profound. Thirteenth law: Conservation of Angular Momentum; simple enough for a child to understand, and yet the implications of it could take a lifetime to explore.

"This, as it turns out, is the great fallacy of physical science. If Ialah is to be found in the details, as many would have it, I say at least that he is in *all* the details together, and not in any single place or thing. The inherent reductionism of science forced me to look always deeper and smaller and narrower, and I realized finally that I could never understand the nature of Ialah's continuum in this manner, that my mind could not contain all there was to know even about a simple thing like angular momentum. Physical science is all about the present, about *now*, but what is now, really? It's nothing, an infinitesimal moment in time, its duration: zero. Capture it in infinite detail, and what do you have? An infinity of nothing.

"I needed a more functional outlook, something that could help me explore the ephemeral but utterly crucial relationship between the present and the future. How do things happen? Before the connections are made, when all the possibilities are still extant, *what exactly happens* to weave the infinite futures into a single liquid present, and frozen past? Quantum physics claims to address this problem, but in fact it simply adds another layer of complexity to it. And so, I turned to mathematics, to statistics, to simulation. I turned to the oracle.

"Some futures are more probable than others; that much is obvious to anyone. But the future is unstable; anything at all can disrupt it. If I cough and disturb the air, I shatter the future that would have been, and exhale a new one in its place. And then that one is shattered when I cough again. But deeper down, there are things about the future we can certainly know. The physical laws do still apply, and so too the forces of history, the terrible inertia of social change, of illumination and transportation and waste processing all rushing forward through time.

"It's possible, even trivial, to gauge the likeliest outcome of a series of events, and around it an infinitely receding cone of lesser probabilities. But *where the present will actually manifest* is not something we can know until it has already cemented itself in the static past. It is this process, the continual selection of the present from the possibilities of the future, that finally seemed more important to me than all the rest of it put together. What is the influence of individual thought and action over this process? I needed to know, and yet it became clear that I could not. During the collapse of the First Colonial Age, a process that all could foresee and none could avert, Pascal Giovanni claimed to have proven, conclusively, the existence of free will. But so very little was known at that time about the metachronics of observed systems. How could they know? And knowing what we do now, how can we claim, like poor Giovanni, to be captains of our fate?

"It boils down to a single unknowable question: the existence of the soul, of free will, of metachronic perturbation at the quantum level. We cannot know, and yet we must, for why else do we even exist? It took me all that time, eighteen thousand days and sleepless nights, to find

that the universe itself is a paradox. And so I learned that
I know nothing at all, and from the purity of that ignorance and innocence I might—"

Viktor paused suddenly, and coughed.

"There," he said with a hoarse chuckle. "I've disrupted
the future and replaced it with another. Such is the proven
extent of my power."

"Names of Ialah," Malye said, touching his arm, feeling cold, intangible fingers groping in her own hollow interior. Viktor's monologue had been offered in a slow but
deliberate cadence that neither she nor anyone else had
dared to interrupt, that had worn on steadily, unvaryingly
through corridors, intersections, doorways. But the awful-
ness of it . . . Viktor's relentless *hope* had been, in the few
days Malye had known him, the most central and significant feature of his character. Had the Congress worn that
away, ground it down to nothing over the years, filling
his head with this nonsense in its place? Had it left anything of him at all? "Oh, oh, Viktor. I had no idea. I
should . . . I should never have let you near that thing."

"No?" Viktor looked and sounded surprised. "Why
not? I feel so much larger than I was before, so much
clearer. The only true way to know your home is to return
to it after long travel." He looked around him, at the
walls and ceiling of the winding, hexagonal tunnel, at
the refugees, at the Gateans, at the children, at Malye herself. And he smiled. "I know this place. I love you, Malyene Andreivne Kurosov'e, and I've come back to help
you in your time of distress."

Well, *that,* thought Malye, was easily the craziest thing
she'd ever heard him say.

"Cease conversation," Crow called back at them.

On the floor ahead, the red stripe took a sudden, right-
angle turn and vanished through a large membrane-
doorway. He vanished through it as well, with Plate right
behind him, and so the refugees followed, as was their lot
in this future time.

In the chamber on the other side, Sasha fainted, and
Svetlane screamed, and Malye grabbed her children and
pulled them tightly to her.

Across the chamber, behind a thick, triangular partition
of glass, stood a group of hideous . . . monsters, arranged

like pieces on a chessboard, poised to make their first move.

Viktor Slavanovot Bratsev simply looked at them and giggled.

Chapter 16

"I'm all right," Sasha said almost immediately. He climbed unsteadily to his feet. "I'm sorry, I'm okay."

Malye ignored him, her eyes riveted to the sight behind the partition. Monstrous figures, twisted and absurd. Waisters? It seemed dizzyingly impossible, and yet what else could they be? A day or two early, she thought, but *what else could they be?* There was a Dog, superficially much like the Gatean ones except for the bulging eyes and darker, purpler skin. But even a cursory inspection showed its long, wide snout to be ringed not with fleshy lips but with what appeared to be dozens of hinged disks, open just wide enough to hint at complex flapping things inside the mouth, a hundred tiny legs groping blindly where the tongue should be. And the eyes—Ialah! They were not bulging at all, but actually mounted on the surface of the head, two solid, featureless spheres of flat brown that squirmed and wriggled, clearly looking around. Clearly looking at the refugees themselves, returning their scrutiny.

And that was the most normal-looking of the creatures. The Queen, for thus she must surely be, looked like a half-toroidal bladder, a kind of C-shaped balloon that had been filled with heavy, viscous fluid. From the top of her curving form dangled a pair of flabby arms terminating in myriad wormy fingers or tentacles, and at the bottom, balanced on four short legs, was her . . . face. Much like a fatter, flabbier version of the Dog's face, except that the eyes protruded even farther, were in fact mounted on fleshy stalks. And the mouth, twitching and flapping in a hundred ways, appeared even more hideously complex.

The Queen's "back" faced forward, Malye realized with a shock. She looked like the Dog, her body essentially a wide, flat roll, but one that had folded back on itself, the rump stretching and lifting behind her like a fleshy, forward-leaning tower. Her arms were really her tail, split in two and arched back over her head until they could easily reach the floor in front of her.

On either side of her, the two Drones followed the same C-shaped body plan. Smaller and leaner, yes, but they gave off an impression of solidity, as if their bulging muscles were springs and cables of steel beneath a resilient outer sheath of tough plastic. Each of them massed easily as much as a Gatean Drone, and looked at least a hundred times more frightening. In a fair fight, there was no doubt which of the two species would emerge victorious.

Flanking the Drones, the two Workers appeared much less formidable. Thin, willowy creatures that looked as if they should crumple under the two-gee gravity here, their twisted backs folding and breaking, their tiny legs crushing atop splayed feet, bodies sagging and flattening. But the bodies held firm, and in fact when they made the small movements that showed they were alive and not mere statues, they did so with an easy grace that made Malye think of weightlessness.

All six of the creatures looked back at Malye and the other refugees with clear interest, their alien features flexing and shifting in alien yet unmistakable ways.

The colors sang high, aching notes in Malye's head.

Images flashed through her: Tyumen splitting open in a hail of unseen projectiles; passenger ferries flashing and dying; the blood streaming from Grigory's nose and mouth, filling his mask, killing him.

Killing him.

These creatures were guilty of murder a billion times over, the torture and murder of an entire star system. Ialah, it dwarfed to nothingness the crimes of the Monster Andrei, who had after all killed only thirty-nine, and that over a period of many years. Did they hear the colors, these Waisters? Did they feel the unclean urging of impulse through the illusion of self-control? Did they feel anything at all?

"Ialah," she whispered. Her hatred too great for expression, and so, too, her fear.

The space back there was wedge-shaped, just a corner of the greater octohedral chamber that had been walled off with a triangle of glass pointing straight up to the ceiling, braced and attached along its three edges with bolted strips of metal. The whole thing looked hasty, functional but lacking in the sort of finesse she'd come to expect from the Gateans. It was not a jewel, or a fog, but a simple glass tank of the sort people once used for algae farms.

So the Gateans had been taken by surprise as well. Which meant that nobody was prepared for this, which meant that anything at all could happen. Anything at all.

The glass was fogged on the far side, as if it were hotter and wetter in there, like a shower stall, and behind the glass hung another haze, thinner and yellower. What kind of breathing air was back there? What was the tank holding in? Not the Waisters themselves, surely; they had a door back there, a white hexagonal membrane covering an opening to ... What, a corridor? Another chamber? A seven-kilometer warship bristling with weapons? How close was this place to the surface of Holders Fastness? At any rate, it appeared the Waisters could leave any time they liked. And no glass she was aware of, metallic or otherwise, was likely to hold those Drones back for long.

The Queen opened her mouth, and through the thick partition Malye heard the sounds of her voice, fluting and scratching in exactly the same way as the Gateans'. That, at least, they had imitated well.

"There is no word for 'hello' in the Waister language," said Crow, standing over beside the tank, lined up with Wende's six in a formation of their own. "But this Queen, whose name is #*Hthw*#, wishes to know whether you are physically well."

Malye turned and eyed Crow sharply, surprised that he should lie about so small a thing. And yet lying he was, and not casually; his posture and facial expression left little doubt. Filled with spite and resentment, earnestly hoping to deceive ... About what? For what possible reason?

"These ... *creatures*," she said to Crow, "are responsible for the destruction of everything we ever held dear.

Names of Ialah, why have you brought them here? Why have you brought *us*?"

He shrugged, glancing up at Wende beside him. "They wished to speak with you. Actually, they insisted."

In all her tightly controlled life, Malye had never once spat on any floor, anywhere, but here and now she did so, unable to contain her fury. She'd aimed for the glass partition, but misjudged the gravity so that her spittle landed instead on the floor, halfway between her own feet and those of Wende's nearest Drone. The Gateans bristled, stiffened, glared. They knew an insult when they saw one.

"I have nothing to say to these monsters. Nor to you, if you will not speak truthfully. What did she really say?"

"As I've told you," Crow said with false calm.

"Then, our talk is over."

Line, the largest of the Drones, whom Malye had nearly spat on, took half a giant's step forward. "It certainly is not," he said in a low, deep voice. "You will not act contrary to the interests of Gate."

"Oh," she said, stepping forward herself, refusing to let her body language surrender for her, "so now your interests are those of Gate, are they? What did we do, have a little territorial dispute? Am I addressing the kings and Queen of Gate, here in audience with the enemy?"

Wende held up her hands, palms down. "Please," she said to Malye, "from you we require help. You will provide help because of friendship? You and I, we have tested one another."

Around Malye, the refugees were half mad with fear and rage and confusion, hating the fact that they could not understand what was happening, and yet not daring to make a move for fear they might upset some delicate balance. All except Viktor, who stood beside her with an infuriating, loose-limbed, almost meditative calm. Damn him, he had not lost his ability to shame her. She strove to imitate his stance, forcing down her rage like half-vomited bile.

"I will not help you, Wende, if I am not told the truth. What did this *Waister Queen* actually say to me?"

Wende made a frightening attempt to smile. "Your people were clever to surrender. Not as stupid as they had expected. That is what she said."

This time, Malye had a clear impression of truth. She

shot a poisonous glare at the Queen behind the glass. "Yes? Tell her she was not at all clever to return here. My husband is dead, everyone I ever *knew* is dead, and I hold her responsible for this. Tell her I wish her only pain."

Wende turned, fluted at the alien Queen.

"Hey," Konstant demanded, "how do we know she's translating faithfully?" The words were confident enough—Konstant seemed to be at his best when he had a technical or semantic complaint to throw in the face of an enemy—but nonetheless he was standing behind Malye, placing her body between his own and the Waisters'.

"I don't see that she's lying," Malye told him.

"Oh, well, that's wonderful then," he sneered.

Viktor turned to face the two of them, holding out the Congress of Advisors in his hand. Damn, how had he gotten ahold of that?

"Actually," he said, "I believe I can help."

And he put his thumb on the trigger and pressed it down.

"No!" Malye shouted. "Viktor, no! Let go of it, let me have it!"

She wrested the device from his grasp. His eyes, which had glazed over, now cleared.

"There," he said, "it's finished."

Malye held the Congress up in his face. "Where did you get this? Why did you take this from me? Damn it, Viktor, you're not to touch it!"

"What's finished?" Konstant asked, and for once his mood seemed more pragmatic than Malye's.

Viktor smiled that same, peaceful smile, as if he were buried deep down inside himself, where none of this turmoil had any ability to reach him. "Enter the Congress," he said to Malye. "I've rigged a translator for you. The parameters may need some adjustment to suit your needs and tastes, but the basics of it are all in place." His grin widened. "It runs in real time, so you needn't worry about becoming trapped."

She eyed him suspiciously, unwilling to believe any good could come of his using the Congress. Surely he'd had enough time—almost a full second—to set such a thing up if it were possible, but ... But what?

"Don't be afraid," Viktor said, and now *that* was the craziest thing she'd ever heard him say.

"If you don't use it, I will," Konstant said, reaching for the Congress.

That decided her. She wouldn't let anyone else even *touch* the thing, not after what happened to Viktor. It was her responsibility. And maybe a large part of her still didn't want to be a leader, to be a Queen, but she'd be damned to Hell before she'd take orders from Konstant.

"Hands to yourself," she said to him, as she might to Vadim or Elle. And she pressed the trigger.

The result was not at all what she'd expected; she did not appear suddenly in the middle of the Senate floor on Council Station, nor in a smaller conference room with a subset of the Congress. Rather, she appeared right where she'd previously been, in the "Interface Station" with Wende's people and the six Waisters and all the refugees. The place had taken on a sculpted, simulated feel, though, and before her stood the familiar figure of Mediator, and in the air between them, just below chin level, hung three flatscreens, marked GRIEF, DENG, and JONSON.

"Hello," said Mediator. "This configuration has been saved by the previous user. You may return to default mode now or at any other time, simply by subvocalizing a command to that effect. In the present configuration, any words you speak aloud will be redirected to your actual vocal cords, and will not be recognized as commands."

"Uh, I understand," Malye said.

Mediator did not react.

"You understand what?" Konstant snapped.

She turned to face him, a sculpted statue of himself, quite lifelike and yet quite clearly not alive. The three screens, which had followed her around, remaining centered in her vision, cut rectangular pits in his body, their edges gray and smooth.

"I understand what Viktor has done with the Congress," she said, and turned to the simulacrum of Viktor. "You've done an excellent job. I had no idea such a capability existed."

Still smiling, he bowed slightly. *You see?* his sculpted features said, *I am not so much a fool as you've come to believe, and though I can hardly demand your love, I may at least hope for your respect.* The image was quite good, full of nuance and detail that was lacking in the true Congressional simulacra. This one, at least, had a real image and a real person to draw upon for inspiration. Malye turned away from it.

'what are these three flatscreens for?' she subvocalized at Mediator.

"The three screens in front of you," Mediator replied dutifully, "represent the best translations of overheard conversation in Waister, as rendered by the three Congressional simulacra who are capable of speaking that language."

'are you capable of speaking that language?'

"Yes, I may be configured to operate in any of fourteen languages, singly or in combination, including Waister, Standard—"

'that's fine,' she told it. 'add a fourth screen.'

Mediator didn't argue or seek clarification; a fourth screen, marked MEDIATOR, simply appeared on the right, shifting the other three slightly so that together they remained centered.

The Waister Queen looked on with obvious interest. She sang a few brief notes.

GRIEF	DENG	JONSON	MEDIATOR
Your fetishism interests.	What a pretty device.	Your use of that object is fascinating to me.	Interest
Fetishism. Explain.	Device for what?	That object is fascinating. What does it do?	Object Employ Object Query

Wende turned to the Queen and replied in a fluting, rattling whisper.

GRIEF	DENG	JONSON	MEDIATOR
Our fetishism listens.	An object for listening.	The object comprehends speech.	Object Listen
Stupid-lings do not speak.	Stupid-lings listen poorly.	Stupid-lings do not comprehend.	Small and stupid Deafmute

The Waisters reached their arms out to touch fingers with one another, in a brief but complicated gesture that

communicated a sense of unease, perhaps of . . . what,
sorrow? It was hard to say—Malye was looking only at
their simulacra, for one thing, and for another their movements and postures and twitching skins resembled nothing she'd ever seen. And yet, they seemed as pregnant
with meaning as any human gesture.

These are also creatures of Ialah, she reminded herself.
Creatures with an animal past, with an aeons-long heritage of preverbal communication. Long abandoned, that
heritage—the Ken Jonson simulacrum had dated Waister
civilization at several millions of years—but since when
had anyone been able to escape the past? It had a way of
reaching forward, to color and shape the future, all the
things you *had been* sharply limiting what you might become.

The Waister Queen spoke again:

GRIEF	DENG	JONSON	MEDIATOR
Perception of that group hallucinating and constructing. Confirmation?	This sphere has dreamed, and piled stones beside the water, yes?	I sense their people have aspired, and achieved much. Is this so?	Perception Sphere Illusion Megalith Shore Query

With silent curses Malye eyed the screens in front of
her. Four interpretations, wildly different. Two were from
green-hairs, of course, and therefore suspect, but they dif-
fered even from one another, hinting that the Queen had
expressed some alien subtlety that did not translate well.

How bizarre a position this was, how bizarre a problem! Mere weeks ago, there had been no Waisters. Humanity the sole offspring of Ialah, with all the universe
stretched out before them, all of time and space and mind
awaiting their investigation. Not lonely, not longing for
company, humanity complete unto itself. The smugness
of it now made her ill—a sin of pride, so easily avenged
by these strong, twisted creatures.

She did not want to be here. She did not want to speak
with the Waisters, or even the Gateans, and for the first
time she wondered if perhaps Tyumen might have been a
better resting place for her, if she should have stayed be-

hind to assist the multitudes there as they gave up their mortal bodies and fled to Ialah. The thought was compelling. But no, Elle and Vadim had needed her more, and needed her still in the here and now. This place held their future, shaped by what Malye and the others would say and do in the next few minutes.

Damn you, Ialah, in all your names.

'mediator,' she subvocalized, 'exit realtime and prepare to reconfigure.'

The scene around her froze, all motion suspended.

"How may I assist you?" Mediator asked.

"These four screens," she said, "the idea was a good one, but it's not working. All these translations are independent, correct?"

"That is so."

"Okay. If possible, what I'd like is a single screen, showing a group consensus translation. Begin with Jonson's sole interpretation and work from there. And give Jonson veto power over the output. Can this be done in realtime?"

"Yes."

"Okay. Another thing: I don't need the translations to be so short. I don't want them to be. If they need annotations or other information for me to understand them, don't leave it out. Is that clear?"

"Yes."

"Reconfigure and return to realtime."

The simulated scene came back to life around her, and now there was a single screen in front of her, labeled CONSENSUS.

She turned to address the Gateans. "Plate, would you please inform the Waister Queen that we refuse to be addressed as 'stupidlings?' We want nothing from her, and if she wishes to speak at all, she must do so in a manner we find acceptable."

Plate and Wende exchanged glances, and after a moment Wende nodded her head, giving him permission to speak.

CONSENSUS

#*Hthw*# (proper name of Waister Queen), that individual wishes you to know that her people are not stupid-lings. The name for her people is #Hua# (closest approximation of "human" available to Waister vocal apparatus). The name for herself is #Ayye# (closest approximation of "Malye" available to Waister vocal apparatus). She wishes you to know that her people will not speak with you unless they are addressed with completion (closest approximation of "respect" available in Waister conceptual realm).

#Hthw# appeared to be thinking hard about that one. After a delay of several seconds, she opened her mouth and said, "Huuuaaa." It sounded like there was a flute shoved down her throat, but the word was recognizable.

"Yes," Malye said to the Waister Queen, with an exaggerated nod of her head. Then she turned to Plate again, speaking bitterly: "Now, tell her that our people consider murder to be a crime. Explain that her people have murdered billions of ours, which constitutes a crime we have no desire nor ability to forgive."

Again checking with Wende, and again receiving permission to speak, Plate relayed Malye's message in slow, careful language. The interpretation on her screen appeared to convey the meaning of it at least adequately, but of course it was just a translation of a translation, and the message itself was aimed at a mind more alien than any criminal's. No way to know what impressions would be generated there; it was like throwing ball bearings into a closed box, never knowing what they were hitting except by the sounds that came back.

The Queen sang:

CONSENSUS

The conflict between our peoples is seen as a mistake *(literally, "poor grasp")*. Mistake. We misunderstand much. Occasionally we had encountered, encountered, encountered Stone Age peoples *(literally, "cairn builders")*, but they were always absent when we returned, so fragile that knowledge of us destroyed them. Destroyed, destroyed them all. The arrival of stupid-lings surprised us. We misunderstood much. Their bodies were blue; they had many hands. They died without surrender, so tragic and strange. You, the #Hua#, we confronted with outrageous force, and still your surrender took long. And we understood that you did not understand us, and we despaired *(literally, "lost air")*.

The song took nearly a minute, and when it was over Malye felt a hand on her shoulder and turned to see Konstant, looking apprehensive.

"Malye," he said earnestly, "are you understanding this? Let us know what's happening, damn it."

Echoes of agreement from the others. For once, Konstant was in tune with their needs and feelings, while Malye ignored them to converse with their nightmare enemy. She knew shame.

"I think we've just received a sort of apology," she told them all. "It's difficult to say for sure."

Konstant snorted in disbelief. "Apology? Let her restore our worlds and our people and then maybe we'll hear her apology."

"Is she here to make reparation?" Vere Sergeivne asked.

A sensible question, and one that had not occurred to Malye until now. The Waisters must have some motive, after all, for their return, and for this bizarre attempt to communicate, after all their silent rampage through the Human Spaces. Malye looked at Plate, who then relayed the question to #Hthw#, whose face rearranged itself again as new emotions played through it.

With the *#Hwhh#* *(i.e., the Waisters)*, there is ignorance, newness, conflict, and completion. We did not suspect a fifth state, in which completed antagonists *(literally, "new things un-newed")* stack together in a single place. This we learned from *#Hua#*. We did not suspect a sixth state, in which a completed antagonist would change to become new again. These people (body gesture indicating Wende's six) are not *#Hua#*. They claim to be *#Hwhh#* and *#Hua#* together, together, but how could this be? They do not coexist *(literally, "stack")* with *#Hua#*? Confusion. We did not suspect a seventh state, to which none of the other states could apply. We misunderstand much. How many states exist? Our presence is for purposes of communication *(literally, "interface," in the physical/chemical sense of the word, i.e., the surface or*

*boundary at which reacting materials come in con-
tact.)*

While the Queen was saying this, and while the translation was growing and rearranging itself on Malye's
screen, she noted a growing agitation on the part of the
Gateans, as if the air on their side of the room contained
some caustic chemical.

Presently, Wende shouted something the translation algorithm didn't catch, something that sounded more human than Waister, and the two Gatean Drones sprang into
action, throwing themselves at the refugees, huge projectiles of gray muscle and sinew.

There was a moment of screaming and confusion as the
refugees attempted to scatter in the close quarters. The
Congress of Advisors was knocked from Malye's hand,
and a moment later she found herself pressed solidly
against the wall, Line's huge hands on her shoulders, his
copper eyes staring straight into her, his sickly sweet
breath in her face.

"Please! Excuse the reaction of the Drones," Plate said
urgently, approaching from somewhere on the other side
of the room. "We've suffered a problem."

"Heard something you didn't like?" Malye heard
Konstant say in his old accusing tone.

"Line," Wende called out, "release the woman. This is
inappropriate."

The Drone looked up sharply at that command, and
took his hands off Malye. Plate strode forward, nudging
Line out of his way as though *he* were the stronger of the
two. In his hand was the Congress.

"Apologies, Malyene Andreivne," Plate said with apparent sincerity. "There is more to understanding than
mere translation. This meeting is difficult for all of us, as
I'm sure you're aware."

"I am very aware of that," Malye replied, in as calm a
voice as she could muster under the circumstances. She
straightened her robe, took the Congress back from him.
"In fact, I can't do this. Take us back to our quarters."

Plate fluted something at Wende, who scraped and
scratched out a reply.

"Yes," Plate said to Malye after that, "I think perhaps

that would be best. We can try this again tomorrow. Perhaps we all need time to adjust."

"What *happened*?" Konstant demanded accusingly.

Malye shrugged, still dazed. "I believe the Waister Queen is suing for peace."

"Peace? Why? I mean, why now?"

She scowled. "Ialah's names, man, how the hell should I know? Let's get out of here."

She turned and leaped through the door membrane with no further delay, and began hurrying at once down the red stripe, putting as much distance as she could between those monsters and herself. This was too much. This was just too much for her to handle. The others followed closely behind, and to an observer it might well have appeared that the Sirian refugees were fleeing in horror from the green-haired Plate, who hurried after them as if to explain a great error.

"I hate your family, Plate. I hate your entire species."

"Madam, what harm have we done, precisely?"

"I don't trust you, I never have. Take this and get out of here. Study the translation algorithm. I want a two-way machine that does the same thing, and that doesn't require any input from you or from your people."

"Madam, I—"

"Do it! Do it, or this whole game is over. We don't want to talk to them anyway, much less with you as our intermediaries."

"Here. Take it back. I've memorized the algorithm."

"Have you? Then get out."

He left her trembling with fear, with rage, with emotions she could not easily put a name to. The pressure, oh, Ialah! Plate was perhaps the most human of his kind, the most willing to see things from a human perspective. But Malye was the *least* human of her kind, the *least* human, and if things kept up like this, she'd soon be showing it, and Plate would be revealing what color the blood was, beneath that ugly gray skin of his.

Chapter 17

"May I borrow the Congress?" Viktor asked when things had settled down a little. Malye shot him a weary look. Enough, enough with the Congress. Couldn't he leave it alone?

Everyone was in the dayroom, lounging together on the couches and the floor, silent for the most part but physically gregarious nonetheless, the bonds between them strengthening as external pressures forced them closer together. Making of them ... not a family, exactly, but something like a small village.

"If this keeps up," Konstant had even joked to her at one point, "you and I may be on the same side."

"We already are," she'd snapped in reply, and he'd said, "I have nothing personal against you, you know," and gone away to speak with Svetlane Antoneve. Which was just fine, because Svetlane had been driving Malye's blood pressure up with incessant demands for things like skin lotion and extra towels, and if Konstant was with her, it would make the two of them that much easier to avoid.

Now she eyed Viktor skeptically.

"What is it you hope to accomplish?" she asked him.

"To answer some questions," he replied carefully. "I'd like to review the transcript of your session, to go over the translations in detail. None of us heard any of that, I'll remind you, and you haven't made any effort to repeat it for us. And I suspect I'm the only one here with even a minimal grasp of Waister psychology and history, so I submit to you that I am the most qualified to make an analysis."

"Indeed," she said, her voice noncommittal. She took out the Congress and turned it over in her hands a few times, examining it minutely, as if its smooth, contoured surface might hold some wisdom for her. But no, the wisdom was all inside, and Viktor was right.

"I'll be as brief as possible," Viktor said. "A few seconds at most."

"Any excuse to get in there, right?"

Malye locked eyes with him, probing for weakness, but he returned her gaze with that same unflappable calm, and after a moment she sighed and threw him the Congress, which he fumbled and caught. Within moments he had the trigger down. It was unpleasant to watch his eyes lose focus, as though he had suddenly died, but he remained sitting as before, his back against the wall, and after a very short time indeed he let the trigger up again, blinked, returned to realtime.

Malye's children edged closer, and Nikolai and Vere after them. And then Konstant and Svetlane and Ludmile turned their attention on Viktor, and Sasha was already sitting next to him, which made it a full house.

"So?" Nik asked, his voice betraying an eagerness Malye had not suspected. And she saw that same eagerness, like a sparkling orange tone, reflected in the eyes of the others. How eager they were to hear the words of their enemy.

"So," Viktor said. Looking around, he blushed with sudden shyness. Unused to being the center of actual human attention, probably, but he spoke nonetheless: "Malyene Andreivne is correct; the Waisters have come here seeking peace. There, ah. . . . Once, millions of years ago, there was a race of creatures that confronted the Waister empire, and was destroyed. The Waisters were afraid they would end up destroying *us*, as well. They still don't understand why it took us so long to surrender to them. They're—"

He ducked his head, cleared his throat, rubbed a hand on the back of his neck.

"They appear to be very hurt and confused by what's happened."

"Oh, my heart is bleeding," Konstant said. "The poor, poor Waisters didn't want to destroy Sirius system, but we made them do it."

Viktor was shaking his head, waving his hands. He was still calm, but there was a thought in his head that he couldn't wrap the right words around, and it clearly bothered him. "They destroyed Wolf and Lalande systems, too, but they didn't destroy Sol, when they clearly could have. Listen, imagine the strangest person you've ever met. Imagine some demented, autistic genius from an old Earth tribal society, who speaks a different language than you do, when he chooses to speak at all. You share almost no cultural reference points, and when you first meet him, he bashes you in the face with his fist. What happened? What's going on in that brain of his? Maybe something very different from what you think."

"I'd lock him up," Malye said flatly.

"I don't care what's going on in his brain," said Svetlane. "If he hits me, I hit back."

Others were nodding, but Sasha appeared to be on Viktor's side. "What if he's too big to hit? What if he's too big to lock up? What if he comes back later and offers to shake hands?"

"You'd be a fool to trust him," Malye said.

"Would I?" For once, Sasha was holding his ground.

"Of course you would!" Malye stood, pulled to her feet by sudden anger. At him, at everyone. "You want to make peace with monsters? With murderers? You can let a man hit you in the face if you want, but if you let him get away with it, I guarantee he'll do it again, anytime he likes."

"Maybe not," Viktor said. "It depends on why he hit you in the first place."

"So what are you suggesting?" Konstant asked, also getting to his feet. "That we roll over and make friends?"

Viktor shrugged, flashed up a feeble grin. "Excuse me, Konstant, but have we been given another option? We can't fight them, and we can't run away from them."

"No, but we can ignore them."

Malye nodded approvingly at Konstant's words, pointing at him for emphasis. "*Exactly* right. Our confrontation with them is complete, yes? We've surrendered, they've gone away, and thankfully we have no further business to conduct."

"Ah," Viktor said, "but it seems we do. They've returned, they've asked for peace, they've asked to speak with us, all very much against their nature. It's as if we all took our clothes off and walked into the autistic man's tribe to smoke weeds and eat animal flesh, holding our noses, as it were, against the stench of a life for which we aren't suited. Why would we do that? It would take something very important to make us do that. If they had something we wanted . . ."

Konstant was shaking his head. "If we had something the Waisters wanted, they could simply take it. What could we do about it?"

"Well, then, why are they back?" Viktor demanded. And suddenly, *finally*, Malye recognized the gleam in his eye, recognized what he was up to.

"You just want to talk to them," she said to Viktor, wonderingly. "They're just like another Congress of Advisors to you, a whole empire, a whole *species* of beings to answer your weird philosophical questions. You just want to find out what they've seen, what they know, what they maybe *suspect* about time and space and superchronic free will!"

"Metachronic," he corrected, as calmly as ever. "And yes, I want to speak with them. What's wrong with that?"

"They murdered our civilization!" Malye flared. "Names of Ialah, Viktor, did you leave your wits behind in the Congress? Would you deal with Saitan, sell your soul to him for the sake of free will?"

Now Viktor's calm began to crack. He scowled. "Malye, listen, the speed of light is constant, even for Waisters, and their fastest ships travel no more than ninety percent of that. The nearest edge of Waister space is thought to be about twelve hundred light-years away. That's a long distance, and it also means this group, this 'peace fleet' of theirs, was launched as much as *eight hundred years* after the end of the war. With all due respect"—and here he swept the room with his gaze, taking in everyone—"we need to develop a *sense* for the magnitudes of time and space involved here. Our grievances, however legitimate, are thousands of years out of date."

That sank in; Sirian law dictated that the gap between commission and punishment of a crime, any crime, could not exceed one hundred standard years.

"Malye," Viktor said gently, "you're an ordinary person, more or less. Does that frighten you? You believe yourself constrained, even doomed, by your heritage, but have you even explored the option of free will? Step outside yourself for a moment. Who and what do you want to be?"

"A collaborator?" she said, shaking her head. "Shall I love and support the Waisters as I did the Monster Andrei? Whatever I may want, that isn't a part of it."

Viktor shrugged. "Peace, like war, is a means to an end. Use your brain."

"Use yours!" she shot back. "Every deviant claims a change of heart, when other defenses have failed. It is no basis for trust."

Silence came over the room in the wake of that remark, everyone taking a few moments to absorb it, to think it through. And then the arguments exploded, the shouting and the fist pounding and the demands for access to the Congress, which were to last for most of the rest of the day.

At Wende's insistence, Plate carried with him a comp jewel linked to microscopic sensors on the walls and floors and ceilings of the refugees' quarters, and some few sensors on the skins of the refugees themselves, and Plate could press the jewel at any time to his forehead and receive a vague, noisy impression of what they were thinking and feeling.

He removed the jewel now, having gleaned as much as he could, and replaced it in his robe's carrying pocket. Alone in an unused chamber, feeling troubled, feeling swept along in the currents of the moment. How far he was from the stations of his comfort, from the exercise of his surest skills! All of Gate was dependent now on Finders ring, and Finders ring on Wende's handling of the human-Waister interface efforts, and Wende herself dependent on Plate's own handling of these humans. And thus far he had not facilitated any improvement on the situation at all. Not at all.

It was very, very important that he regain the refugees' trust. By speaking with them frequently? By explaining the true importance of what was happening around them, and to them? They were so difficult to handle, to speak with, to predict. In a way, he almost admired this about them, but for now the disturbance of it was intolerable.

Crow, of course, was no help. His expertise lay mainly in other areas, and his interest still more so. "Why not simply force them?" he would often ask, showing how very little he understood of the situation, and how fortunate Wende was not to have granted him greater discretionary liberty. The other Workers knew and understood still less, and the Drones, even among Finders ring, seemed to accept only grudgingly the humans' right to exist at all.

No, this situation was his own responsibility, and if it were to evolve in a favorable way it must be through his own avoidance of error. But what error? Where and how would he recognize it?

Had he practiced the human art of cursing during his life, of using language to release and express emotional tension, he would now have exercised it. Instead, he stretched his lips wide, pulling the corners up and leaving them there, practicing his smile until it hurt.

He came to realize, after a time, that he was not alone. Turning, he saw that a foreign Worker had entered the chamber. Warders ring, the patterns of his scalp announced. Young, probably trained in the handling of complex and dangerous equipment. He was looking at Plate with undisguised, unmitigated hatred.

Plate nodded at the Worker, neither alarmed nor annoyed nor surprised. He'd been expecting visits like this one, underlings sneaking off to express their Queens' feelings to other underlings, to *influential* underlings who clearly should know they were not in the right.

"Yes?" Plate said in Standard. "Finders ring has destroyed Gatean society, and your life in particular? Communication with the Waister empire is our only function, and Finders ring has handed that over to a bunch of humans. Is that what you wish to tell me?"

"Yes," the Worker said, echoing Plate's use of Standard.

"Very well, then," Plate said, "you may tell me that."

This joke, poor though it was, angered the Worker still further. "You will not succeed! Warders ring has arranged a signal to the Waister fleet, and even now it is being broadcast. A signal of surrender! They are strong and clever, but naive, and so we will join them, and lead them away from this misguided endeavor."

Plate dared to laugh. That was the stupidest, most insane plan he'd ever heard in his life. If the Waisters paid any attention at all, they could only regard Warders ring as a newness. What advantage could be gained by such a maneuver? His eyes narrowed, breath deepening. Did Warders ring know something he himself did not? Certainly, the Waisters had thus far been acting contrary to expectation. Had Warders deduced some new pattern?

"Why inform us now?" Plate asked, falling into a very human tone of suspicion. "Why not after?"

The other looked bitterly pleased at that. "Finders ring is not without influence. We do not wish an alienation, merely an adjustment of priorities. That Finders ring should have some brief warning is very much to our advantage."

Plate sighed, putting a hand to his brow, relieved that he'd begun this strange conversation in Standard. In Waister it would have been cumbersome in the extreme, and even Teigo, often described as a language of intrigue, lacked the brevity of Standard, which had been born, after all, in an age of turmoil and upheaval, and forced on an immense, diverse, and often unwilling population.

"Your plan will likely fail," he said now, relishing the compactness of the words and concepts, "but I thank you for the warning."

The Worker signaled his understanding, turned, and departed.

"Shit," Plate said, trying out the concept of profanity after all, as he fumbled for the other comp jewel, the one that would let him warn Wende and the others. Hadn't the day proved interesting enough already?

Chapter 18

When next the refugees entered the Interface Station, changes were evident. Seats had been added, for one thing: three gray couches in the usual Gatean style sat off to one side of the glass barrier, and directly in front of it, eight large chairs of some shiny, orange, soft-looking material, and two smaller ones sized just right for Elle and Vadim. In front of the chairs was a large flatscreen, rising up from the floor on a slender post. It looked very Sirian, very familiar, so much so that Malye had to wonder if Finders ring, in their function as archaeologists and historians, had found something like it in the ruins of some world or other. Certainly, it looked like nothing they would design on their own.

To her further surprise, she saw that Wende's Drones had remained in the corridor, rather than following them inside here. Guarding the door? Simply staying out of the way? Wende occupied the central couch, her Dog curled up at her feet, and Crow and Plate took the couches on either side, looking carefully harmless, as though they wished to convey their good intentions more openly, but were afraid of giving offense. Plate, especially, looked deferential and flighty; Crow let an edge of annoyance creep through for her to see. But he was clearly trying not to, and she supposed that was significant by itself.

Wende was harder to read, more alien. Not so much Waisterlike as simply blank, like she wasn't thinking anything at all. But Malye doubted that very much.

Movement behind the glass partition. The Drones absent there, as well, the Queen and Dog and Workers sitting on couches of their own. The design of the couches

was different—they were low and strangely shaped, and
the Waisters draped themselves over them in what looked
like a very uncomfortable way, particularly in the high
gravity. Malye revised her opinion of what the anatomy
must be like, inside those skins.

"HHEEOO," the Queen said, in a voice that was
strangely musical but very clear nonetheless. "HHEEOO,
AYYE. HHEEOO, HUA."

The refugees gasped, and Malye, too, when she realized the Waister Queen was attempting to speak to them
in Standard.

"She is saying hello," Plate offered politely. "We have
informed her that this is normal and expected when
meeting with someone in peace, and though it is strange
to her, she appears to have understood the concept."

"Hello," Malye said back, without really thinking.
Maybe it wasn't a good idea? But the flatscreen in front
of the chairs went green for a moment, beeped, and then
began producing the tones and scrapes of the Waister
language. Behind the partition, the Queen and Workers
shifted, turning their heads, clearly listening to the words.

"Please," Plate said, gesturing at the chairs, "sit, if you
wish to. We hope these accommodations will comfort you
sufficiently. We were not entirely sure what you would
prefer."

"Why don't you ask?" Konstant snapped. But he took
a seat, as did the others. There were two parallel rows of
four chairs each, with the smaller two off to the right by
a wall, and Malye thought it significant that while
Konstant chose to sit in the front row, he took the end
seat and let Svetlane sit behind him. Nik and Vere also
took the back row, and Sasha, leaving the older Ludmile
to sit on the other end in front, and just like that it had
been decided that Malye and Viktor should sit front and
center, with nothing separating them from the enormous
Waister Queen but two meters of space, and a spindly
flatscreen, and a heavy glass partition. And some funny
breathing air on the other side of it, that was not quite
completely transparent.

They sat.

Malye looked hard at Wende. "What are you people up
to?"

Wende nodded, as if perhaps acknowledging that the

question was a fair one. "We desire the facilitation of peace. You are necessary to that process. Are you in comprehension of this?"

"Only partly," Malye said. And then, all at once, she caught something in Wende's manner, a sliver of readable emotion, and she read it and felt relief. "Something has happened. Again, I mean. Something has changed in the last thirteen hours."

"Yes," Wende agreed, and once again she was blank.

Plate stepped in, though, with reassuring tones. "Our . . . political situation is somewhat . . . unstable, I suppose you would say. It's hardly a surprise, under the circumstances. There have been . . . well, a series of intrigues, all working at cross purposes. None of this initiated by Finders ring, but in the absence of clear coordination we have benefitted from the confusion. Our position is stronger than it was; the other rings are not certain whom else to trust. Consequently, we feel a greater liberty to allocate resources. Your comfort was thought to have been too long neglected."

"That's very kind of you," Malye said, not entirely without sincerity. Plate was lying, but only a little, and that was normal enough in any dialogue. Nothing untoward was happening here, so far as she could tell.

She turned to the Waister Queen, and spoke experimentally: "We are willing to speak with you, though it is distasteful. Coming here without your Drones was an admirable gesture. What do you wish to tell us?"

The flatscreen flashed, beeped, spoke. The Waisters listened, and after a pause, the Queen replied. Words appeared on the flatscreen:

#	This is no thing with which we hold	#
#	familiarity. It is not new, for we	#
#	have completed. It is beyond completion,	#
#	and of the nature of this you must inform.	#

Malye blinked. "You want *us* to talk? We have nothing to say. We did not ask for this contact."

"How do your starship drive motors work?" Viktor asked suddenly and with a leading tone that said he knew his speaking would displease Malye.

She turned. They shared a look, he shrugging: *they*

want to talk, so, let them tell us something useful, and her scowling back: *what are you doing? These creatures are unimaginably dangerous!*

But the question was asked, and the flatscreen translated it promptly, without stopping to ask Malye's permission. And one of the alien Workers replied:

#	Broad littoral zones, fractally infinite	#
#	Every principle affects every other. I	#
#	inquire regarding the time scale of this	#
#	song.	#

And irrepressibly, Viktor replied to that, leaning forward and nodding just as though the comment had made sense to him, had fed some nugget of information directly into his learning centers. "Yes. What I want to know is, where does the energy come from? When you create relativistic mass out of rest mass, or the reverse, you must emit energy. And yet, the mass of your ship remains almost constant. That should violate the eighth law of physics. Where does the energy come from?"

"Viktor, stop it!" Malye physically reached for him, thrust him down in his chair. "Do not reveal our knowledge or ignorance, do you hear me? Are you mad? In the years of your Congressional education, did you forget just how we got here?"

"It doesn't matter what they think we know," Viktor said patiently. "It doesn't matter at all. If they wished us harm, you and I would not be speaking."

Curiously, the flatscreen still hadn't beeped. And then, suddenly, it did, after a total delay of something like ten seconds. About twelve hours, in Congress time? She assumed the Congressional simulacra were still involved in the translation process somehow, and if so they had had a tough time with Viktor's question.

The Waister translation that emerged was a continuous stream of clicks and scrapes, with only the occasional fluting sound. Malye and Viktor exchanged looks again, he: bemused, she: still angry. And still the translation went on, and finally it broke with a series of trilling notes, more scraping, more notes, then silence. The total message had taken over a minute to deliver, and the

Waisters themselves appeared dazed by it, as though deafened.

"Ialah's names," Viktor said with a chuckle, "it looks like I asked them something hard."

"This isn't a game, Viktor," Sasha said from the back row. "Stop it, before you cause problems."

"Problems?" Viktor said, turning, a look of mock amazement on his face. "Yes, of course. Ialah forbid that we should have problems."

And with those words, Malye knew they had the old Viktor back, or at least an aged version of him. But what she said was "Be quiet, both of you."

Finally, one of the Workers sat up higher on his couch, and framed a long reply. The translator held onto that one for several seconds, as well, and then said:

> # Artificial instinct, operating by agreement. #
> # Difficulty obtains. Your concepts and logic   #
> #   confuse. Alternate logics are possible.   #
> # Confusion. The compressed summation of   #
> #   universal operatives is understood.   #
> #   Prediction holds value. Conceptual   #
> #   intersection appears empty. Difficulty is   #
> #   therefore created. Temperature? Is   #
> # temperature understood? Attempted pooling   #
> #   yields observations that all temperatures   #
> #   may be reduced, universally.   #

For a moment nobody said anything, too deeply confused by that reply. But then Viktor, his eyes on Malye, apologizing to her for not keeping silent, spoke: "Too abstract. I think I see what's happening."

"Do you?" she said, arching an eyebrow. "Do you really." Already, this exchange had grown tiresome. What did these creatures have, that humans needed? Nonsense? Humanity had always had enough of that.

"The Waisters are animals," Viktor said. "We're fortunate that they communicate verbally, but of course, if you're a terrestrial, air-breathing organism of any size at all, that's really the best way to do it. If they were gas giant dwellers or something, I expect we'd have a much harder time. But really, they're not *so* terribly different; they breathe, they speak. I'm sure they eat and drink and defecate, too, just like any other animal. Well, I'm not *sure* they do, but it seems logical that they would. Even the Gateans have to eat, right? They've made extensive modifications to their metabolism, but that's just not a problem biomechanics can solve."

"What is your point, Viktor?" Konstant asked, his voice impatient and hard, like a gas pistol firing the words one after another. "We're all getting very tired of this obscurity from you."

The words disrupted Viktor's calm, sent quiet ripples through him. "And I grow tired of your impatience, Konstant. Can you sit still for one minute and let me speak? Are you capable of that? My point is that we have commonalities, even with Waisters, but the further we move from these commonalities, the higher the level of abstraction we attempt to communicate, the less likely the concepts are to translate. Really, this is obvious if you think about it."

"So we should ask them about the state of their bowels?" Konstant sneered. "Is that what you're saying?"

"Stop it," Malye said to them again. She'd noticed that the translator was sharing their argument with the Waisters, and she didn't like that at all. No clear reason, she supposed, but it struck her as a very bad idea indeed.

Presently, the Waister Queen spoke:

We defecate. We are capable of defecation.

Behind Malye, several voices broke into laughter. "Look, we've made a breakthrough," Nikolai chuckled. Beside her, Konstant was choking back an embarrassed laugh, and across the room, even Plate looked amused. Malye saw the humor, vaguely, but felt more annoyed than anything else. Now, of all times . . .

"Be quiet, please," she said, but that just made *every-one* start laughing, even Viktor. She was reminded sharply of the old days, of Elye and Kromov joking with her in the Atrium at Tyumen. Then, as now, she'd been powerless against the laughter. It was a weapon she'd never been able to defend against, a weapon Andrei Brakanov had used again and again to disarm her, to allay suspicion, to misdirect. That it had worked so well and for so long was a disgrace with which she had never made peace. She'd been *fifteen* when they finally came for him, and she'd never suspected a thing, not really.

Laughter's legacy, the discomfiture of the monster. Helpless, she simply sat and waited for it to subside, which it soon did.

The Queen spoke:

\#   You are very strange to us. I am confused   \#
\#   by this activity.   \#

You and I both, Malye thought, and for the first time, she looked at the Queen, really *looked,* and saw behind that corpulent, bruise-colored face an actual person, with thoughts and feelings and a desire, however misplaced, to communicate. Impulsively, she leaned forward.

"You are strange to me as well. And they"—she pointed at Plate and Crow and Wende—"are strange. Everything is strange to us here. We're visitors, as much as you."

The Queen shifted posture, her C-shaped body tensing, the dangling arms seeming to draw upward and inward toward her spine. Or back, or front, or whatever. Did Waisters even have spinal columns?

\#   These ones are strange to you? We believed   \#
\#   that they and you had completed. Is there   \#
\#   newness? Are we obligated to destroy?   \#

Indeed? Malye thought. This explained the Gateans' uncharacteristically obsequious behavior of late. And suddenly she had to revise her opinion, that the Waisters had nothing useful to tell her. How to use this knowledge? Not now, that was how. She needed time to think, to put things together. What she said, a little angrily, was, "There is no obligation to destroy anything. We do not approve of all your destruction! This Queen and I have fought, and she has surrendered to me. That does not mean I understand her."

\#   I comprehend.   \#

There was silence for a few moments, but then, without warning, Crow sat bolt upright on his couch, and then

Wende did the same, and the Dog jumped up from the floor and began barking. Malye watched Plate produce a green jewel from somewhere, and press it against his head. He lowered it after a moment, and fixed his anxious eyes on the Waisters behind the glass partition.

By now, Malye was accustomed to this Gatean excitability, but there was something different about it this time, something altered in the focus of it. They were not, she perceived, upset about anything she or the other refugees had done or said. Nor were they upset at the Waisters. No, she had the distinct impression they were receiving news somehow from a remote source, and the news was bad.

As if the mood were infectious, the Waister Queen suddenly stiffened as well, her face pudging inward and outward, expressing nameless emotions. She began to bob up and down, her thick, short legs flexing and straightening, flexing and straightening, much too quickly for the gravity and the bulk they had to support. And then the Workers caught the hysteria and began imitating her actions.

"What is happening?" Malye asked of no one in particular.

Plate looked sharply at her. "Take your people and go," he said quickly. "Return to your quarters and stay there, please! For your safety."

"What's *happening*?"

He fixed her with a blank copper stare that nonetheless conveyed a sense of urgency and fear, white as static in Malye's synesthetic brain. "It's the Waister fleet," he said. "I do not believe this. I do *not* believe this. Somebody is attacking the Waister fleet!"

Chapter 19

"Show me," Malye said without hesitation. "Put it on this flatscreen of yours."

Wende had gone glassy-eyed, her face limp as a mask, a red jewel clenched in her huge, meaty fist.

Plate was shaking his head. "No, no, you've got to get out of here. We're too close to the surface. Go!"

"Show me! Do not give us orders, Plate. Show us what's happening."

Anxiously, casting glances over his shoulder at the still-entranced Wende, Plate hurried to the flatscreen, put his hands on the back of it. He, too, went blank and distant for a moment.

"Who would attack the Waisters? *Why* would they?" Konstant asked the empty air. On his face was a look of horror, a reflection of all he'd been told about the fall of Sirius, through which he'd been fortunate enough to have slept.

But it was Viktor who answered: "I suppose it makes sense, in a way. Stand up and be recognized, force the Waisters to deal with *you* rather than Finders ring and a bunch of human refugees . . . Assuming you survive the encounter, I suppose, and that's a big assumption."

The flatscreen came to life, opening out like a window on the depthless void of space. Against a backdrop of stars hung a long, irregular world, its shadow side gridded with lights, the Beeward and Ayeward faces reflecting harsh, blue-white sunlight. Artya. Holders Fastness. Around and in front of it hung the smaller forms of the Waister ships, oxide-red and phallic in design, like the Gatean ferry but clearly much, much larger. Seven

kilometers? It was hard to say for sure, but the shadow of
one was clearly visible on Artya's surface, giving a feel
for the range and relative size, and certainly it was no
small thing against this Lesser World.

Malye wondered where the rest of the fleet was; she'd
had the impression there were once again hundreds of
ships swarming into Sirius system, but here only five of
them were visible. The space around them flashed and
flickered. Malye thought of the passenger ferries, dying
one by one as they fled a shattered Tyumen. But these
things, these dying things too small for her to see on the
screen, were not fleeing but attacking. Did it matter?
Could they have any effect at all?

Apparently so; the surface of one Waister ship flared
brightly, a searing pinpoint near its stern that faded
slowly, leaving behind a red-hot smear down the side of
the hull, fully as large as the Atrium of Tyumen.

"What are we seeing?" Malye demanded of Plate, who
had taken his hands off the flatscreen's back but who still
looked vague, as if he were listening to something she
herself couldn't hear.

Behind the glass partition, the Waisters, too, had gone
limp and unresponsive, something turned inward in their
attention.

"At least eight rings are involved," Plate replied distantly, without looking at Malye. His troubled eyes had
wandered back toward Wende, whom Crow was now ca-
ressing briskly, as if he meant to clean her shiny-smooth
skin with his hands. "Warders, Watchers, Testers . . . I
don't know who else. Activity is scattered throughout the
system, and only some of the information is coming to us
FTL. Slowlight images are trickling in out of sequence,
which has caused confusion. This view you see is from an
ansible repeater station in trailing libration behind the
Fastness."

"What are they doing, these eight rings?"

"They've commandeered all the weapons of Gate system. All of them, the product of fifty Earth-standard
years' labor. The waste is unimaginable."

"Are they winning?"

"No. They have destroyed one ship, and they are demanding the Waisters' surrender, but the clear advantage
is against themselves. Every minute a year's production is

destroyed, and sixes of lives along with it. Oh, the resources they are squandering! This conflict will resolve within the hour."

At least the battle seemed more equal this time, Malye thought. A handful of individuals, probably no more than ten thousand, and they were managing to punish the Waisters as all the hapless billions of Sirius had not. A military debacle, no doubt, but as an act of defiance she had to admire it, and the waste be damned.

But behind the glass, the Waister Queen appeared more puzzled than frightened or upset. Her movements were slight, tentative.

"They have destroyed another ship," Plate reported. "Their last, I think; the greater part of their weaponry has been incapacitated."

The image on the flatscreen told a different story, though; the damaged Waister ship had been struck twice more by whatever weapon had burned its hull initially, and now its drive motors, clearly identifiable, had begun to flow and melt like ice sculptures left beside a heating vent. And the flashing around the other ships had intensified, as if the Gateans had called in a wave of reinforcements, a wave of new ships lurking silently in the space around Holders Fastness.

How would they look, like ferries, like miniature Waister ships? Like small, stealthy rescue pods with escorting swarms of automated weaponry? Or perhaps they were simply fogs and jewels. Perhaps a fog of tiny surgical machines was *disassembling* those drive motors—that certainly seemed a more Gatean way of handling the problem.

But presently, the character of the battle shifted in some subtle way. The flashes went on as before, but the pattern of them had altered, so that Malye was certain something important had changed, some turning point had come, but just what it might be she could not discern.

"The rings are surrendering," Plate said. "Finally. What is wrong with them?"

The Waister Queen seemed to come to life. Her little brown eyes swiveled and focused on Plate, and she spoke to him. The flatscreen blanked for a moment, and then said:

Your rings do not stack? There are as many
of you as there are rings? Comprehension #
begins. A surrender occurs, despite
completion, because completion does not
apply universally.

Plate said something back to her in Waister, but the translator had not been equipped to respond to his voice, so the next thing it relayed was the Queen's reply:

You are not this group. Neither newness nor
completion applies. We are the superior
force, and yet this occurrence is of no
consequence to us. Response appears
limited.

And Plate spoke again, and the Queen said to him,

This strangeness shall be resolved through
its removal. Piling of stones beside the
water, the first steps in spatial and
material manipulation. You and we are
complete, and practicing the *#Hua#* instinct
of *#Pfeesh#* between us. These others have #
removed from that process. Instinct does not
obtain, but variegated logics indicate that
we will remove them from processes
universally, for convenience. This
capitulation completes nothing.

"If they want a fight," Viktor said, translating the translator's message, "they can have one to the death. Serves them right for mucking up the peace process, I suppose. Not that my opinion matters, but I agree with you, *Hthw*: sometimes aberrant behavior calls for more than censure or punishment."

With those words, he glanced very deliberately at Malye, forcing her to recognize his point. What to do with dangerous criminals? See, how the Waisters accommodate us? Malye looked away.

Plate appeared neither happy nor unhappy at the Queen's words, but simply calculating. How would this affect his plans, he seemed to be thinking. How would it

affect Wende's, and those of Finders ring as a whole?
Thoughtfully, he pressed the green jewel to his forehead.

On the screen, the flickers and flashes had taken on a
distinctly different look, for now the Gatean forces were
fleeing, and the Waister ships had begun to pursue them
in a lackadaisical manner, turning and accelerating and
turning again, as though it were the easiest thing in the
worlds, as though hunting down every last Gatean
weapon were a necessary chore, but one that required no
great attention from them.

The Waister Queen turned her eyes on Malye.

#	These ones listen too much to the counsel of	#
#	their Drones. They are operating always	#
#	within the anxiety of newness. They relate	#
#	that they have copied our minds, but they	#
#	have copied our minds of war, our minds of	#
#	newness. Did they think us capable of no	#
#	other emotion? You small ones are superior.	#
#	#Hua# contain much that interests. Do they	#
#	obey you? Can this be arranged?	#

"Cease a moment," Plate protested, his attention drawn
back, albeit reluctantly, to the Interface Station around
him. He shot Malye an angry look, then fluted something
long and complex at the Waister Queen.

"What are you saying to her?" Malye asked.

"Nothing of your concern," he snapped back.

"What did you say to her? I can ask *her*, if you like,
but I'd rather hear it from you."

He sighed in a very un-Gatean way, and looked at her
as though avoiding offense had been a great strain for
him, which he would now put aside in favor of untem-
pered honesty. "I told her to stop upsetting our balance of
influence," he said. "Her presence in this world, and
yours, have already disrupted our society intolerably. The
idea that humans should *command* Gate system is absurd.
No one commands here, least of all a small, ignorant
group like yourselves.

"And she insults us, additionally, by refusing to acknowledge the extremes to which we have gone to
accommodate Waister goals and ideals within our society.
If she finds us so irrelevant, I told her, then she is free to

speak to you without our assistance. As far as I'm concerned, she is free to take you back to the Waist of Orion with her."

Malye allowed herself a slight smile. "You're so much more human than the rest of your kind, Plate. I've always liked that about you. If it makes you feel any better, I wouldn't dream of doing this without your help. Peace? I'd rather they simply leave us alone, but if they insist on talking, better that you are here. I mean you, specifically, as an individual. That's one thing you people don't do well: recognize the individual. You've made all this possible, haven't you? Without you, we'd all still be frozen, probably forever."

"Do you have a point to make?" he snapped, his tiny mouth frowning, copper eyes narrowed, smooth gray brows furrowed beneath sprouts of blue-green hair. His frustration sang through her, almost refreshing.

"Not at all," she said. She glanced at the screen, on which only one Waister ship was now visible, the space around it silent and still. "But Gate is presently being stripped of its weapons, it seems, and this *small, ignorant* group of humans is on better terms with the enemy than you are yourself. If word of this gets out, it could be very upsetting to your poor, unstable society. You should remember this while you see to our comfort."

"Word has already gotten out," Plate said darkly. "Finders ring remains a contributive force for Gate's betterment. We do not operate in secret."

So much for leverage, she thought. Her smile fell away. "That's unfortunate."

"Yes," he agreed. And then he crossed his arms as any human being would, and simply scowled at her. *What are we to do?* he seemed to be asking.

But Malye was far from home, operating with little guidance and no clear goals, and Ialah damn her if she knew what to do now.

Plate found some other images of the battle for them to watch, but by now it had wound down considerably, and there was not much to see, except when the Waisters tracked a group of their attackers back to a tiny world that none of the refugees recognized. #Hthw#, apparently in contact with the Waister forces, asked Plate whether any noncombatants lived there. He denied it, and soon the Waister ships were carving the world to pieces with the beams of their drive motors.

"Gamma ray lasers," Viktor explained. "Very powerful. Most of the worst destruction at Sirius was accomplished with those."

"Thank you for letting us know," Malye growled at him. Who was interfering with the peace process now?

But the little world was all rubble and molten fragments in a very short time, and once again the fight against the renegade Gateans was too slow and subtle to be observed well on a holie screen. Conversation with the Waister Queen started up again, in a grudging and desultory manner. Probably, it was too soon for any of them to be doing this, to be attempting any sort of negotiation at all, but really, what else did they have to do? She wasn't about to sit around Holders Fastness, begging the Gateans for food and other necessities. No, it was better to have a job, even an awful one.

Dispirited, she even let Viktor try his physics questions again, but the results this time were not appreciably better. The Waisters seemed sometimes like insane or fevered children, unable to focus, prattling and raving about imaginary worlds that worked by strange imaginary rules. At other times they were more like withered geriatrics, wise but slow and sullen with years.

Eventually, Malye called Viktor off, and asked Sasha if he'd like to try some questions about biology. This worked a little better, eventually bringing forth an intelligible comment about food: theirs was wholly synthetic, but reminiscent of "dead things beside the water." The Waisters also explained, with painful indirectness, the vast number of "life places" they had encountered in the galaxy, all wildly different and yet somehow all the same.

The exchange was slow and difficult, but at least it proved that meaningful dialogue was possible, with these creatures who had destroyed so much without any communication at all. Old Nikolai, thus encouraged, voiced the opinion that religion should be the next topic of conversation. What did the Waisters know of Ialah? Of origins and creation in general? But Konstant insisted that

political and social organization should take a much
higher priority.

"Obviously, they don't really organize the way the
Gateans do. There must be important differences, and
understanding these may prove crucial to our survival."

Malye had opened her mouth to retort, just on general
principle, but at that moment she noticed movement out
of the corner of her eye, and turned to see a small, irregular hole closing up in the doorway behind them, as if an
invisible hand had passed through the membrane. No, not
invisible! She could see a kind of smear moving along the
floor, like an irregular lens, or a blob of extremely transparent gel. Or a fog. Yes, it looked very much like the security fog that surrounded Wende, that was so nearly
invisible that Malye barely noticed it anymore.

"Hey," she warned, standing and pointing. She had a
bad feeling about this. "What is that thing? What is that?"

Plate, who in his foul mood had gone back to stand by
the silent Wende and Crow again, now peered and
squinted, stepping forward to inspect the intruding sub-
stance.

"That's . . ." he said, squinting. "It's a low-grade surgical fog, but the model has been—"

Suddenly, Plate was falling, his legs collapsing under
him, his arms flying up in the air, and for a moment it
seemed a hole had opened up in the floor and he was disappearing through it. But there was no hole, and he was
spreading as he fell, as if his flesh were melting on a hot
surface. The blood was bright red, like any blood, anywhere, and a wide, irregular pool of it splashed out
around him as his body dissolved. His mouth opened to
scream, his copper eyes wide with alarm, but the head
had fallen nearly to the floor already, the last bit of him,
and in a fraction of a moment that was gone as well, dis-
mantled, dissolved, and there was nothing left of Plate
except the splattered crimson pool. And a barely visible
mound of fog at its center.

Malye had seen several deaths in her life, even before
the Waisters, and she thought herself a hard woman because of it. But she'd neither seen nor imagined anything
like this before. There was *no question* of her enjoying it.
She found she could not suppress a shriek of horror.

Nor could the others, it seemed. The room erupted with

screams, and rising high above them was a sharp, shrill, impossibly loud wail from Wende, whose voice then exploded into a torrent of Waister sounds.

The fog, moving like a self-aware but slightly stupid animal, scooted along the floor toward one of the walls, leaving no blood trail behind it, and then changed direction sharply, heading for the refugees' chairs. Heading, specifically, for Elle. Malye's scream cut off abruptly, and without any conscious thought at all, she was in motion, leaping over the back of her own seat, climbing straight over Sasha and Nikolai as though they were stairs or ladder rungs. She leaped across the gap to where Elle sat, dazed, apparently unaware of her peril.

Just as the fog made contact, Malye grabbed her daughter's arm and hurled her forward out of the seat. Elle's face lit up with shock, and then with pain, and as she landed in a heap she squawked, and then suddenly there was blood flowing again, and Malye saw with vivid, surreal, synesthetic clarity that a major piece of her little girl's foot was missing, the sandal sliced in half right along with it, and blood had begun to fountain from the stub.

Hurriedly, she leaped after her daughter, throwing herself on top, careful not to crush her in the heavy gee but grabbing the injured foot with both hands and squeezing tightly, to slow the hemorrhage.

What happened next was all a blur of half-seen, half-understood images. Everyone was running, tumbling, escaping. Through the corner of her eye she saw Viktor go down, and Ludmile, saw their blood defy the heavy gravity to splash high across the walls and ceiling. The screaming never stopped, not for a moment, and then something was happening to the partition that separated the Waisters from the rest of the chamber. The glass groaned and cracked, and the air began to sting Malye's eyes and nose and throat and lungs.

"It's dead," someone called out to her. "Malye, it's dead. Come on!"

Strong hands were helping her up, and she let them, though she kept a tight grip on Elle's foot, and on the rest of her as well, to keep her from struggling. Her scream was a low, animal keening unlike any noise Malye had ever heard her make before, heard any human make.

Coughing now, she caught a glimpse of the Waister Queen and her two Workers, fleeing in obvious fear through their membrane-door behind the partition, but she was not really permitted to see. It was Konstant who had helped her up, and now he was behind her, urging her forward, toward the doorway that led outside. Everyone else had gone already, even the Gateans, leaving the room empty and bloody and foul with strange gases.

"Come on, the air is bad," Konstant rasped. "The Waister air is leaking. Ialah, what *is* this crap?"

He pushed her through the membrane. Outside was turmoil, and a lot more blood. Vadim, she saw with relief, was safe and whole, as were all the other refugees save Ludmile and Viktor, and without even asking Malye knew those two would not be turning up anywhere. The Gateans were out here as well, Crow and Wende and the Dog. Plate, of course, was absent, and the places where the two Drones had stood guard were now great ponds of red fluid, deep on the floor, oozing up over everyone's sandals to color their toes, to stain the hems of their robes. It was as if a huge drum of paint had been spilled and splattered. There were no other traces.

Crow appeared dazed, but Wende was simply hysterical, whining and howling with each fast, shallow breath she drew. She appeared unnaturally sharp to the eye, and Malye realized with surprise that the security fog normally surrounding that flabby body was now absent.

"What happened?" she asked, turning to Konstant. "Where did the fog thing go?"

"It's killed," he said. "Wende killed it. Malye, two of our people are dead."

An eerie calm had settled over her. Now she knew: the Waisters were capable of fear, and the Gateans, of grief. And Viktor Slavanovot Bratsev was capable of dying, and the people of this future time were as capable of murder as any people anywhere.

She made a futile attempt to shush Elle, brushed damp hair from her little forehead, and over the screams she said to Konstant and Wende and Crow, "My daughter is injured. Medical arrangements must be made right away."

Wende continued to pant and grunt. Crow continued to look blank, and Konstant said, "Did you hear me? Two of us have been killed!"

"Yes, I heard you," Malye said impatiently, "and I will see that the persons responsible are brought swiftly to justice."

And suddenly the thought was there in her mind, fully formed and bright with sharp edges: she would take advantage of Wende's distress to do some bullying, demanding an armed escort and the full cooperation of Gatean society. Demanding even a black and burgundy uniform to replace the one she'd lost, for even here, even now, with all that had happened and all that no doubt soon would, there was still monster's work to be done. Perhaps the future was not so strange after all.

Chapter 20

218::10
HOLDERS FASTNESS, GATE SYSTEM:
CONTINUITY 5218, YEAR OF THE DRAGON

Malye's body was one giant ache as the Gateans first arrested Elle's bleeding, and then brought in a surgical fog to begin reconstruction of the flesh. There was some protest at this, from humans, from Gateans, from Malye herself, but assurances were made that the fog would be carefully monitored and supervised, protected from misuse. Since the alternative was to leave Elle crippled, Malye finally relented.

It took effort to keep her mind focused. Without constant attention, it would wander off into grief and rage and worst of all a kind of blank confusion. Fugue state.

Wende's own grief was astonishing; she seemed ready to tear Holders Fastness apart, physically, with her bare hands. Only with great risk and difficulty was Malye able to urge her toward a more sophisticated response, but as with the fog, there was really only one correct answer, and eventually Wende adopted it as her own. The investigation began only a few hours later.

Alas, it quickly became mired in the complex twists and confusions of reality. Malye's first thought had naturally been that the attack was politically motivated, simply a part of the battle that still raged here and there in Gate system, that one of the eight insurgent rings had directed weapons inside Holders Fastness as well as outside of it.

She was soon disabused of this notion: there was strong sentiment in favor of punishing the rebels in any case, but for reasons whose explanations Malye never quite caught, an attack of this sort could only be arranged and executed from within certain regions of Holders Fastness, and none of the eight rings had representatives in the proper places at the proper times. Of this, at least, they were innocent. However, the attack was considered extremely devious and clever, requiring the perversion of numerous housekeeping systems away from their normal functions, and it was agreed by all and sundry that only Workers could have accomplished it, and that probably at least two would be required for the task. Which still left fully a third of this Lesser World's population on her suspect list, almost two thousand individuals representing several hundred separate rings. The investigation did not promise to be an easy one.

Who and why? Who and why? She ached with the need to know. If only her C.I. staff could be here with her! Even in worlds far more familiar than this one, the legwork of detection had never suited her as well as the interrogation phase. Typically, by the time she became deeply involved in a case, a suspect had already been identified, and must simply be caught and made to confess. Less frequently, the truth must be sifted from a larger handful of suspects, to determine which of them had played a part in the crime. But the principle remained the same, regardless of the number of suspects; sooner or later, she would discover the truth.

Right now, she was starting in the most obvious place, interviewing the more influential Workers of Holders ring, who after all had lost the most when Wende and her people seized power. Or influence, or prestige, or whatever they chose to call it. And the Holders had apparently suffered a humiliation at Malye's own hands as well, her surrender to Tempe having been followed so closely by the Waisters' request or demand to speak with actual humans in preference to candidates the Gatcans might pick from their own ranks. It was not known whether the attack had been directed at the Sirian refugees or at Wende's six or at the Waisters themselves, or perhaps at some combination of these, but in any case Holders seemed to have the strongest, clearest motive.

Monstering her way through the Gatean equivalent of a bureaucracy, Malye had caused certain preparations to be made. The Gateans were not happy about it, but with Wende's full weight and fury behind her, she was a force indeed. An office and interrogation room had been set up, and to her great satisfaction they had appeared almost immediately, and were neither white nor octohedral, but rectangular and gray, with floors of bare metal and blue-white lighting stripes crisscrossing the ceiling, in lieu of the hazy, immovable, intangible lighting globes the Gateans so favored.

The Worker across the table from her now was named "Chip," which she found vaguely amusing because there had been a cartoon character by that name in one of the holie comedies of her time. But they didn't look the same, and Malye wasn't in a laughing mood, and so they began.

"I trust you're comfortable?" she asked indifferently. In fact, Chip looked distinctly unsettled by these environs, which was of course her intention. Even the chair on which he sat was of Sirian design, and probably none too comfortable for him. And so he eyed her with no small measure of resentment, this talking animal who had somehow gained power over him. But in deed if not in thought, he was kept meek by the two Finders Drones hulking behind her, culled from two different sixes and instructed by their Queens to protect Malye and to obey her in all things.

"What is it you want me to tell you?" the Worker asked sullenly. "I have nothing to tell you about these deaths."

"That may be," Malye replied. "I'm just asking around, building the framework for a proper investigation, and I thought perhaps you could help. I'm told your ring is knowledgeable and clever."

Chip looked puzzled and put off by that remark, not the approach he'd been expecting, and Malye pressed the advantage, seeking to cow him as quickly and completely as possible.

"Listen, you don't like my being in charge of this investigation. That's fine, but recognize that recent events have strengthened Finders ring. My activities are backed by their orders, and by over twenty years' experience in exactly this sort of work, as a member of what you might call an Enforcers ring."

"What is it you want me to tell you?" he repeated.

She spread her hands. "I don't know. What is it you're able to contribute?"

Through her weariness and grief and Investigator's curiosity, she felt a low anger burning, threatening to flare up at any moment, and she could let that show through, so long as she tempered it with calm and fairness. The combination was effective: C.I. uniforms for herself and the Drones, but otherwise a soft touch. Intimidation and invitation all at once; it is easier if you cooperate, my friend.

"Well," he said, looking uncomfortable, and began the slow process of spilling his guts.

Malye had him for a little over an hour, and while she was quickly satisfied that he knew nothing about the murders, she took the time and trouble to empty him out just the same. He was, after all, the first suspect she'd interviewed in over two millennia, and the right questions here and now could provide the context needed to narrow her investigation. Who wants what, and why can't they have it? And yes, this Worker reminded her much more of Crow than of Plate, and she took a vague pleasure in punishing him for it, in making him feel small and stupid and inadequate while seeming to have quite the opposite intention.

He left even less happy than he'd entered, and Malye, with grim pride, complimented herself that his view of humans would never be the same.

The next few suspects were less interesting, and she let them go quickly. As the evening wore on and her established bedtime came and went, she'd made up her mind that Holders ring was not involved even peripherally in the murders. It seemed routine enough to keep secrets from other rings, and certainly from humans, but *within* a ring there seemed to be a strong tendency toward consensus and resource sharing, and with the pseudo-telepathic communications they seemed to employ, secrets were unlikely to remain that way for long. So a one-percent sample, a mere dozen Workers, was in all likelihood sufficient to clear the whole ring, and in a way Malye was glad, because this probably meant their status would plummet still further when the finding became known. How could they let such a thing occur in their own stronghold? How could they fail to know anything about it? And yet, that seemed to be precisely what had occurred.

They did have their secrets, of course, things they refused to discuss with Malye, things they refused to be questioned about. The keeping of secrets was an almost pathological condition among Gateans. But they were clearly not the secrets she sought, and so she let them be. This job would be difficult enough without her stirring up random resentment, without her poking into every corner and crevice to see what lurked there. Most of it would be meaningless or irrelevant to her, anyway.

When the interviews were finished, she let the Drones escort her back to the refugees' chambers, and was grateful for the security fogs that surrounded them, and for their angry alertness. They were not her friends, not even to the extent that Plate had been, but they didn't want another incident any more than she did, and if anything happened to her it would go badly for them indeed. Assuming they survived, of course, as Wende's own Drones had not.

Once back "home," however, finding that everyone had waited up for her, waited up to share their grief, she found her mood crashing down in pieces around her.

Ludmile had been nothing to her; they had exchanged at most a hundred words between them, and those mostly in the first few days. But even so, the loss of her made a visible hole in the group, an absence in what was already too small a community. And Plate, too, had been at least an honorary Sirian, appreciated for his efforts if not always his deeds. How empty the future seemed without him! His loss was perhaps the very worst thing that could have happened, for without him they were left with no genuine allies at all, left among strangers and enemies, forced to lever and coerce rather than simply asking for the things they needed.

Of course, it was Viktor she would really miss. Her eyes misted at the mere thought of him, and that was strange, because she'd really only known him for five days, barely long enough to understand anything about him at all. But he'd loved her, or said he had, and as with Grigory, she'd given him little warmth in return. *How we repeat the same mistakes,* she thought, *how incapable we are of learning anything at all from our lives.* Was it that way for Gateans and Waisters, too? Was life a great cosmic joke, Ialah's continuum nothing more than a loop that curled forever back on itself?

"Why are you crying, Mother?" Vadim asked her as she leaned back on one of the couches, drinking water from a cup, wishing it were vodka or beer or even milk. Could the Gateans manufacture something that would resemble milk?

"I'm very sad," she told her son, "about the death of Viktor Slavanovot."

"I'll miss him, too," he said. And then more pointedly: "I'll miss a lot of people."

And at that, she *really* broke down, sobbing uncontrollably, the tears streaming down her cheeks, staining the edges of her hair, wetting the front of her robe as they fell. Vadim hugged her, and had Elle hug her as well, and then in a rare moment of thoughtfulness, Sasha came over and sent the children to bed.

"Your mother is very tired," he told them. "You can speak with her in the morning. All right?"

The other adults seemed to regard Malye with an infuriating pity, as if she had lost much more than a casual friend. As if she had lost a lover, which Viktor certainly had not been. And that thought simply made her cry all the harder. Still, there were only so many tears inside her, and eventually they trailed off. As did the adults, who found they would also benefit from a little sleep. Soon, Malye and Sasha were alone in the dayroom, and the lights were down low, on their night-shift setting.

"He was a good man, wasn't he?" Malye asked. Oddly, she found Sasha had become an old friend. The first human she'd seen and talked to in this place, and present for so many of the early developments that he surely possessed an insider feeling the others did not. It had been herself and Sasha who, along with Viktor, first faced the Gateans, first stood up to them, first took a place, however tenuous, among them.

"Yes he was," Sasha agreed, sitting down beside her, and in his tone she heard the confirmation she'd been seeking. Yes, he and she were the only early ones left, the only ones who really knew what was going on, knew how all this had started.

"I hope he likes it in Paradise," she said. "I'm sure he has a lot of friends there."

Sasha chuckled a little, not politely but with genuine amusement. The emotion was so fresh and so welcome, it swept through Malye like a shower of mist, cooling, soothing. All at once, the tensions of the day fell away, the tensions of the week and the month and the millennium, and she was chuckling a little, too.

Sasha was right next to her, his leg almost touching hers, and impulsively she put her arm around him and kissed him. He reacted with surprise, but did not pull away. After that it was easy; they fell together on the couch and did what humans had always done to comfort one another. He proved a gentle and considerate lover.

She wished the same were true of her, but in fact she was rough, hurried, impersonal, taking what she needed from him and providing little in return. And the whole experience tasted of ashes anyway, because whoever she was really with, in her heart and mind, neither of them had any illusions that it was Sasha himself.

But she had stopped herself, at least, from crying out the wrong name, and she supposed that was a victory of sorts.

Impulse control, Malye thought. Oh, how she needed it today! Someone had found an ink stick somewhere and decorated the dayroom wall with an image of Skato, the shitting boy, and her reaction had been spectacular and entirely uncalled for, frightening everyone into silence. No one would admit to the deed, and small wonder, for even Malye herself didn't know what she'd have done to the perpetrator. Something rash, certainly.

And when Konstant had asked her whether the talks with #*Hthw*# would resume today, whether Malye would press the issue one way or the other, she had erupted again, coming within a hairbreadth of striking him. "Handle it yourself," she'd told him. "You're in charge." But it had been more an exile than a delegation: get thee from my sight, smartass, and busy yourself however you please.

The refugees, even Sasha, even her own children, had rolled their eyes with unmistakable relief when she'd donned the burgundy uniform and left them to pursue her old job once more. Waves of yellow-white anxiety chasing after her down the hallway, echoing from the walls

and the bodies of passing Gateans. Hands clenched into
fists—she badly wanted to smash something, anything,
but the only things here that might be fragile enough were
the Gateans themselves. The Workers, of course, not her
own hulking guards.

In her new office, halfway between the refugees' quarters and the Interface Station, she settled in and ordered
the flow of interviewees to resume once more. Talkers
ring, today, and Shapers, and a couple of others whose
names refused to stick in her mind. No matter.

The first victim was named Chain, and when the
Sirian-style door slid closed behind him and he sat down
across from her, a palpable wave of hostility passed between them, his disdain and dislike and displeasure written clearly in his features, and evident in every little
gesture. She wasn't the only one having a bad morning,
all right, but she sincerely hoped he would cooperate
nonetheless, because there was a serious danger she'd kill
him if he didn't. At least he had the sense to be afraid.

"Do you know why you're here?" she asked as calmly
and evenly as she could, her voice sliding out as if the
words had been oiled. It cost nothing to be polite.

"Nominally, to answer questions," Chain replied.

She cocked her head, stifled a growl. "Nominally? Is
there another purpose?"

"Yes."

"Would you share it with me?"

"Yes." He looked behind her at the Drones. "But in
confidence only. Not in the presence of these two, whose
interests cross sharply with those of my ring."

Malye thought for a moment, and then nodded. She
sensed no immediate harm from this Worker, and anyway
it would hardly be her first time alone with a suspect. She
turned to the Drones, huge Olympian figures swathed in
black and burgundy, imposing as the minions of Saitan.

"Wait outside for a few minutes, please. I'll come get
you when we're finished."

"We are to protect you," one of them said in a low,
thundering voice.

"And to obey," Malye said, and turned her back. After
a moment's pause, she heard their heavy footfalls, heard
the door open and close.

"Will you speak with me now?" she asked Chain.

He looked at her for a moment. "Perhaps. Perhaps I will."

All at once, Malye was poised on the knife edge of fury, barely able to contain herself. Breathing deeply, she counted to five, and then said in a warning voice, "Please don't waste my time like this, citizen. I'm sure you understand that time is of the essence in investigations of this sort, and"—she leaned forward, standing, hands on the table, hoping to violate some near-human concept of personal space—"I have more efficient methods than this at my disposal."

She couldn't read the expression on the Worker's face after that, but she knew it wasn't a happy one. She sat, crossed her hands.

"Talkers ring has suffered tremendous reversals," he said to her in a tight voice. "We are charged with the care and operation of Gate's exocommunication devices. Our job has been to transmit slowlight signals to the Waister civilization, and to hunt for any accidental emissions from that region, and to hope one day for deliberate replies. When the approaching fleet was first detected, it was we who hailed them, we who mediated all communications with them. Until four days ago, when this function was subsumed by the trash gatherers of Finders ring, and two days ago, when your own people took up a role."

"I'm aware of this," Malye said, watching him closely, picking her careful way through his emotional structures. He knew something, his body language *screamed* that he knew something she wanted to hear, but he had not yet decided what to share of it, what to withhold, what to distort. He was reading her, they were reading each other. "I'm aware of a great deal. All our functions are changing, and the adjustment has been difficult, not only for you. Why do you mention it?"

"For purposes of clarification. I will assist you not in munificence, but only because our two interests align." His copper eyes narrowed. "Are you wholly the tool of Finders ring?"

"I am the tool of justice," she answered without rancor, without pride or artifice. "If Finders ring opposed that imperative in any way, then no, we would not remain allied."

"In that case," Chain said gravely, "we possess information which you desire."

"Really," she said, letting no hint of eagerness show. *This is all routine, boring, passé*, her posture informed him. "And how do you know it will interest me? I hear a great deal."

"You must comprehend that Talkers ring also controls the ansible array, which enables communication with the Suzerainty."

Malye nodded. She hadn't known that, but certainly it made sense.

He went on: "Gate system has been in unceasing contact with the Suzerainty since the array first became operational, over five decades ago. Outgoing content has been trivial, and in many cases, false. Does this surprise you?"

"No, not really." *Get on with it or go away.*

"You should comprehend that the Suzerainty has not been informed of the Waister presence here. Only Talkers ring has spoken in favor of their enlightenment, and in return we have received anonymous warnings in great number. Plans are deploying all around us, and none in Gate system wish humankind's ignorance to be lifted."

Now Malye was surprised and let it show, let it leak from her like breathing air from a sundered hull. "Why?" she demanded. "Why don't they want that? The Suzerainty is so far away, I can't—"

And then suddenly she knew.

"To the Waisters it is not far," Chain said, confirming her blackest fears. Local gravity seemed to increase as his words settled into her. "If they can be tricked, or coerced, or subjugated, or befriended, if they can somehow be convinced to help us, Sol could be in Gatean hands within a decade, and the rest of the Suzerainty by a decade after that. Hasha would be the last to fall, would have many years of warning before we came, but they are the youngest colony, barely older than we, and they would be powerless before us."

"Why?" Malye asked, standing again, placing her palms flat against the tabletop. "Why would you do that, attack the Suzerainty? Because it's different? Without humankind, you have no purpose, no one for whom to serve as intermediaries."

"Talkers ring does not desire this thing," Chain assured her.

"But the plan exists, yes?"

He spread his arms wide. "A thousand plans exist, madam, at least as many plans as rings. Do you know so little of us? Always jostling for influence, for attention, always working at cross-purposes. Holders ring was a catalyst for alignment, a remover of barriers to cooperation and consensus, but they have lost stature, and Finders ring lacks experience with these matters. I can tell you that at least seven promises have been made, to destroy the ansible array if we use it to warn the Suzerainty. Truthfully, I expect someone will destroy it anyway—few will gain advantage by its existence—and while most of the strategic weaponry has been nullified, many rings possess the tactical and personal resources to overcome any defense Talkers ring is capable of erecting."

Malye was shaking her head. "What is to be gained by attacking the Suzerainty? What threat is it to Gate?"

"Not a threat," Chain said, "but an irritant. We Aggressors have never been welcome among humans. Lacking influence, lacking even respect, we've skulked always at the edges of their society, unable to penetrate, unable to flee. As you say, the Human Spaces are where we belong, for we bridge the gap between human and Waister minds. It is our only function, and we will not see it disregarded."

"You will have respect from the Suzerainty, even if you must conquer it," Malye said wonderingly.

"Talkers ring does not agree with this outlook," he reminded her. "We are not soldiers, but facilitators of communication, and as such we occasionally overhear what we are not intended to. I warn you that the deaths you seek to avenge were engendered by these plans of conquest, though there are others who wish you to live. Some would see *you* as intermediaries, between Gate and the Suzerainty. Or as hostages, or puppets, or icons. It was felt that you should be warned. Though you have aggrieved us, the interests of Talkers ring are not furthered by your elimination."

Concepts were falling together like polybricks, interlocking to form tough, durable structures. Chain believed almost everything he was telling her, which was a goodly chunk of everything he believed he knew, and suddenly a great many things flashed clear in Malye's mind. Her mood opened out, her bitterness expanding to encompass this new view of the worlds.

"Damn," she said. "Damn me for ever waking up in this hell. Can you get a message to the Waisters? In secret, I mean? I can't believe I'm asking this, but can you send a courier, or stuff a note in a bottle and throw it at one of their ships? It's very important."

Now it was Chain's turn to look puzzled. "In concealment? I believe that would be possible, yes, but why do you query? Would you trust us with such a task, after all that I have told you?"

"Citizen, we have no need for trust between us. Your manipulations are not so deft that I cannot see them, and I rather suspect your own information sources are tainted. Whose tool are you? But we are not so powerless, you and I. We can constrain one another, so that I further your interests even as you are furthering mine, and betrayal can only doom us both. And if some third party has been shifting us toward this, well, that doesn't mean we cannot surprise them."

Chain looked completely aghast. "Madam, Talkers ring is not a human tool, is not anyone's tool. We felt it would go better for us if you had been warned, and this has been accomplished. Beyond that, what can you expect of us? We cannot defend you; we dare not even try. What is it you conceive?"

She stretched her back, putting her hands on it, massaging where it hurt. Four days of high gravity, with no relief. Her back got so sore just walking around, and sleeping on it only made things worse.

"There are times when an enemy's strength becomes your own," she said quietly. "You exploit it, without interfering directly and without attracting notice. In a training exercise once, a surface navigation and survival course, I grabbed an officer's air tank and simply rode him back to the rendezvous point. In the low-gee, he never even guessed I was there, though I could have opened him up to the vacuum at any time. What we must accomplish is something very much like that."

"What message would you wish conveyed?"

"I don't know all of it yet. I'll need some time to think it through."

"Time," Chain warned, "is not a thing I can guarantee."

Chapter 21

"There's going to be trouble," Malye said to the ghost of Ken Jonson. "I can smell it, I can see it coming, like a riot about to break."

"What kind of riot?" Jonson asked her.

They were in their little conference room again inside the Congress, just the two of them. And Mediator, of course, but she'd learned how to keep him in the background, watching without jabbering and interfering every minute or two. Everything was flat and sterile around them, a world of dim colors and muted senses, a mere approximation of a world. *Ialah save me*, she thought suddenly, *from ever becoming one of these Congressional simulacra*. Soulless and yet almost alive, enslaved in this shadowy purgatory, answering questions over and over and over again like suspects whose interrogation would never end. Viktor, at least, had dwelt here willingly, and tasted reality again before he died. No such opportunity would befall Ken Jonson, who would remain here forever, with no hope of reprieve.

"Ialah," she wanted to say to him, "what a tortured existence you lead! Would you rather I destroyed this unit, and sent you to oblivion?" But she needed him too much. Slave he might be, yes, but *her* slave, whose advice might save countless lives, might save all of humanity from sharing his own fate.

What she said was this: "Gate has flown to pieces, with rebellion and murder and everyone working their plans in secret. I trust none of them, and even if I did, they are as trapped in the chaos as we are. I have never seen a society in such turmoil."

Jonson was nodding, looking thoughtful. "Yeah, the greatest danger of created entities is that they'll outlive their original purpose, and seek madly for a new one. Machine intelligence was an outlaw technology in my time, for precisely this reason. Unstable, untrustworthy, although I suppose human beings are just as susceptible to that. And we Aggressors"—he grinned humorlessly— "have always been a dangerous breed."

"We humans are trapped," Malye said, her simulated brain buzzing with the feeling, claustrophobic and terrifying. "We're caught in the middle of everything, with no way to escape, and no way to protect ourselves. Who can protect us? Not Finders ring, certainly; I expect they're as much a target as we are, and yet they're still so eager to please. They'd have no compunctions about turning us over, trading us like supplies, and even then they might not be safe. Names of Ialah, the only *stable* force in this system is the Waisters themselves."

"And have you spoken with them?" Jonson asked.

"No. Maybe. I've initiated a communication, but . . . What can they do? They're monsters, aliens, they have no concern for our petty affairs. Do they? Will they intervene?"

He shrugged. "Who knows? If they have a particular interest in you, who's to say they wouldn't move to eliminate a threat? During the war, we studied them until it was coming out our ears, but they were always full of surprises."

Malye felt herself growing angry, a strange thing for a simulacrum to do, but there it was. "It was a surprise," she said, "when they annihilated us for no reason. I watched them hunt and destroy a hundred fleeing ships. I watched them crack an entire world. I saw my husband die, Ken Jonson, and an entire civilization along with him. Are those the surprises you mean?"

He paused, regarded her for a long moment before speaking. "A misunderstanding," he said finally. "It's true, the Waisters' attack on humanity was a mistake of monstrous proportion. I think they realize that now. Why else would they have returned, after all this time? But their genes tell them to fight with a stranger, just as yours tell you to fight for revenge, for justice. Will you let instinct betray you, as they've done, or will you calm yourself and actually *think* about this for a few minutes?

"My job is to give advice, and here it is, unfiltered: put the past in the past, and make the most of the opportunities God shoves under your nose. The Waisters killed *my* family, too, you know, but now they're holding out the olive branch, and if I were you, I wouldn't hesitate to accept it. Why keep them as an enemy? You said yourself, you trust them more than you trust the rings."

"The rings did not eradicate the Sirius colony," she said, her voice sounding petulant and defensive even to her. She realized she had her arms crossed, broadcasting her obstinacy. She uncrossed them. "The rings saved my life, in fact. How can I trust Waisters to protect—"

"I've given you the only sound advice I can think of," Ken Jonson said with a touch of condescension. "Either follow it, or don't."

"Fine," she snapped back at him, and took her thumb off the Congressional trigger.

The view changed suddenly. She was in the dayroom, in the refugees' quarters at Holders Fastness, with Sasha Petrovot staring her full in the face, his glance flicking briefly down to his palm chronometer and then back up again, as per instructions.

"Less than a second," he said.

She nodded. "Good. Don't ever let me stay too long."

His look turned anxious. "Did, uh, you find what you needed?"

"Oh, yes," she said acerbically, "I got all sorts of good advice in there. We're going to war, it seems, and this time, the Waisters are on our side."

Sasha blinked. Blinked again. "That's a joke, right?"

She took his hand, tugged, and helped herself up off the couch, grunting with the effort. "It is a joke," she told him seriously. "It's very much a joke. But it's happening anyway. Get everyone together; it's time for a meeting."

"You desired to question me again?" Chain asked, entering the interrogation room and taking the proper seat.

"Leave us for a moment," she said to her guards, and this time they obeyed readily. Too readily, she thought, as though they meant to lull her, to reassure her that all was well, at least for the moment. Malye had often behaved similarly, with convicts who were soon to die but had not yet been informed of the fact.

Earlier, Malye had demanded a fully functional, Sirian-style flatscreen from Wende, claiming she needed it for recordkeeping in her investigation, which certainly was true. Wende seemed to have a better grip on things now, though, and Malye had sensed that same easy agreement, that same kind of wistfulness. *This is given in friend-ship,* Wende had seemed to say, *though it be my last favor to you.*

Well, what of it? What could Malye do differently, knowing this? Not much. She held the flatscreen up now for Chain to see, and she asked him, "Is there a chance we are being monitored?"

"There is a certainty," he replied absently, "but the eavesdroppers will receive false data. Whether they will know it to be false, I cannot say."

"But they can't see and hear us now?"

"No."

She nodded, and touched symbols on the screen, switching its display. She laid it flat on the table then and slid it across to him. "This is the message I'd like you to send. And there's more; I need some manufactured goods. Nothing massive, but some of it is complex. I think the need is rather urgent. How soon could you get them to us?"

He frowned. "What is it you require?"

"Touch the screen," she said.

He did so, and then leaned closer to study the list and explanations which had replaced Malye's message text. Still frowning, he raised his copper eyes back up to her face.

"I see what you intend," he said, "but I do not compre-hend your rationale. How can this escape benefit you? Why should we assist?"

"If we succeed," she told him, "it will go well for you. If we fail, who will know what role you played? By all means, grovel and fawn before our mutual enemies, be-cause *that* will go well for you if my people are killed. But if you bring me these things, then either outcome is to your benefit. Do you see?"

He thought for a moment, then took out an azure jewel and touched it to the side of his head. His face slackened briefly, then came once more to life. He slipped the jewel back into his sleeve pocket. "Your proposal has been accepted. I will say, madam, that you surprise us. Our culture cannot closely resemble your own, and yet you endure among us."

"Thank you," she said, nodding, accepting the compliment in the intended spirit. "Surviving in lethal environments is a knack we humans perfected long ago. You would do well to remember your roots."

"There is an additional datum I wish to share," he said, dropping his voice. "Two names: Shim and Vent of Striders ring. I have no authorization to speak of this, but harm toward you is imminent, and I felt you should know."

"I never heard it from you," Malye said. "Ialah, I think my investigating days are over anyway. Justice is patient, and we need to move quickly if this is going to happen at all."

"Indeed," Chain said, and rose from the chair.

"See you again sometime," she said, holding out a hand.

He stared at it uncomprehendingly, and said, "I find that very unlikely."

Chapter 22

"Waiting is what makes it hard," Vere Sergeivne said to Konstant. "For *all* of us, yes; you needn't take it out on Malye like that. You *shouldn't* take it out on her."

"No?" Konstant said. He looked across the dayroom at her, his eyes slitted at first and then relaxing. "Well, I suppose not, but I'm very unhappy with this plan. If I could think of a better one . . . Well"—he turned his gaze on Malye, and his nervous energy was a bright, sharp reek in the air—"the moment I think of a better plan, you'll know it."

"I'll be waiting," Malye said. She was fidgeting a little, herself.

It was night shift, and ordinarily they'd all be asleep by now, but nobody seemed tired, and in fact, they'd been going on like this for hours, bickering lightly, finding fault without finding solutions. Nothing to do but wait, really, and as Vere had pointed out, waiting was not a skill that came without practice. But Malye's children, behaving with uncharacteristic patience, served as an example to all; she'd told them to amuse themselves quietly, and thus far they had done a commendable job.

They were playing Viktor's finger game, and she saw that Sasha had joined them at some point. They were all giggling together, nervous but still managing somehow to enjoy themselves, and in a way it felt as if Viktor, with his durable enthusiasm, was with them still. She wondered who was winning.

Svetlane Antoneve, who was curled up with Konstant on one of the room's many gray couches, stroked the side of his face with mingled gentleness and reproach. "At least, darling," she said in her deep, almost scratchy voice, "we'll be getting out of here. That's all we've wanted all along, our freedom. I'm not thrilled about breathing masks—I never have been!—but we've all agreed it's the only way. And it is, the only way."

"Yes, well," Konstant grumbled.

And then, finally, without warning, a Gatean Worker stepped through the outer door's membrane, with a huge burgundy-clad Drone—one of Malye's guards—trailing behind him. "Pierce," the Drone's name was. The friendly one, who once had said three words to Malye for no reason at all. The Worker was not familiar, but she'd learned that the patterns of blue-green hair sprouting from Gatean scalps were as distinct as fingerprints, though on a clan rather than an individual level. This one came unmistakably from Talkers ring, a fact that was confirmed by the large bundles he carried under each arm, and under whose weight he staggered.

"Hello!" Malye called out, hopping off her couch.

"Madam," Pierce said, "this Worker professes a delivery for you."

"Yes, we've been expecting it," she told him. She turned to the Worker. "Thank you, citizen, this will be very helpful. Is everything . . . going well?"

"I do not know what you mean," the Worker said, dropping the bundles unceremoniously to the floor. "I am hurried. Is our business complete?"

"I suppose so, yes. Thanks once again."

The Worker did not reply, but turned and exited. Pierce stood looking at the assembled refugees for a moment, like a father taking notice of his children's suspicious behavior. But not like a father, no, for there was no love in him, nor even respect. Had Malye forgotten that look so quickly? The look of a greenbar about to break up a juvenile gathering. But Pierce held there for only a few moments and then, with a warning glance in Malye's direction, withdrew from the room.

Everyone dove for the piles at once, sorting through them, looking for the size tags. Malye held back, but she understood the feeling; they had nothing of their own here, so that every time a Gatean brought something other than food, the gift was magnified all out of proportion. The refugees' material wealth had just increased fourfold or better. Soon, everyone was trying on the masks, holding the garments in front of them, double-checking the size, looking for rips or flaws. There appeared to be none; when called upon, these Gateans could do good work, and very quickly.

Finally, Malye took up the two remaining bundles, and checked over the smaller one as the others were doing, and then the larger one, which was unique, its contents only marginally familiar. A paint stick, some oxygen bottles, a climbing platform ... When she'd parceled these items out and finished inspecting her own equipment she looked up and saw, to her surprise, that all eyes were on her. Even Konstant was looking to her as if for guidance, for encouragement, as if she knew anything more than he did, as if he could draw strength from her in some ill-defined way. Well, perhaps he could.

She focused her attention on Vadim and Elle, and gave them a smile like she hadn't given anyone in thousands of years. They came to her, and she tousled their hair and hugged them. "I'm very proud of you both. This has been a hard time, and some children would have made it harder still by refusing to cope with it. But you both have been very brave, and I know you'll be brave tonight, as well. This time, I don't have a rescue ball to stuff you into!"

"Thank you, Mother. You have our trust," Vadim said, and Malye thought it was probably the most heartfelt compliment she'd ever received.

She turned her attention to the others. "You all know the plan. Head straight for the Interface Station. Remember to stay together, and look out for each other. We've been told that harm is imminent, and I fully believe it. What we're about to do is dangerous and difficult, but it isn't something we can practice, and we can't afford to bungle it. Most importantly, remember to stay calm."

She stopped, but they still seemed to expect something of her. Well, damn it, she was no military woman. She'd led a few arrest teams in her day, but what a very different thing that was!

"Uh," she said, reaching for the protocols in a disused corner of her mind, "are there any questions?"

There weren't.

"All right then. Take a deep breath, and follow me."

She made a final quick inspection of Elle's repaired foot, and then rose and grabbed one of her little hands, and one of Vadim's. She moved to the door membrane, paused a minute to let everyone line up behind her, and stepped through.

Pierce and Frame, who stood on the other side with their backs to the wall, turned and looked at her with obvious surprise.

"What—" Pierce started to say. Then he saw the children, and the others filing out behind her, and his surprise gave way to doubt.

"We have an appointment at the Interface Station," Malye said without slowing down for them. "It's very important for the investigation."

The Drones hurried to catch up with her, an easy enough task given the length of their stride. "This is not authorized," Pierce said to her. "We have no instructions regarding this."

"Don't you?" Malye said, and kept walking.

The Drones were not stupid, they knew something of fundamental importance was happening right in front of them, but they had no idea what to do about it. Drones were quick, she'd found, where the threats were clear and the solutions involved smashing or pounding on something. And they were clever interpreters of orders, bending them to suit whatever mood or desire happened to strike, and in this respect, they were very much like children. But when the instructions were absent or ambiguous or in conflict, when the true desires of their Queens were not known and could not be guessed, the Drones froze up, terrified of making the wrong decision.

It was a trait Malye had been counting on, for together Pierce and Frame could easily gather up the refugees and return them forcibly to the dayroom, or even individual quarters. As it was, it wouldn't be long before the two called up for some advice. Indeed, they were already taking out comp jewels, already pressing them through layers of security fog to kiss smooth gray foreheads.

Malye took advantage of the distraction to quicken her pace, rushing down the twisting corridor now, dragging the children along and dodging the occasional Gateans who got in their way. Following the red stripe to its inevitable destination. A quick look over her shoulder confirmed that everyone was right behind her. Their colors sang, the breath whooshing in and out of them in near-visible whorls.

She caught a glimpse of the Drones, now in motion once more, now striding forward purposefully, grim expressions on their faces. "You must stop this!" Pierce called out. "Immediately, you must submit yourselves to me. Stop!"

"Run!" Malye said to the refugees, and promptly followed her own instructions. Not that the humans could hope to outrun Gatean Drones, but the distance was only a little farther now, a hundred or two hundred meters at most, and much of that downhill. Indeed, she thought she saw the red stripe's end up ahead, just around that far bend in the corridor.

"STOP!" Pierce boomed. He had almost caught up with Konstant, who was last in line, and Frame was coming along right behind.

Malye's legs slammed and jarred with each impact, the high gravity driving twice her normal weight down upon them. It was less awkward than carrying another person, but no less difficult for that. The weight of the children half dragging behind her threatened to tear her arms. But up ahead now, she could definitely see the Interface Station. Another group of Gateans stood outside it, a Queen and Worker and Dog. It was Wende, she saw, and the remains of what once had been her six.

"Wende!" Malye called out, gasping now. "Wende! Stop these Drones, I need to talk to you!"

She slowed her pace. She *had* to. Behind her, Pierce had seized a struggling Konstant and lifted him off the floor. Half a stride in front, Svetlane Antoneve was in the hands of the other Drone.

"Release them," Malye huffed. Still moving forward, she turned back to Wende. "Wende, make him release them! We have to talk, urgently. We have to *talk!*"

Musical tones cut the air, a shouted exchange in Waister.

"Wende!" her voice aggrieved, reproachful.

"You will approach," the Gatean Queen said, her voice commanding but not unkind. She spoke as if Malye had proved an embarrassment after all, despite weeks of promising behavior, and would now have to be . . . what? Punished? Incarcerated?

"Wende, call off the Drones. This is important."

"It has been done. The Drones are called off."

Malye turned to see Konstant and Svetya released, to see all the refugees streaming in behind her one by one, puffing and sweating and groaning.

"This activity is inappropriate," Wende said impatiently. "What communication do you desire?"

"I . . . I . . ." Malye was still panting, still hadn't caught her breath. Probably, it would be a few minutes before she did, and really, she didn't have a few minutes. Instead, she took out the orange ink stick Talkers ring had created for her, the stick that did not contain orange ink at all but a special solvent she had heard about from one of the Workers she'd questioned.

Wende frowned at the ink stick, clearly displeased. "This is what?" she demanded.

Having secured the release of Vere and Konstant, Malye had concluded her business with Wende, and with Gatean society in general. So rather than explaining, Malye simply demonstrated the stick's purpose by uncaping it and drawing it sharply across the Interface Station's door membrane. Where the solvent touched, the membrane shrank aside and opened. Instantly, a long crescent-shaped hole appeared across it, and it quickly spread, the membrane parting, dissolving. Within a second the hexagonal doorway stood completely uncovered.

Foul air swirled out of it. The Gateans shrank back.

Malye shouted: "Masks!" and quickly fumbled for her own, spreading it and pulling it down over her face as her eyes and nasal passages began to sting. The mouthpiece shoved its way between her lips, between her teeth, and for a moment she gagged breathlessly before it gave her the air she demanded. Her view began to fog slightly as the mask sealed in place, smelling of rubber in her nose.

Next she grabbed Elle, made sure *her* mask got seated correctly. Vadim seemed to have done all right on his own.

And still the Gateans shrank away.

Malye had no access to weapons, no way to penetrate the Gateans' security fog. It would be impossible, she'd been told, for her to control a fog of her own, and really, what else was there to defend with? Except the air. Security fog was almost entirely empty space, and could no more hold air molecules in, or out, than a strainer could hold water.

The Waister air, as toxic to Gateans as to humans, would therefore serve as a buffer between the refugees and those who might oppose their escape. Please, Ialah, let the Waisters do their part! *Meet us at the spin axis,* she'd told them. *Pluck us from this deadly world.* Weightless, they could hold out there as long as necessary.

She stepped through the open doorway, into the slightly hazy chamber beyond. Konstant never had arranged another chat with the Waisters; it turned out their ship had already pulled away from Holders Fastness, and anyway the Gateans' self-absorption had put repair of the Interface Station at rather a low priority. The chairs were still toppled and scattered, the walls and floor and ceiling still stained with dried blood, which for some reason had faded to a glossy black. What chemicals hung suspended in this air, she wondered? What exactly did they do? Well, her skin still felt all right, and hopefully they wouldn't be in here very long anyway.

With an overhand gesture, she invited the others to follow her through. Meanwhile, she tried not to think of what had happened here so recently, tried not to think at all as she stepped over a single overturned chair on her way to the glass partition that had once separated Waister from human. The glass was ebbed with cracks now, and one corner of it had gone white and pitted. Had the rogue surgical fog tried to burrow through there?

Well, it was Malye who would burrow through it now. She hit the whitened spot with her ink stick, rubbing it on hard, and then traced a line all around the edges of the triangular partition, and as high as she could reach along the top, and then for good measure she made a wide X across the center of the glass as well. The solvent wouldn't actually damage the glass, as she understood it, but it would get in between the molecules somehow and render the whole thing brittle, at least for a little while. Well, a little while was all they needed; she gestured to Nikolai Ilyovot, who picked up a chair and smashed it hard against the partition, which shattered easily, not so much breaking as turning to powder at the impact. The granules rained down together like a glittery-white curtain cut from its moorings, falling quickly in the high gravity, and the chair flew through and bounced against the angled walls before coming to rest.

Age had done little to wear down Nik's hard, construction worker's body. Which was good, because they needed it still.

Malye checked her people over once more, making sure no one was choking or bleeding into their masks, and then nodded her approval and turned toward the partition's empty frame and stepped across. Another two paces carried her past the bizarre couches on which the Waisters had lain, to the white membrane-door on one of the two walls. Without ceremony she penetrated it, stepping through to another hexagonal corridor on the far side. This one, though, was bright red inside, the diaphanous light spheres hovering along the ceiling glowing the ruby color of fresh blood. The walls were probably still white, though it was hard to tell. In any case, they had markings all over them, orange and black chevrons and stripes, and messages printed large in a language she didn't recognize, though the characters were clearly from some human alphabet or other. Farther ahead, perhaps a hundred meters down the hallway, she could see another membrane-door, glowing red in the warning lights.

She moved a few meters in to give everyone space to come through behind her, which presently they did, one by one. Sasha was carrying the oxygen canister, and as soon as he was through the door, everyone was grabbing up the thin hoses from him and connecting them to the masks' inlet valves, refreshing their air supplies lest the recyclers go foul on them. The children managed this task as well as any of the adults, and once again Malye felt a surge of pride. She gave them a childish "high sign," wishing she could actually *say* something, but of course she didn't dare take the mask off for even a moment.

In fact, the moment had arrived for them all to get into their pressure-equivalence garments. And quickly, for the Gateans might follow them in here at any moment. No time for modesty; she undid the sash and shrugged her shoulders, dropping her robe to the floor. Despite repeated whining from the refugees, they had never been given any undergarments to wear, and for once this was a good thing, as there was nothing left for her to remove. She unfurled her orange emergency suit, found and undid its zipper. The air *was* starting to bother the more sensitive parts of her skin, so she pulled the suit on over her feet and knees and thighs as quickly as she could without actually hurrying, and then got her arms through the sleeves and hauled the zipper up all the way to her chin, just under the bottom of the mask. A little Waister air leaked under the edge of it, stinging her eyes momentarily.

Around her, the others were stripping and dressing as well. There was a bit of furtive ogling going on, probably normal enough even in circumstances like these, but mostly everyone was focused on the task at hand, focused on survival and escape and the distant hope of rescue.

Malye still felt naked, vulnerable. The suit was porous, really just ordinary cloth that pulled against the skin with an atmosphere's worth of pressure, and despite its toughness it was thin. The last time she'd worn a suit like this, as Pinega succumbed to the Waisters' fire and flew apart around her, she'd taken an extra few seconds to throw her uniform on for protection, to help guard both herself and the suit's all-important fabric. But now, the idea of pulling on that loose, flapping robe seemed ill-advised, even ludicrous. They would have to face the vacuum bare-arsed, an unpleasant prospect.

But what other prospects did they have? The alternative was to sit around in the dayroom until somebody murdered them, which she felt sure would not have been a long wait at all.

When everyone was dressed, they began buddy checks, just like an emergency drill. Air meters, seals, zippers, loose articles ... Really, they weren't ready for this at all. But the checks were finished in another minute, and they left their robes on the floor behind them and moved on down the corridor, secure in the knowledge that nobody was in a truly panicked state, that nobody was going to bleed out and die the moment they hit vacuum.

The door at the corridor's far end had a curious look to it, stiff and shiny as if it were thicker than an ordinary membrane. Even so, it bulged outward slightly at its center, and Malye thought she could hear it creaking faintly with the pressure, just at the edges of audibility. Perhaps it was her imagination. She often wondered if a great deal of what she sensed around her might not have its roots in imagination.

Hear the colors, little Malye!

Again, it fell to Malye to step through the doorway first. She did so, and immediately felt herself pushed through the membrane with considerable force. She saw stars, literally; the blackness of space whirling out in front of her, all around, and she was thrown out into it by the pressure differential across the door membrane. Full atmosphere on one side, full vacuum on the other. Damn! But presently, she felt herself slowing, and through the slightly foggy mask she could see that she was surrounded by tendrils of structural fog, or mechanical fog, or whatever it was they called it. It had a gentle grip on her, and was reversing the push she'd been given.

She looked down, and, seeing nothing but stars beneath her feet, gasped in a sharp breath through her mouthpiece. The air lock's exterior was just a wide, oval-shaped depression in the side of the planetoid, no wider than a train car and no deeper than Malye was tall. Waving with barely visible fog tendrils, like something from a holie documentary about ocean life on Earth or Astaroth or one of the Barnardean worlds. And she was looking straight down, past the lip of the depression and down along the world's rocky face.

Holders Fastness was a vertical wall from which she hung like a decoration, and at two gees' worth of spin gravity, the stars whirled past her with alarming swiftness. If she fell, it would be in a straight line and at a constant velocity, but the world would spin on without her, the surface receding, falling away. From the world's point of view, Coriolis forces would whip her down and out into space. Would she fall past the cucumber's tip, fall forever into the void? Or would the tip beat her to it, swinging around in a few minutes to smash down upon her, a wall of rock from which there could be no escape?

She shuddered and moaned, but she did not fall. And since she did not fall, she calmed, realizing that the fog tendrils' gentle grip was going to hold her up.

As she was thinking this, something soft and heavy slammed into her back, knocking the breathing air from her lungs, shoving her another meter forward. The stars reeled, and she half expected to fly out to join them. But again, the fog held her up. Awkwardly, she turned to see Nikolai behind her, jerking and struggling among the tendrils.

She drew a ragged breath. Ialah's names, they had to get away from the doorway, or else the next person through would slam into Nikolai, shoving him into Malye once again, and in all probability knocking her past the ends of the fog. Or could the tendrils stretch to catch her? No, that wasn't something she wanted to test.

Instead, she moved her arm upward, feeling the fog roll out of her way and then close behind the arm once more. Well, that was fine; she moved the other arm up there with it, and in a moment she was climbing, if awkwardly, up along the center of the depression. It was like air-swimming in a weightless tank, like water-swimming in gravity, like climbing a ladder made of soft gelatin ropes that oozed and parted and rejoined in her grip. Against the skin of her fingers the fog was a pressure and nothing more, no sensation of mass or texture, and the only other feeling was the disturbing numbness of the vacuum itself. Hands could survive an atmosphere's worth of pressure differential well enough, but there was nothing natural about the sensation.

The stars wheeled past.

Seeing her climb, Nikolai copied her movements just in time to get out of the way of Vere Sergeivne, who exploded through the membrane like a human projectile and was quickly seized and halted, only a part of her shoulder striking a part of his foot. Which was good, because while the two had become lovers, Malye doubted they shared any mad desire to fly off into eternity together.

Behind the mask, Vere's eyes were wide with sudden terror, but Malye and Nik both made reassuring gestures at her, and demonstrated the art of climbing. She was no fool, and her near collision with Nik had demonstrated the potential danger. She climbed out to the side, almost fast enough to avoid the next person through the membrane.

It went on like that until everyone was out, until they all clung to the surface of the depression like the peculiar creatures they were, far out of their normal element. Bugs nestling in a hole in the wall ... There had been a close call there at the end; for some reason the children both came through the door more slowly than any of the adults had, and Konstant burst through right behind them, his collision sending them all flying. The fog seemed ready for this, however, and it caught and halted them all before they'd moved a meter.

So here they were, at the very edge of the world, dangling out over nothing at all. Malye was not at all happy with the situation, because in the long hours the refugees had spent planning their escape, this was supposed to have been the easy part.

Chapter 23

219::18
HOLDERS FASTNESS, GATE SYSTEM:
CONTINUITY 5218, YEAR OF THE DRAGON

Nikolai was able to put the platform together with a speed and ease that Malye found surprising. It was largely a self-deploying mechanism, of course, folding out from its tiny package and taking firm grip upon the rock face with its three strong piton wheels, but the process required considerable human supervision, lest something mechanically sensible but otherwise disastrous occur. Or so Nik had earlier insisted.

But he'd climbed up to the top of the depression and fired in a few spikes, and then it had seemed to take only a few minutes before he was dropping the guy wires down and opening the platform's floor gate.

Above them, about a hundred meters up and two or three meters off the cliff face, hovered one of the Gateans' light globes, spilling white light down through that wire-mesh ceiling, as the refugees climbed up toward it, one by one. At least they were not on the dayside, blasted and blinded by sunlight! Every now and again, an object would swing past with the starscape, a nearby ship or a distant world, fully illuminated and reflecting brightly, and even that was enough to hurt the eyes that lingered too long.

Nikolai, kneeling above on the platform, helped each climber through the gate's square opening, sending eerie shadows cascading all around. The platform was nothing but slender, telescoping rods and mesh screens that supposedly rolled and flexed in one direction but not the other. It was like a larger version of the frying baskets people used for sliced potatoes and such, and under two full gees it certainly looked too spindly to support the weight of eight people. But Malye, who climbed aboard last, felt it bend and tremble beneath her only slightly.

There wasn't really *room* for eight people, however, and it was only a moment before she began to feel both claustrophobic and seriously in danger of falling. Bad enough to have a mask over her face and a breathing tube in her mouth, without elbows and masked faces pressing in from all directions, and nothing but a waist-high railing protecting her from the infinite void. Uneasily, they broke out Sasha's oxygen bottle again and shared from it, but the procedure was difficult and awkward and probably quite dangerous.

Malye was relieved when Nikolai finally pointed at the gate opening, and then lowered himself through it and back down into the fog tendrils. There was room enough for seven here, just barely. Malye watched the top of Nikolai's head bobbing as he climbed down, his bald, vacuum-bruised scalp gleaming each time it crossed the barrier between shadow and light.

He had to attach the guy wires, of course, and tighten them, or the platform would have nothing to press it firmly against the rock face, nothing to keep it oriented as it climbed upward toward the spin axis. Malye tried to watch what he was doing, but the shadows down below were simply too deep, the contrast too sharp for her to see. Until the bright object swung by again, briefly illuminating the air lock's depression like a bowl of foggy light, and Nikolai down in it, carefully unreeling the guy wires. But then the brightness was gone, the shadows returned, and it was much easier to look *across* the air lock, at the expanses of rock below and on either side of it.

The surface of Holders Fastness was smooth, almost glassy, which fit with her impression of what had happened to it in the war, back when it was still called Artya, and this was still Sirius system. Melted, distorted . . . In all, this world had probably fared better than most, else the Gateans would never have chosen to reoccupy it. And really, the surface was rather pretty with the starlight and globe-light gleaming off its highlights and inclusions. Like a semiprecious stone of gigantic proportions.

Movement caught her eye. She turned. To the left, just at the horizon, something was happening, something was moving. She peered through the moisture on the inside of her mask, straining for a better view.

Oh, Ialah.

Two or three Gateans were out there, Drones in silver-colored pressure suits. Three of them, yes. They were tiny in the distance, impossible to make out in detail, but it seemed they were not quite in contact with the world's surface. Rather, they drifted along it in hazy bubbles of fog, as if it were doing the climbing for them, as if they were being carried along with no particular effort of their own.

And then Malye realized why they were so difficult to see—it was not the distance so much as the haze. Human-size globs of fog raced alongside and in front of them, making shimmers and rainbows of the stars that swept past the horizon. Ialah, there were dozens of them, much larger than the surgical fog that had killed Viktor and Plate. And coming this direction!

She pointed, waving her finger urgently to alert the others. Weapons, attackers! When she was sure they'd seen, she threw herself down on her knees and peered through the floor gate. Nik! She couldn't see him, but down in the shadows of the air-lock depression, something appeared to be moving spasmodically, as if he were down there dancing or fighting. And then suddenly there was a spray of dark liquid, breaking at once into tiny droplets that froze and danced and fell in the starlight, and Malye understood at once that Nikolai Ilyovot Kuprin was not down there anymore. The dust of bloodred jewels spinning out into the light simply confirmed it for her, as she searched madly to see whether the guy wires had in fact been spiked to the surface.

They had.

Slamming the gate shut between her knees—as if this wire mesh could keep out a fog weapon!—she threw herself toward the back of the basket, toppling Elle and Sasha out of her way against the rails, and she fumbled for the controls that hung there at the back. Three fat buttons, marked UP, STOP, and DOWN, on a slim pendant controller that hung flat against the mesh wall. She slapped the UP button as fast and hard as she dared, her fist pushing pendant and mesh up against the unyielding rock.

The platform lurched and shuddered and began to rise,

its three piton wheels firing pins deep into the rock, then expanding and roughing their surfaces for unshakable grip, then rolling a notch upward and firing again, the first set of pins collapsing on themselves and rolling back up into the mechanism. The motion was jerky but surprisingly swift, carrying them upward a full five meters in only a couple of seconds. The guy wires spooled out on their reels. Malye bit down again and again on her mouthpiece as the basket shook.

Ialah, what this would sound like if it weren't in vacuum! Malye knew a moment of raw, red terror, mingled with exhilaration and amazement that this contraption should work at all. Never had she seen such a thing, though Nikolai has insisted they were common enough in Sirian times. Her tongue tasted not of batteries but of cinnamon, sharp and biting but not unpleasant, not really.

But that moment passed, and once again she was helpless because the platform wasn't climbing *nearly* fast enough, and the fogs were swirling up on all sides. Ten seconds, maybe twenty, and—

Bright light flashed down from above, seeming to freeze everything in place. Malye could see each individual fog weapon standing out like filmy lenses against the rock and stars, and she could see the Gateans, now only seconds away, and she could see something else, as well: a wall of huge, flailing objects tumbling down the rock face from above.

After that, everything seemed to happen at once.

The light was reflecting off the hull of a ship that looked very much like a Gatean ferry, orange and phallic and vaguely organic in appearance. But it was enormously larger, and Malye understood it to be a Waister fleetship coming up over the horizon, so far away that it was in sunlight and yet still it filled a quarter of the sky.

The falling objects were Drones, Waister Drones, dressed up in gray hardsuits of some sort. Space armor. They looked like plated sausages with arms and legs attached in all the wrong places, and they were not falling at all, but *running* down the surface of Holders Fastness in full defiance of the laws of gravity and centrifugal motion.

Here and there, the glassy surface flashed and kicked

up sprays of grit, which promptly fell out and down into infinity, and at some point Malye noticed that all the fogs were gone, and the Gateans as well, though she hadn't seen quite what had happened to them.

The Waister drones swarmed down all around them, shaking both the platform and the rock face itself with their passing. The air-lock depression, now brightly lit with the reflected sunlight, filled up with Waisters. They swirled into it and cast themselves through the air-lock membrane, not one at a time but by the dozens, almost as if they overlapped one another in space.

It was at approximately this time that Malye began to doubt her senses. What was happening around her was insane, impossible, and also too quick for the eye to follow, like it was all a series of optical illusions or—admit it!—hallucinations. And then, as suddenly as everything else had happened, the cliff was cast once more into relative darkness, as the Waister ship, growing huger and huger with each passing second, slipped into the shadow of Holders Fastness.

And still the ship approached, now a wall of shadow above them, illuminated in diffuse circles where the Gatean light globes reflected, but these circles kept shrinking and sharpening and the ship was like a world unto itself and it seemed it must crush them all against the rock face at any moment. And still it approached.

Malye and the others ducked, shrank back, cowered against the back side of the basket. Not even afraid, really; human brains simply weren't equipped for an experience like this. There was no programmed response except confusion, and that was not really a response at all.

Finally, the great ship slowed and stopped, a wall that filled all but the very edges of the sky, and Malye found her senses returning. She could turn and look straight across at the alien hull, its orange, ripply-smooth surface shot through with orange, ripply-smooth threads. Like a leaf, sort of.

She noticed there was an opening in it spilling out purple light. It was well below the level of the platform and slightly off to one side, and suddenly her brain kicked in at full power. Despite appearances, the Waister ship was not hovering at all, but accelerating in a mad circle that kept it parallel to the ever-retreating face of Holders Fastness. Her binocular vision engaged as well, so that the range and size of the opening became clear, as well as its purpose.

No citizen of a spin-gee world could survive for long without a clear grasp of Coriolis forces, and this was doubly true of the police, who must after all learn to fire projectile weapons accurately, no matter which direction they were facing or which level they were on. One simply developed an instinct for it, and right now Malye's instinct was clear on the fact that a leap from this platform would carry her right into that open doorway.

Lately she'd been having a problem with impulse control anyway, so she motioned for everyone to follow her, and then went ahead and jumped.

Chapter 24

Events followed one after the other with a dreamy-soft focus, and afterward Malye was never quite sure of the order in which they'd occurred. There was much moving from place to place, much communication between Gateans and Waisters. At some point the refugees had all taken off their breathing masks, though they kept the orange emergency suits on.

Much later, Malye would begin to understand how carefully orchestrated their rescue had been, how inevitable, really. They had begged the Waisters to pluck them from Artya's equator, which seemed the easiest place for it, but they'd neither expected nor received any reply. From the beginning it had been a gamble, based on her intuition, and Ken Jonson's, and everyone else's for that matter, even the children's. They had tried doing nothing, after all, and that hadn't worked, so what was left?

For a while it had seemed this mad plan couldn't work either, that they were doomed no matter what they tried, but in fact they had been under close observation all the while, and their rescue would have been that much easier if they'd simply thrown themselves into empty spaces.

But on that morning, in the Holders throne room thronged with Gateans and Waisters and orange-suited Sirian refugees, Malye knew nothing of this, knew only that they had been brave, that though the probabilities were stacked against them they had pressed on, suffering losses and yet emerging alive from their ordeal. Most of them. In truth, she suspected the hand of Ialah, and even years later, when the facts were well-known, this suspicion lingered within her. *Twice* they had survived against all odds. Twice!

The chamber in which they all had gathered was a high, vaulted space, a single octohedron with three smaller copies branching off to the sides. In its center was a hexagonal dais, flat and smooth and empty. This might have been the same throne room in which Malye had confronted and surrendered to Queen Tempe and the rest of Holders ring, or it might not. These things were hard to tell with Gatean architecture.

In any case, the Waisters had caused a gathering to take place here, with representatives from most of the major rings inhabiting Holders Fastness. Tempe was here, and Wende and Crow, and the Worker, Chain, from Talkers ring. Nobody else that Malye recognized, but as on the earlier occasion, Queens were disproportionately represented in the Gatean crowd.

Not so for the Waisters, who had brought along a single Queen, plus her Dog and two Workers, all dressed up in peculiar, awkward-looking pressure suits. The rest were Drones, dozens of them, standing huge and imposing in the gray battle armor they had worn outside on the surface. Their alien, bubble-enclosed faces were near the floor, it was true, but their bodies and arms rose high into the air, and even without the high gravity it seemed they could smash any being to pulp, anytime they wished. Even the Gatean Drones, with their marble-gray Olympian physiques, looked feeble by comparison.

Fortunately, though, the Waisters did not seem to be in a hostile mood any longer.

The chamber was deathly silent. Every little creak of space armor or shuffling of sandaled feet echoed and rang off the high walls. Everyone was looking at the Waister Queen, waiting for her to do or say something. Surprisingly, though, when she spoke it was not in Waister but in Standard, the words leaping crisply and without inflection from a translation module of some sort built into the bottom of her helmet bubble.

"WE," she said, and then paused, waddling her fat body around in a quarter circle, so that she was facing Malye and the other humans. "WWE LEARN NOT ONLY FWHEEESH BUT WWAR FROM HUA PEOPLE. HUA ATTACKED US WWITH THIS MANNER. IT

MEETS CLEVER LOGIC UNSUSPECTED. OUR
METHODS WASTE NEEDLESSLY. WWE DREAM OF
HUA PEOPLE, UNCLOTHED AND NAIVE, PILING
STONES BESIDE THE WWATER. DO HUA DREAM?"

She paused, looking around with her brown, stalk-
mounted eyes. No one felt like speaking.

"ABSENCE OF STABILITY WWITHIN THIS CUL-
TURE PRECLUDES PRACTICE OF FWHEEESH." She
paused, tried again: "OF *PFEACE*. STABILITY HAS
BEEN IMPOSED. WWE OCCUPY ALL INHABITED
BODIES WWITHIN THIS STAR SYSTEM, AND WWE
HAVE DESTROYED THOSE WHO RESIST OR
THREATEN. THIS WWE LEARN FROM HUA. FROM
HWWUMAAN. FWHEEESH WWILL NOW OCCUR."

Somewhere in the crowd, one of the Gateans began to
laugh. Others turned that way with sharp looks, though,
and the disturbance was quickly silenced.

Peace will now occur? Peace will now occur? The
Waisters were ordering peace within Gatean society? The
idea was too strange for Malye to know what to think
about it. Or for anyone else, it seemed; there was more
shuffling and fidgeting, a bit of whispering here and there
in what she was pretty sure must be the Teigo language,
but as a population the Gateans appeared utterly at a loss.
Had they never faced a superior enemy before? Had they
never received an order? Perhaps not.

Konstant was elbowing her in the side, sharply, but
when she turned to glare at him she saw only a look of
urgency on his face. He looked at her, then up at the
empty dais, then back at her again, nodding his head sideways. Behind him, Sasha was nodding, and so were Vere
and Svetlane, the sole remaining adults of the human
population. What did they want of her now?

"Get up there!" Konstant snapped in a low whisper.
"Now, you idiot! This is our chance!"

Get up on the dais?

Suddenly, their reasoning was clear: the Waisters had
in effect forced the surrender of all the Gate, but having
obtained it, did not have any idea what else to do.
"FWHEEESH" was an alien concept, after all, with
which they had no prior experience. Thus, a power vacuum had been created, and all Malyene Andreivne

Kurosov'e had to do to fill that vacuum was climb up there and start talking.

Well, that was easy enough. With hands and elbows and glaring eyes, she cut herself a hole in the crowd and strode toward the dais with slow dignity. Even the Waister Queen edged out of her way, as if afraid somehow of giving offense. The dais was barely half a meter high, and Malye hopped up onto it easily, even at two gees. The crowd was at her feet, silent, watchful. A little curious, she thought, and a little afraid. How right they were, to be afraid.

"All right," she said, looking around at the Gatean Queens and Drones. There was no question in her mind about what she would say. A little speech had written itself in her mind, and all that remained was to recite it. "It's time we all had a talk. Names of Ialah, people, what kind of society are you trying to run? You want to live like the Waisters, well, I suppose there are reasons to do that. I suppose a lot of good can be accomplished. But do you think the Waisters live like this? Stabbing each other in the back, cutting each other's knees off at every opportunity? I don't think so. Even as they destroyed Sirius system around us, they seemed a single entity, bent on a single purpose. With themselves at least, they operated in harmony.

"Let me explain something to you, all right? It's something my friend Viktor said, before you people had him killed. He said, 'these Gateans really have shit for brains, don't they?' And indeed, that appears to be the case. You know how to imitate Waister hostility and human fractiousness, and you think somehow that this will bridge the gap between the two species? These are the *very worst* attributes of us both. Better that you had chosen human kindness and Waister determination, or even drunkenness and apathy, or greed and reticence. There are a thousand other ways to do what you are attempting.

"The first step toward reform, I think, would be to shuffle the membership in these damned rings. Maybe that kind of society works for the Waisters, I don't know, but it doesn't work here; your brains are simply too human for it. How long has it taken humanity to shrug off the curse of tribalism? To return to it, as you have, like a bunch of youth gangs ... We should see half the membership of every ring scattered throughout all the others. Let's level out the gravity contours, let everyone become everyone else's best ally and worst enemy all at the same time. If this doesn't work, we may need to phase out the rings altogether."

A storm of quiet protest met that remark, and a single voice rose up above the crowd. Crow's; he stepped forward from Wende's side, his copper eyes and flattened nostrils flaring wide. "You cannot do that!" he cried. "Who are you, a human whom we rescued from death, to tell us what to do?"

Confronting the monster directly was always a mistake, for it was here that her greatest strengths came into play. In this particular case, she simply stared down at Crow as if he were no more than a minor distraction. She was surrounded by armored Waister Drones, and she was up on this pedestal, and she was the only one in this great chamber to whom anyone was paying any attention. And in addition, she was being "contributive" in precisely the Gatean style, sharing crucial insight and plans for the benefit of all, and yet doing so in a fundamentally self-centered, self-aggrandizing way.

The combination was irresistible; she felt their acceptance, felt power and influence flowing into her like a chorus of enthusiastic notes, filling her, confirming and vindicating. Just like that, an entire society was under the monster's thumb. Her father's laughter blossomed inside her. Ialah's names, did these people know what they'd done? Did they know whose monstrous ideas they had just agreed to submit to?

For a moment the anxiety was a blinding yellow wave, but it passed quickly, leaving a kind of purity behind it. *It boils down to a single unknowable question,* Viktor had told her: *the existence of the soul, of free will, of metachronic perturbation at the quantum level. We cannot know, and yet we must, for why else do we even exist?*

If the Waisters could change so dramatically, could Malye not change as well? If she occasionally heard and saw things that others did not, even if she'd somehow inherited the twisted instincts of Andrei Brakanov himself, did that mean she must behave as he did? Her life thus far indicated otherwise. Her presence here, among the Waisters, indicated otherwise. And suddenly, she knew the answer to Viktor's riddle: free will not only existed, but outmatched the power of instinct by orders and orders of magnitude. Only if she wished it to be so, of course, but that was the whole point, now, wasn't it?

If she were *sufficiently determined* to stop the madness here, to mete out justice, to dig a tunnel toward lasting peace, would these things not occur? Who, exactly, was going to stop her?

"Citizens," she said to the crowd, in a quieter voice now, "the Waisters are correct. Peace will now occur. Together we can create a new Gate, with"—what was that old Earth saying?—"with liberty and justice for all. Oh, and speaking of justice, will somebody please arrest Shim and Vent of Striders ring? They are, ah, suspected of the murders of at least five people."

Epilogue

ARTYA PEACEHOLD, GATE SYSTEM: CONTINUITY 5220, YEAR OF THE HORSE

"Mother," Vadim said as he entered, "the festival is about to begin. They're asking for you before they open the swimming tank."

"Well," Malye said good-naturedly, "tell them to start without me. *#Hthw#* has something she wants to talk about, and we'll be at least a few minutes here."

"Oh," he said. "Very well, I'll tell them."

And he turned on his heel, and slipped out through the door membrane.

"HE MATURES RAPIDLY," *#Hthw#* said, watching the door. "OUR YOUNG, WHO ARE RARE, GROW AND LEARN VERY SLOWLY. EVERYTHING ABOUT HUA HAS BEEN ACCELERATED. WE FIND IT STRANGE."

Malye and the Waister Queen were separated by no more than a thin, clear membrane through which they could speak, and even pass small objects back and forth. Once upon a time, they had come here often, but the passage of months had placed increasing and mutually incomprehensible burdens on them both. Being back here again gave Malye a reminiscent feeling that only served to remind her how very far she'd come from her old life. It seemed she'd always been here in the future, and the time before was nothing but a kind of dream, or a practice life where she might learn a few of the skills she would need when her real one came around.

Not that she didn't miss it; even now, she'd awake from bad dreams and expect to find Grigory's comforting presence there beside her. Or Viktor's—the two had gotten very mixed up in the part of her mind that dreamed.

But the ache had faded with familiarity, becoming simply another part of her new life, one burden among many.

Speaking with #*Hthw*# was another. The conversations were rarely fascinating; things tended to wander rather quickly toward the obscure and ambiguous, and while there was a learnable trick to keeping them in the comprehensible realm, to creating the illusion of free, unfettered conversation, it required considerable effort. Still, Malye thought the common ground of their understanding grew a little wider every year, which probably meant she was slowly becoming more alien, and ‖*Hthw*‖ more human.

The Gateans, pulled equally toward both poles, had begun to grow stubborn, prideful, independent. *This is what we are,* they seemed to say. *If we change, it will be for our own reasons.* They were almost a species unto themselves anyway, with their own unique history and ideals, and Malye found herself welcoming the return of their confidence. Better that they find their own sort of peace, than that humans or Waisters find it for them.

Probably, they would all remain strangers forever. But they weren't fighting anymore, which was a lot to be thankful for, and Malye herself was happier, more fulfilled than she'd ever been. She'd been a diplomat at heart for all those empty years, and never once suspected it! What would her father think?

"You know," she said to #*Hthw*#, "sometimes I feel like you people came all the way back here just to help me make peace with myself."

She knew right away what a dumb thing that was to say to a Waister. #*Hthw*# thought for a long time before replying, "FWHEESH IS FOR ALL OTHERS. FWHEESH IS NOT EXCLUSIVELY FOR YOURSELF. HAS THIS NOT BEEN UNDERSTOOD?"

Sighing, Malye smiled and shook her head. "It's just ... it's a figure of speech, an idiom. I apologize; I'm out of practice for this. Peace for all, yes. Obviously that's understood."

"I COMPREHEND. PFEACE FOR ALL. HOWEVER, ADDITIONAL REASONS EXIST FOR OUR RETURN."

"Really?"

"BLUE STAR DISEASE. HAS THIS BEEN DISCUSSED?"

Malye sat up straighter. Something in the Queen's body language alerted her; this was more than an idle question.

"Blue star disease? What is that?"

"ERR, DISEASE, NO. BLUE STAR ... CONTAMINATION? GALACTIC REGION WHERE STARS CHANGE COLOR AND LOSE LIGHT. VERY DISTANT. SLOW LIGHT IMAGES HAVE NOT REACHED THIS PLACE."

"#*Hthw*#, what are you talking about?"

"IN OUR HISTORY THERE HAVE BEEN EIGHT CAIRN BUILDERS. ALL DIED. THERE HAVE BEEN STUPIDLINGS, WHOSE BODIES WERE MANY-HANDED AND SMALL, WHOSE MINDS WERE MANY-HANDED AND SMALL. ALL DIED. ONCE THERE WERE FAINT VOICES FROM GALACTIC CORE, BUT THEY STOPPED SO LONG AGO. SO LONG AGO. WE BELIEVE THEY DIED. ONLY HUA HAVE NOT DIED, AND SO CLOSE TO TIME OF HUA ARE THE BLUE STARS."

"What are the blue stars?" Malye asked, feeling the hairs prickle erect on the back of her neck.

"THEIR LIGHT WILL ARRIVE IN SIX-POWER-THREE ORBITS OF THIS WORLD."

Malye calculated. Twelve hundred orbits of Artya ... four thousand Standard years? Something like that. "What are they?" she asked again. "Why are they blue?"

"SURROUNDING OF WATER. LIQUID. THIN LAYERS OF LIQUID WATER ORBIT THESE STARS IN WAYS THAT CANNOT OCCUR UNINTERVENED. SOMEONE IS THERE. DO YOU COMPREHEND?"

"Someone is surrounding the stars with water? That's crazy. How could they do that?"

#*Hthw*# didn't answer.

"You came here because of that? Is that what you said? I don't understand what you're talking about."

The Queen's face pudged in and out. Her breathing was heavy for a moment, her eyes pinching together and then relaxing.

"BLUE STARS LIGHT WILL ARRIVE, BUT THERE IS NO QUICKLIGHT TRACE. WE AND HUA AND STUPIDLINGS AND CORE-SINGERS VIBRATE UNI-

VERSALLY. QUICKLIGHT EMITS, DO YOU UNDER-
STAND? BLUE STAR SICKNESS EMITS NO UN-
NATURAL QUICKLIGHT. THUS WE COMPREHEND
NOTHING."

"Huh," Malye said. This was starting to worry her
more than a little. "So there's something very strange
happening, yes? What makes you think we can help
you?"

"NOT HELP," #Hthw# said quickly. "HELP LEARN.
IN SIX-POWER-SIX ORBITS OF THIS WORLD,
BLUE STAR SICKNESS WILL ARRIVE. IN TWO-SIX-
POWER-SIX ORBITS, BLUE STAR SICKNESS WILL
COMPLETE GALACTICALLY."

Malye couldn't immediately convert those numbers,
but they were large. Millions of years, she thought. Huh.
What matter if something new came along in a million
years?

"That's a long time in the future," she said.

#Hthw# became visibly agitated. "NOT LONG, NOT
LONG. FOR US, ALWAYS THERE IS A CONFRON-
TATION AND A COMPLETION. ALWAYS THERE IS
ANNIHILATION OF THOSE WE ENCOUNTER, EX-
CEPT FOR HUA. BUT BLUE STAR SICKNESS WILL
BE TOO LARGE. NOT CONFRONT, NOT ANNIHI-
LATE."

"You're afraid of it!" Malye said, surprised and obscurely pleased. Not that there was anything pleasant
about this; she'd seen individual Waisters act startled or
afraid, if some immediately dangerous stimulus were
right there in their faces, but it had simply never occurred
to her that as a species, as an overwhelmingly powerful
species, they would be capable of fearing anything.
Maybe this blue star sickness would be a *serious* problem, in a million years or so.

"AFRAID," #Hthw# said, shrinking into herself
slightly. "WE ARE AFRAID OF IT. WE DESIRE TO
GREET SICKNESS BEFORE IT SPREADS FURTHER.
WE DESIRE TO PRACTICE PFEACE UPON IT, BUT
OF THIS WE KNOW NOTHING. OF ALL SPECIES
KNOWN, ONLY HUA DEMONSTRATE PFEACE. WE
MUST LEARN FROM YOU, QUICKLY."

"Quickly," Malye mused. "Your perception must differ
greatly from mine. If you send them a slow light signal,

it will be thousands of years before you get an answer back. That's hardly cause for alarm."

"ALARM," #*Hthw*# agreed, completely missing Malye's point. "SIGNALS WILL ARRIVE HERE FIRST. HUA ARE CLOSER. BLUE STAR SICKNESS WILL TOUCH HUA FIRST. YOU SHOULD KNOW THIS, AND PREPARE."

"Thank you," Malye said sincerely, "I'll let my people know. But really, I'm not very worried; I'll be dead before their *light* even gets here."

#*Hthw*# made a face that Malye had learned was associated with confusion, or possibly disbelief. "THIS CRYOSTASIS ADAPTATION IS INTERESTING, FOR A SPECIES SO SHORT-LIVED. ARE YOU NOT MANY-SIX-POWER-TWO ORBITS OF THIS WORLD IN AGE?"

"I—" Malye stopped, letting the idea sink in. She *was* thousands of years old, and could easily live to be thousands more, if for some reason she went back into cryostasis. So perhaps a million years was not so long after all. Perhaps her children would still be alive, when the blue star sickness swept down upon the Human Spaces and did, well, whatever it was. She frowned, not liking that idea at all.

"I don't know," she said finally. "Maybe you're right. Maybe you're right. But we're not going to solve the problem tonight."

"WE WILL DISCUSS IN DETAIL?"

"Another time, yes." Malye smiled reassuringly, a gesture she knew #*Hthw*# would recognize. "Meanwhile why don't you get a pressure suit on and come to the swimming festival with me? We can pile some stones beside the water."

But #*Hthw*# had no sense of humor, and Malye wasted another half hour explaining the joke.

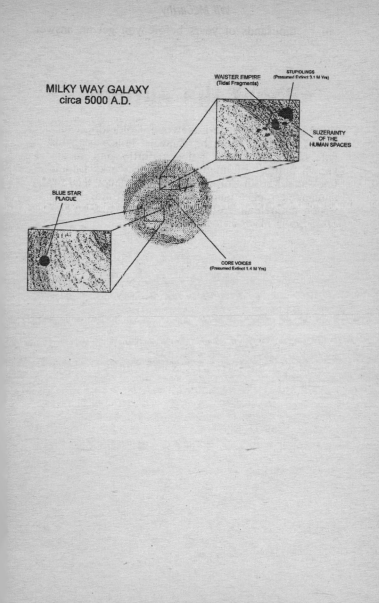

MILKY WAY GALAXY
circa 5000 A.D.

WAISTER EMPIRE
(Tidal Fragments)

STUPIDLINGS
(Presumed Extinct 3.1 M Yrs)

SUZERAINTY
OF THE
HUMAN SPACES

BLUE STAR
PLAGUE

CORE VOICES
(Presumed Extinct 1.4 M Yrs)

About the Author

Wil McCarthy lives in Lakewood, Colorado, a suburb of Denver, where he shares a house with his wife Cathy, two cats, a dog, a turtle, and an unknown number of mice. By day he works for the Lockheed Martin Corporation as a guidance lead for unmanned rocket launches. At other times he's a writer, handyman, rescue diver, and bum. *The Fall of Sirius* is his fourth novel.

If you and/or a friend would like to receive the *ROC Advance*, a bimonthly newsletter featuring all the newest and hottest ROC books and authors, on a complimentary basis, please fill out this form and return it to:

Penguin USA
Mass Market
375 Hudson Street
New York, NY 10014

Your Address

Name _____

Street _____ Apt. #_____

City _____ State _____ Zip _____

Friend's Address

Name _____

Street _____ Apt. #_____

City _____ State _____ Zip _____